THE CRAFTSMAN AND THE WIZARD

Joel Newlon

Silver E

Paperback ISBN: 978-1-7362211-0-5
E-Book ISBN: 978-1-7362211-1-2

Cover art by Kevin Sardinha
Cover design by Silver Eel Publishing
Printed in the United States of America

For Sophie

CONTENTS

ACKNOWLEDGEMENTS

I must take this opportunity to acknowledge that this book would never have been a success without the incredible hard work of Ashleigh at Silver Eel Publishing. Her editing, understanding, her encouragement, and sometimes even harsh criticism were crucial to its success.

My deepest gratitude also to Michelle, whose commentary and diligent work as proofreader went above and beyond anything I could have hoped for.

Special thanks to Kevin for allowing me input on the cover art and blowing me away by bringing a slice of the world I created to life.

Thanks is also due to the beta readers, whose advice and enthusiasm were invaluable.

Under ancient carven arch

Kept he faithful dwarfen watch

Baited still for hammer song

That snares right from baleful wrong

FROM THE OLD NORSE

AUTHOR'S TRANSLATION

CHAPTER ONE

*T*he old gray horse stopped walking before the top of the hill and whickered indignantly. She had served faithfully for many years, and thought it quite improper for the man to ask so much of her. "Please," said the man in the cart as he flicked the reins. His voice, which was usually so sweet and filled with cheer, sounded sad and rough. She had heard him weeping many times during the long journey.

  Reluctantly, she trudged ahead once more. As they reached the top of the rise, she heard the man's excited gasp and felt the cart shift as he abruptly sat up straight. She looked down from the crest of the hill and spied what had caught his attention. Ahead, not very far away, the road led straight through a tall, open gate and ended in the courtyard of a mighty structure. Sensing the long journey would soon be over, she forgot her weariness and quickened her pace to a trot.

  The man stepped down from the cart and stretched his stiffened joints with relief. He lifted a sack from the back and approached the towering doors.

Once, many winters ago, he had seen the longhouse of the king. This building, whose wide steps he now ascended, seemed twice the size of that. Unlike the dwelling of the king, which had been a bustling hive of activity, this place was completely still and silent.

He had traveled all day, and the sun was now setting, casting long, heavy shadows through the empty courtyard. All around him he saw evidence pointing to long years of abandonment and disuse. He felt a stab of despair trying to take hold, but he fought it off. *Maybe they will still be here. Maybe they will help me,* he told himself.

He climbed the cracked and weathered steps to the entrance. As he reached the massive doors of iron bands and ancient timbers, he saw that the right one hung open slightly, some of its hinges having succumbed to years of unhindered rust. With a hard push he was able to open it wider. It let out a loud squeak as it moved, voicing its protest at having been disturbed from its long, peaceful slumber. The waning sunlight invaded the gloom, showing him a glimpse of the dusty interior. He stood motionless for a long moment, feeling lost, until the gray horse behind him paused from eating the tufts of grass near the steps and snorted. Snapping out of his momentary stupor, he stepped inside.

Instead of a feast hall, or throne room, or indeed anything he might have expected, he found himself in what appeared to be a vast workshop. It contained all of the tools for the forging and smelting of metals, the carving of wood and the weaving of wool. Every trade, every craft the man had ever seen – and even some he hadn't – had its place here. There was only one thing missing: the people. No craftsmen were here to fill the room with the din of their hammering and turning and chiseling. There was no hum of voices to break the perfect silence. The man could detect no sign of life at all in this vast empty hall. This place was like a tomb, long ago forgotten. Now at last he was forced to face his sorrow. This quest, this dream, had allowed him to put it aside, but it could no longer be avoided. It came rushing down on top of him and nothing could stop it – no one was here, no one could help him. He was truly and utterly alone. Not one sliver of hope remained.

All alone in this forsaken place, he broke down and wept, the sound of his grief echoing in the huge chamber and filling his own ears. His weeping was no longer the tears and gentle sobbing that had afflicted him over the last few days; it was now a torrent, a downpour of mourning. It was not until he paused to fill his lungs in preparation for a fresh wail that he finally heard the irritated voice that had been trying to get his attention. His tears ceased abruptly.

"Excuse me?" he asked sheepishly. The grumpy voice spoke again.

"I said, it's damned hard to work when I can't even hear myself think, and if you are going to continue crying, kindly go back outside."

The man stood dumbfounded for a moment. He looked all around, but saw no one.

"I'm sorry," he said. "I did not think anyone was here."

"That's preposterous! Do you mean to tell me that you have nothing better to do then roam the countryside, looking for vacant buildings to cry in?" asked the voice.

"No, I, uh, it's just..." stammered the man, still searching for the origin of the mysterious voice. "Why are you hiding?"

"I'm not hiding. I'm over here." The echoes in the massive room made the voice seem like it came from everywhere at once.

"Where is here?" the man asked.

"To your left. Come to your left."

The man did as instructed, setting off along a path between the rows of workbenches to his left. His footsteps echoed in the cavernous building. He skirted around a giant loom, then rounded a crucible that was taller than he was. He marveled at the cunningly crafted machines as he passed. At one point he found himself in a dead end formed by a collection of lathes and had to retrace his steps. He chose a new direction and passed through a long aisle of racks, containing row upon row of hand tools. As he explored, he continually scanned the room, but still could see no sign of the mysterious speaker. "Where are you? I still can't find you," he called out hopelessly.

"I'm right here," the voice replied. It sounded much closer than before.

The man hurried forward, spurred by the nearness of the voice. He arrived at a large anvil with beautiful carvings embellishing its sides. Turning to his right in order to navigate around it, he stopped in his tracks and beheld his objective. It was a craftsman with a long beard hanging down over his leather apron. He was using a delicate hand file to shape a small golden box. His arms and legs, his chest, and shoulders were thick and heavy, suggesting that he was possessed of great physical strength. The reason the man had been unable to see him was also revealed. The craftsman stood no more than three and a half feet tall, and the workbenches he stood between, though themselves not very high, did an excellent job of concealing him. The craftsman stopped filing the edge of the box and looked up as the man approached.

"Have you finished crying?"

The man nodded and rubbed the back of his hand across his still-soggy eyes.

"Good. Come with me."

The craftsman led him from the huge workroom into a long hallway. "Where is everybody else?" asked the man as they passed several closed doors.

"There is no one else. Just me."

"Oh," the man said, then remembered the sack he held. "This is for you."

The craftsman stopped and turned around, eyeing the man who was now holding the sack out to him. "What is it?"

"It's payment," he replied uncertainly. "I did not know how this worked, and I just wanted to, um..." He trailed off.

The craftsman took the bag and looked inside. He pulled out a chalice made of silver. He grunted in mild disapproval as he looked closely at the workmanship.

The man said, "These things are all I have. I am not a wealthy man. I am just a farmer."

The craftsman was now examining two candle holders, turned from a dark wood. He nodded his approval.

"Those were passed to my wife from her mother upon our marriage."

The craftsman looked into the sack once again. It

now contained only two loaves of bread. He removed one and smiled. He carefully tore it open and pressed his face into it, inhaling deeply. He pulled some of the bread from inside the loaf and squeezed it. Then he rolled it between his fingers. Smelling the bread again, he closed his eyes, and took a bite, chewing slowly.

The man watched the craftsman in confusion. Finally, he cleared his throat. "So... the payment is acceptable?"

The craftsman broke from his reverie. He held up the chalice. "This was crudely made by a tawdry peddler of wares. I will accept it for the silver it contains. These–" indicating the wooden candle holders – "were carved with care but not much skill by a poor farmer who did not have the proper tools or training. I will accept them because of the love they contain." He held up the loaves of bread and paused, closing his eyes again. "These, however, were made by a master in their craft, unsurpassed in skill and devotion to detail. They contain flour from wheat grown in the river valley region north and east from here, six days' journey from the sea."

"That's right!" said the man. "That is the region I come from. As for the hands that created them – my wife baked them and sent them along with the candle holders that were her only inheritance. She said she was sorry there wasn't more."

"Wasn't more," echoed the craftsman with a touch of disbelief in his voice. He held the bread to his chest, shook his head, and whispered, "Sorry there wasn't more." He stood a few moments more, then abruptly deposited the items back into the sack and turned. "You should have told me about this earlier!

Now we must go back the way we came." He walked past the man, heading back down the hallway in the direction of the grand workshop, calling, "We must take the payment to the treasury."

The man stood, watching him go, until the craftsman's voice sounded from down the hall.

"Hurry along now!"

The man shook himself and ran to catch up. They entered the workshop and he started in surprise. The machines, the tools, the workbenches – they were gone. In their place mountains of gold reached up to the distant ceiling, dotted throughout with bright, glittering gemstones – white ones, red ones, green ones, and some in a color he did not know a name for – almost like the color of summer skies. Some were as big as a man's fist. There were piles of chains wrought of gold and silver and an almost white metal, more silver than silver. He saw heaps of bejeweled swords and armor, furniture and chests of wood, all crafted and carved so cunningly that he felt sure no mortal hand could have fashioned them.

The man stood still, amazed. He opened his mouth to speak, then closed it again, then repeated the process. He observed the craftsman placing the loaves of bread on a golden table filled with dozens upon dozens of every kind of cake and pie and bread imaginable. They must have been there for ages, yet somehow not a single item seemed to show any signs of spoil or decay. The craftsman turned, and seeing the expression on the man's face, said, "What are you gaping at?"

"Wasn't this the workshop before?"

"Perhaps, but it is the treasury now. Come, let us head back the way we came to a place where we can talk."

Yes, need to talk. To tell him, the man thought, regaining his focus. He spun around to head back down the hall and almost walked into a wall. He stumbled back in confusion. "Where did the hallway go?" he asked, stepping back and examining the solid wall before him.

Here and there were hung beautiful tapestries, finely woven and colored with dyes so vivid that he thought his eyes must be deceiving him. Vibrant greens, sunny yellows, deep reds, and that color again which was almost like certain skies. The scenes they depicted were marvelous – gods and monsters and mortal men, mighty battles and heroic deeds, stories of love and loss. There were also paintings rendered with so sure a hand and so keen an eye that it was as if he were actually there watching the scenes unfolding before his very eyes. These were mounted in frames which were themselves so masterfully crafted from wood and bone and precious metals that they were works of art unto themselves.

"Come on now," called the craftsman from behind him.

"Come where? The hallway is gone!" he retorted.

"No, it's not. It's over here now."

The man turned and saw the hallway directly across from him on the far side of the vast treasure room. The diminutive workman was already heading toward it. He shrugged his shoulders and ran to catch up. They entered the hallway. The craftsman took six steps, stopped, and said, "Here we are," as he opened the first door on the left.

◆ ◆ ◆

They stepped into what appeared to be a neatly kept cottage. The man glanced back as the craftsman was swinging the door closed behind them. To his surprise, there was no longer a hallway beyond the door. Instead he saw a farmyard touched by the last colors of sunset. The craftsman directed him to a simple chair and began to stoke the fire. Once the flames were crackling, he poured the man a horn of mead and said, "This will help calm your nerves, that you may tell me why you've come. For no one can come here who does not mean to, and in truth, I did not know that any still knew the way." With that the craftsman poured himself a horn and sat down in his own chair. The man, who had decided that he would no longer be surprised by anything in this enchanted place, watched placidly as a colossal boar trotted into the firelight, circled once, and settled down on the rug next to the craftsman's chair. It gave out a short yawn, leaned its head sleepily against the craftsman's leg, and shut its eyes.

The man squeezed his own eyes shut and took a gulp of the mead. A sense of warmth and calm washed over him. The man had tasted mead on occasion before. The finest one he had ever enjoyed had been given to him and his wife when they married. But the memory of it was now eclipsed by the sublime elixir he was tasting. It felt as if a golden beam of sunlight ran through his insides, relaxing him completely. For the first time in two days, the tight knot of fear in his chest loosened and he was able to draw a full breath.

"I am Balder, son of Ake, son of Einar, son of Arvid, and it was my father's father's father whose father Haldor knew the way and passed down the knowing and said: it has been granted unto the sons of Haldor that the path and the door of the Great Hall will be opened to us, and we may ask for aid in an hour of need."

The man's gaze fell upon the craftsman and he said, "I must admit I did not truly believe the tale could be true, and even when I found the hidden path – even when I saw the Hall draped in mist – I thought: so many years have passed since the deeds of my great, great, great grandfather, no one will still be here to remember."

"One still remains," said the craftsman. He gazed thoughtfully at the pale golden liquid in his drinking horn. "Tell me your tale, farmer. I will listen."

Balder paused and sipped his drink once more, considering where to begin.

"Ours is the Village of the Two Rivers, where peace and plenty have reigned for generations. Five winters ago, an old farmer who had lived there died. He was the last of his line, having produced no sons. The farm was left to his only daughter, who was known in the village as a spinster. She had never shown any interest in marrying, but she was a practical woman. With her father gone, running the farm was proving too much for one person, so she married a man from the village of the South Lakes. He, too, had never married, and thus they seemed a perfect fit. The arrangement was made all the sweeter when they found to their surprise that they truly loved one another. The little farm had but one small field, and at its center was a rather large pale white stone. It had lain there for countless generations. The new husband found it difficult to work around the big stone. The wasted space confounded him.

"He went to his wife and asked her why her many

forefathers had never moved the stone. The only answer she knew to give was that it was forbidden. From father to son down through the ages it had been told that to move the stone was to bring calamity upon the village.

"She told him that abiding by this had always served them well, even in the long year of ice when she was only twelve – some in the village had starved, but her family had been blessed. A ring around the stone would not freeze. Her mother and father had planted there, and even without much sunlight, crops grew and they survived.

"The wife entreated her husband not to move the stone and to leave the farm as it had ever been. He listened to the word of his wife and they were blessed. The crops were abundant and their animals were fat and healthy. Then last spring they learned that she was with child. They were very happy there on the farmhold of the white stone.

"Then fate took a hand. The winter was cold and long. The wife took ill. Bearing children once you had seen more than fourty winters is dangerous enough in itself – but then to also have caught a sweating sickness – well, a son came into the world and a mother left it.

"At last the long, cold winter finally broke. The bereaved husband with the newborn babe to care for prepared for planting. His wife's voice was no longer there to counsel him, and in his bitterness, he no longer believed the farm held any blessing. He hitched a team of oxen to the big white stone and ripped it from its place. Even as he did, he felt the wrongness of the deed, but he embraced the feeling of wrongness and did not turn aside from it.

"He could not yet see that he had not been personally singled out by misery. Life gives and takes away from all in equal measure. But the wounds to his heart were too fresh, and so he ripped the stone away. Then he spat and said, 'I care not! What more harm can be done to me?' He did not have to wait long before learning the answer, for that very night, the farmer's infant son was carried off into the darkness, never to be seen again. Two weeks later he hanged himself in the barn.

"The disappearance of the child was seven moons ago. Every new moon since, a child who has not yet seen five winters has been taken without a trace. They are taken even though the doors and windows are barred. Even though the family watches over them. We dragged the stone back into its place – myself and the other farmers. You can see if you look closely that runes of the old tongue are carved in its face, and where it had always been bright white stone, it now is a dull gray and covered in a foul brown fungus. Putting it back in its place was useless, for every month, at the coming of the new moon, another child is ripped from its bed and carried away into the dead of night!"

Balder did not realize he had begun shouting his narrative, sitting on the edge of his chair, hands shaking, brow sweating, staring with horror into the fire. He blinked, slowly regaining his composure, and drained the last of his mead. "Two nights gone, on the new moon, I sat before the barred door of our cottage. My axe was across my knees. My wife leaned close over our only child – my three-year-old, Sassa, with the honey-colored hair.

"At the hour the moon would be highest in the sky, the good strong timbers of our door burst open! In came a wraith cloaked in black! Just as Dag the sheep-herder described from two months prior when his son was taken. He had told us all, standing in the meeting hall, that he had tried to wrestle with it, but could not hold it. The men of the village scoffed. They called him a liar, called him a coward." Shamefacedly, he added, "I joined in with them. I think it felt better not to believe him." He moved to sip his mead, and found he had finished it already.

"I swore that I would be more prepared if the wraith visited me, and so when the door gave in and that black, faceless demon stood before me, I was on my feet, swinging my broadaxe with every bit of strength in my body."

Silence hung in the air. Balder's eyes were far away, reliving that moment from two nights earlier. He came back as the craftsman refilled his horn from the small red jug.

"My axe went right through it. *I* went right through it. It paid me no heed. Ragna screamed at it. Struck at it. Tried to cling to our baby as she was seized. But it paid her no heed either. It took our Sassa from her bed. Ragna changed her strategy. She fell to her knees. Clasping her hands, she begged, 'Oh dear spirit, please no. Please take me instead!' The wraith was unmoved, and swept my Sassa out the door, and with her my heart."

Balder hung his head and prepared for fresh tears, but found that none came. He felt wrung out. He had had just enough will to follow the directions passed down from father to son for generations and travel the hidden path to tell his tale, and to see all the strange things that confronted him in this place, and now he found he had nothing left to give.

After a time, the craftsman rose in silence and left him gazing numbly at the fire. He returned some time later with a great many skins, which he piled on the floor to create a makeshift bed by the hearth. "I have fed and stabled your horse. Sleep here, and in the morning, rise and return to your home."

Balder stood, feeling heavy and ready for slumber. The mead was working in him; he was filled with warmth and peace in spite of all the horrors that had been plaguing him. He lay down before the fire and asked, "And what will you do?"

"What will I do?" echoed the craftsman. "I have less than one month before the new moon and much work to do. I have not followed my brothers across the bridge, because I knew there was one last promise to keep, one last thing that needed to be made. Now at last Haldor Helmbreaker's heir has come to me, bringing with him the coal of vengeance and the fire of justice, saying, 'Light your forge one last time.'"

Balder pulled the skins over himself and closed his eyes. In moments, he was asleep.

Asmund moved as swiftly as he could over the uneven terrain. The desire to turn and flee in terror was great. He wished fervently to give in to this desire, but to his horror, he found that he could not. To his right was a road running parallel to the strange field he was traversing. He could see the signpost identifying the village he was entering to all those who could read it. What was he doing in a place called Kalbaek? He had never heard of it. What was he doing, scared and alone, walking across a farm field in the

dark? And why was he heading toward the sounds of a battle? This was not like him. None of this was like him.

Now he could see the battle. A short man – no, a dwarf, he judged, by his size and shape, and by the dwarfen battle armor he wore. He was fighting a creature of shadow and smoke, the sight of which drove the spike of fear even deeper into his heart. He watched the creature rear back and attack, striking down the dwarf. Asmund was pulled irresistibly toward the scene, but then something struck him, and all went black.

Some time later, he knew not how much, he opened his eyes. Seven faces were looking up at him from the darkness. All at once they spoke to him in a whisper. "Asmund, help us."

He sat up, trembling, and wiped the sweat from his face. He jumped with fright at the sound of fluttering wings. He looked at the window, but nothing was there now. Toward the horizon he could glimpse the first rays of morning. He swung his legs out of bed and sat still for a moment, trying to recover himself. He squeezed his eyes shut and tried to banish the memory of those three words whispering in his mind. *Asmund, help us.*

Why must he have this same dream night after night? It was so vivid, so real. What did it mean? All he knew was the name of the place. He remembered the faces and whispers of the seven children. He could still see the knotwork carved into the dwarfen armor and the way the creature moved like a rushing wave. Worst of all, he saw himself in the center of it all. Did it mean anything? And if it did, then what? He opened his eyes and stared out at the brightening horizon.

He rose from his bed, walked to the basin and washed. Then he donned his brown robes and ate a small breakfast. He left his chamber behind and moved quickly down the hall, his staff clacking heavily on the stones, as it always did when he made haste.

He entered Master Rangvald's outer chambers and found the old, white-bearded man in the rumpled gray robes sitting at his desk. He was studying his books by candlelight, as the early morning sun was still not strong enough to brighten the room. Asmund scrutinized Master Rangvald's candle to see if he had just risen and begun work, or if he had been at it all night. The candle was not far from being spent, and the rivulets of wax were a silent witness pointing to the latter.

"It's Asmund, My Lord," he announced as he entered, even though he knew his clacking staff and unique shuffling gait were all the announcing his master's keen ears required.

The old wizard lifted a hand, forbidding distraction, without raising his eyes from the page.

Asmund waited in silence. After a time, Rangvald closed the book. He gazed out the window, lost in thought. At last he nodded slowly and turned to regard the young man in the brown apprentice robes. "Asmund, my boy, good morning to you. Sit down here and tell me, why do you race the sun into my chamber this morning?"

Asmund sat across the desk from his master and swallowed hard. "A dream, My Lord."

"You had a bad dream, Asmund?"

"Yes, My Lord."

"Well, bad dreams can be most distressing," said

the master, his voice sounding slightly annoyed. "But I must say, Asmund, you have passed your seventeenth winter; you are a young man now, and while I want you to know that I am here for you and you can come to me with anything, it is important for you to be able to face your own fears. You are an apprentice wizard. The people look to wizards for wisdom and courage. Am I making myself understood?"

"Yes, My Lord. I did try to deal with it myself," the embarrassed youth said.

"Well, I confess, I cannot say I'm very impressed with how long you tried. The sun is scarcely up before you leave your bed and run to me."

"But, My Lord, you do not understand me. I have had this same dream every night for the last seven days."

Rangvald sat up in his chair, looking at the boy. He saw the dark circles which had formed under his haunted eyes. "Exactly the same dream?" he asked.

"Down to the tiniest details," Asmund answered.

Master Rangvald sat back slowly, stroking his long white beard. Then he rose without a word and disappeared into his inner chamber, returning moments later carrying his distaff. This reassured Asmund that the master was taking his problem seriously. The short staff with its bundle of unspun flax and hanging spindle was a common sight in every house across the land, but in the hands of a practitioner of the magic arts, it meant something quite different. It would help the master to interpret what, if anything, his recurring dreams signified. "Tell me the dream. Leave nothing out," Rangvald ordered, returning to his seat.

Asmund related all to the wizard with precise

detail, as it had been etched into his memory by sheer repetition. When he had finished telling it, he felt a vague sense of relief. It was as if simply the telling had made the weight of it a little easier to bear. He took his first deep breath of the morning, letting it out slowly and relaxing. Everything would be all right. Just as soon as Rangvald told him what to do.

"You must go to this Kalbaek and face the demon," Rangvald said.

Asmund stared at the wizard without blinking. *I'm still dreaming,* he thought. *Yes, thats it. In this new version of the dream, the children whisper, I dream I wake up, come for help, and my teacher tells me I must go be devoured by the demon. The remedy is simple. I must somehow make myself really wake up.*

"Asmund," the wizard said. "Asmund! Did you hear what I told you? This dream does not come from inside you. It is sent to you, to call you. You must go to this place and use your powers to fight the evil. It is your destiny."

So this wasn't a dream. This was really happening. Asmund felt as though he were standing at the bottom of a deep well, looking up at Rangvald, who was calling down to him from a circle of daylight high above. He could feel the stone walls of the well closing in on him, squeezing him. He felt the water in the well rising up around his ankles, his knees, his waist, his chest. Now it was drowning him!

"Asmund! Asmund!" Rangvald stood by his chair, shaking his shoulder.

Asmund turned his pale face up to him and blinked slowly. "I can't."

"You must," answered Rangvald.

CHAPTER TWO

The craftsman entered the sunny orchard and walked the green path, which was lined on both sides by trees whose limbs were heavy with fruit. This kingdom was hidden, just like the Great Hall. You could not come here without knowing the way. This place was the very wellspring of fertility. It was perpetually in harvest here, and that was because of her.

He passed through the orchard, and then, following the distant sound of falling water, he made his way down the hill. He arrived at a pool with a tranquil waterfall that fell to the rocks on the far side, casting tiny rainbows in the sunshine. She stood looking into the pool, her back to him.

"Aren't you a little short for an elf?" he called out, smiling.

"I am only Vanir on my mothers side," she said, turning and matching his smile. "My father was a dwarf."

"Well, anyone could see that," he laughed. "That's where you get your incomparable beauty, my sister."

They embraced, both still laughing joyfully. "If you are here, then it means you have been called upon at last," she said. "You are the last of our brothers, and your hands the most skilled. Whatever you must make, if my wisdom and farsight can be of aid to you, then they are yours."

The craftsman stood back and bowed. "Oh, Idunn, you who are the fairest of all, I am unworthy of your gifts, but my quest is not. It is my hand that must make a mighty weapon, strong enough to slay an ancient evil. If you would see all that must be done and give me your guidance, then I would show you." At a nod from her, he stepped forward, and grasping her slender wrist with his big hand, he placed her palm onto his head.

In scarcely a moment she had seen all. She withdrew her hand and said, "Yes, it can work. It will take much effort, and time will be your enemy. We must look to find what will be needed. Fill the basin from the dreaming pool and come with me."

He fetched the hammered copper basin his father had made many ages ago from its hook and filled it from the pool. As he dipped the basin into the water, the ripples flashed images, images that dragged at his eyes and pulled at his mind, trying to trap him with their fascination. The ripples coming toward him flashed a scene of a fallen giant. He saw elves and dwarfs new born crawling out from under it at the founding of the world. He wrenched his eyes away, but they were immediately caught by the ripples moving away from him. They showed him people who bore themselves like kings and queens, their robes brightly dyed. They boarded a strange white longship and sailed through the sky. He squeezed his eyes shut and stood, bearing the filled basin.

When he turned, Idunn was watching him, with a

look of surprise. She shook her head in wonder. "You are strong, brother."

He laughed. "Did you think I could not still lift a basin of water?"

"No. I meant your mind. Your mind is strong."

"Oh, now I know you are jesting," he chortled.

"I love our jests, but this is no part of them. I know your mind must be strong, because your goodness and your belief in goodness have been tested by all the darkest hatreds of the world, and for them to still live so strongly in you, there are only three possibilities, and as you do not have a feeble mind, and you are not a blind zealot, that leaves only the third."

"And that is?"

"Well, that you've examined the evidence, weighed it carefully, arrived at the only possible answer, and then rejected it – and continued to believe in goodness anyway."

"Well, I may not be as smart as you give me credit for," he said. "You see, what you said is true, except at the part when I was weighing the evidence carefully, I discovered an anomaly with my scales. When I placed a single day of true happiness on the one side, I discovered that I would have to heap at least two or three of the world's darkest hatreds upon the other side to try and outweigh it. As time passed and I continued the experiment, I learned that this outcome was variable depending on what version of myself was conducting the test that day. But then I added one last element to the exercise. I asked myself if I could influence the final outcome with an act of will. Could I stare at the one good day, the one moment of happiness and force it to always outweigh the bad? And do you know what I found out?"

"That you could?" she asked on cue.

"No," the craftsman admitted. "Not all the time. But a lot of the time I can. It also means that I've trained myself on how to look at things. I think back to times in my life that I remembered as bad, and I can see that there was joy there as well. And now as I encounter new things, I am more sensitive to what is good and less worried about what is not. So I think perhaps you may be right. Maybe my mind is strong enough to choose to believe in goodness in spite of the evidence."

Her face broke into a big smile. "I've listened to your explanations, and now I know for a fact that I was simply mistaken. You are both feeble-minded and a bit of a zealot."

"How can everything be so fertile and healthy around here when you are so completely rotten?" he laughed. "Perhaps you will see further wearing the water in this basin!"

"Don't you dare!" she shouted, holding up a commanding finger and giggling. Then she grew serious. "The water in the pool is the real reason I spoke of your strength. I have everyone who would far-see draw their own water from the pool of dreams. And always – without exception – I have to wake them from the trap they fall into. Everyone, that is, but you. The thing you are to face has a mind and will so fortified by terrible hatreds that it defies the very laws of life and death. It may attack your mind as well as your body. When you stood up from the pool on your own, I knew why this task had been reserved for you. You can prevail."

She led him around the pool. At a wave from her dainty hand, the curtain of the waterfall parted and they entered her home. There is a feeling known only to craftspeople: that of being reunited with things they have made and not seen in a long time. He felt it now as he saw his hand in many of the things around him. The bed, the shelves, the chairs. And this... he sat the basin in its hole that he had many ages ago built into the round table. He ran his hand over the inlay of dark woods that were set into the pale surface. The inlays were carved characters enacting the saga of how Idunn had once learned the secret of bestowing immortality – and how it had brought her to sorrow.

She who was both elf and dwarf had once loved a human man, and dreaming of love everlasting had made him immortal. The tale of the saga told by the intricate wooden figurines ended right where her chair sat. Thus as she looked into the basin and saw the hidden things therein, she would be reminded of the cost of changing things that should not be changed. Right at the lip of the copper bowl, as carved by the craftsman at her request, was an image of the pile of dust her beloved had turned into when she had brokenheartedly revoked his endless life and the many years came rushing back upon him. Instead of remembering her love for the kindhearted man he had once been, she now must always live with the memory of the jaded monster he became. The table reminded her of this each time she sat and took a hand in what might be.

"I always rest my scales on this table when I perform your test, brother. My results are always the same."

The craftsman sat down at the table. "Well, there is the problem. I never could make anything level."

She sat in the chair across the basin from him

and rested her left hand upon the pile of dust depicted there. "Before we find what is needed, I must ask a deeper question. This will tell us if the plan is worth the undertaking. If it is not, there may still be time to devise another." She moved her hands above the surface of the water and spoke the words of the old tongue. A blur of images danced across the water before the craftsman's eyes. He saw rivers and oceans, trails and roadways, beasts and giants, swords and blood. He saw a fierce woman standing in the rain. He saw a boy wearing a gray robe. He saw tears and laughter – but none of it meant anything to him. The images flashed by too swiftly for him to focus. Idunn studied it all in silence. At last she looked up and addressed him. "There are things I can see for certain and others I cannot. I cannot see the dead thing. He is hidden from me. I do not know what hand he will play. But I do see your path. Before you begin this undertaking there is something you must know. Success can be yours, but not without sacrifice. Ultimate sacrifice."

The craftsman thought for a moment, then said, "I have no wish to die, but I do not fear it either. I will willingly make that sacrifice."

"Then it is not your ultimate sacrifice, is it?" she said, staring into his eyes.

"I do not understand," the craftsman said.

"You are willing to sacrifice your own life. But are you willing to sacrifice other people's lives? If you begin this quest, others will die."

The craftsman could not look her in the eye any longer. He stared into the basin, but the water was now still. At last he spoke. "If I do nothing, then does the evil go unchallenged? Do the children continue to be taken?

Their families left broken?"

"Yes," she said. "No one who would help can prevail against it, save you. But you cannot get there alone, nor without their sacrifice."

He swallowed hard at the lump in his throat; then, clenching his fist, he said, "If they choose to fight for what is right and this evil creature kills them, then that does not rest on my head."

"The creature does not kill them. You need to know before you begin this – it will be because of you, because of the times that you fail, that others will sacrifice themselves. They will choose to die so that you may live. You must know this, and you must make the choice."

The craftsman sat in silence for a long time. He could not look at his sister or at the basin of water. His head was turned to his left and he was staring at the blank wall, but he was not seeing it. All he could see was a scale with one side pinned down. No matter what he heaped onto the other side, he could not get it to budge. The moment before his spirit retreated completely into itself, he paused. A few indistinct figures fell onto the raised side of the scales. The direction of the scales reversed, and now the opposite side was firmly planted on his imaginary table. He felt a touch of wonder. Finally, he turned back and faced her, saying, "I freely enter into this quest, even knowing that it will cost more than I want to pay, and I vow that I will not rest until I vanquish this wretched enemy, and bring peace to those who suffer at its hands."

She paused for a moment, then, "I believe you," she said simply. "Now, we must find the first ingredient." She moved her hands once more across the surface of the water and a single clear image filled the basin. A great rock engulfed in flames was hurtling from the night sky. It was approaching the distant land. It moved so swiftly that in the blink of an eye, the land was no longer distant. In another blink, the rock had vanished from sight. All that was now visible was a great gash of toppled, broken trees and a cloud of dust which rushed up to hide their view of the stricken land.

She moved her hand again and their viewpoint widened. Now he could see the shape of the coastline. It was unfamiliar. The image kept backing away further until other lands came into view. Now he knew where the flaming rock had struck. It would be somewhere outside of Jorvik.

"That is very far," he said. "If I journey down to the Angles' land by hoof and ship, the new moon will have come and gone before I can even claim the first ingredient."

"It is even farther than you know, brother. It is not just the where of it, but also the when. No mortal path will be able to take you there." She rose and crossed the room, retrieving a small Eski box made of ash from a stand by her bed. "Here," she said, reaching in and bringing out two small red apples. "Eat the first one as you lie to sleep by the pool; you will dream of the place you saw the burning rock fall to earth." She traced a sigil on it with her finger and handed it to him. "This one you must take with you. Eat it once you have found the rock. When you do, you must dream of the Great Hall of our father." She traced a sigil on this one as well. He took it from her and carefully placed it in his purse. "You must go now. Only, first tell me..." She paused.

"Anything. I will tell you anything. Do not be

afraid to ask."

"When I looked into the future and told you that others would die so that you might live... I read in your face that all the sorrow and unfairness of it had tipped your scales toward the real truth of the world. Then, right before my very eyes, I watched the scales in your mind tip back."

"Yes. That is precisely what happened."

"Then may I ask, what was so good that it could shift the balance?"

The craftsman smiled. "It was just a small change of perspective. Instead of focusing on how sad I was to be the cause of someone's death, I was struck by how much goodness must still be left in the world that someone would care enough about me and what I was fighting for that they would willingly sacrifice their lives. Who could ever believe that darkness was stronger than that?"

She stood looking down at the table without saying a word. Then she looked up with a fragile smile and placed her hand in his. "Come, it is time," she said, and led him back out through the curtain of the waterfall. They rounded the pool, but once they had reached the far side, the craftsman stopped.

"My gloves!" he exclaimed. "I left them by the chair. You go on. I will get them and come right back." Without waiting for a reply he ran back into the house. A moment later he re-emerged saying, "I forgot – I have dwarf's hands. I don't wear gloves." She gave him a strange half-smile as he hurried around the pool to meet her.

"Here, lie down and eat and dream of the far-off Angles' land."

They embraced. He heard her saying words over him and felt her finger tracing something on his back. He sat down on the grass and took a bite of the apple. He felt instantly drowsy.

"What did you really do when you went back into the house just now?"

He settled back onto the grass and said, "I did something to show you that I love you, and to remind you to focus on the good things that happen in life – not just the bad ones." He closed his eyes and then he was gone.

Idunn stayed there for some time, eyes lingering where he had been. She raised her gaze beyond the spot and looked into the pool. Then she sighed and returned to the house. She walked slowly through. How had he left her his message? Had he left a note or some gift? She walked through a second time. She saw nothing. Nothing new, nothing moved. What had he done? How strange.

"Oh well," she said. She sat down at her basin and as always moved to touch the pile of dust. Instead, her hand fell upon the carved characters of a girl and a boy as they were meeting and falling in love. Suddenly, she could see that day clearly once again. It stood alone in her heart as if no days preceded or followed. Her brother had simply turned the table around, making her look at the happy instead of the sad. A joyous tear fell onto the tabletop and she laughed.

Asmund sat by the fire, sipping from a cup of watered wine. He was feeling more himself now. "There is simply no way I would be called for this quest."

"Why not? You are a wizard," replied Rangvald, who was standing nearby, looking into the fire.

"*Apprentice* wizard," corrected Asmund. "Apprentice wizard who failed at his chosen path. Actually, it wasn't even my chosen path. It was simply the only path that I had a ghost of a chance at succeeding in. I have no gift for seeing what may be, so that was out. I would never be strong enough to march into battle and call forth lightning or cast fireballs. So that left healer as my default option."

"You mastered healing magic with ease. You are speaking nonsense."

"Oh, yes, I can perform the spells. But one must take and bear the hurt themselves before dispelling it, and my body is so weak and feeble that I cannot take on any real hurt without losing consciousness. Instead of dispelling the hurt, I would get killed by it. There is no way you've forgotten that. That had to have ranked among the school's proudest moments – having an apprentice use the magic he was trained to use and fall almost dead to the ground. Had you or Gert not been there to save me, we wouldn't even be having this discussion."

"Do you think it uncommon for students of magic to be imperiled? You are overlooking that there are many lesser hurts that need healing as well."

"Oh yes, remember all the songs about the wizards who cured a toothache? No, that's right, no one cares about that. It doesn't matter. Only the wizards who are strong enough to mend broken bones and sword wounds are remembered."

"You are wrong, Asmund. The man whose tooth-ache you healed last week was sick with it. He was so distracted he could not work. His entire family owes you greatly for what you did. You have mastered spells to help crops grow and charms to keep items from being lost. These are helpful to people in their every-day lives. You obsess too much with what you think of as 'bigger magic.'"

"Yes, master. I concede that all you say is true. I help the farmers and the shopkeepers with all my small magics. But that makes my point, not yours. I cannot be the one who has been chosen for this quest – chosen to fight some great evil."

"That," said Rangvald, "is not for you to decide."

"I did not decide it! This did!" Asmund shouted, jerking his twisted right leg in front of him. "And this did!" he repeated, lifting his withered left arm. "All of this did!" He waved his right hand over himself, indicat-ing his whole frail form. Hot tears were running down his cheeks as he yelled.

Rangvald stood impassively, watching as the youth struggled to regain his composure. Once he finally succeeded, he asked calmly, "Are you finished?"

Asmund nodded his head, avoiding his master's eyes.

"Good," Rangvald continued. "You will leave at once for Kalbaek."

"You haven't heard a word I've said, have you?" Asmund exploded again. "I can't go! Send one of the other apprentices!"

"They were not chosen. You were."

"I don't care! I am not strong enough to do this!"

"You want songs to be sung about you. You want to accomplish deeds of note. But then when you are called, you say you will not go."

"Because I can't! You know the only reason I am at this school is because my family is the richest in the city. Einarshofn was built around the port, and the port was built around my family's trading business. I could not work or command workers, so I was put here and forgotten, along with their shame for me. I was happy to be put here. To learn that I had the spark, and that maybe I could be of some use after all was a great relief. But no, I can't even be a proper wizard. If I had been born to a poor family, they most likely would have seen such a twisted little infant and left it in the snow to die. If anyone thinks that my escaping that fate was a kindness, they would be mistaken."

Rangvald looked into the fire for a long moment. "Very well, I understand," he said. He returned to his desk and sat.

"You do?" asked Asmund, relieved.

"Yes, I do. I understand you. You, who have been given so many gifts, and who appreciates none of them. You, who believes no one else has ever suffered but you. You, who can perform so much magic, but who only cares about what magic you cannot do. Yes, I understand you. You have been summoned by the universe to go and learn all that you could be. But instead, you can go back to your parents' big house; they can keep you in enough beer and mead that you can forget the great injustices that have been done to you. Now here, take this and go." He finished writing on a small piece of parchment, which he rolled and tied with ribbon.

Asmund stood silently for a moment, then came

to the desk and received the scroll. "I..." he started, but the master wizard held up his hand for silence, just as he had done when Asmund had first come in.

"Take that back to your chambers and read it there. I am sorry life has been so unkind to you. Farewell."

Asmund left with no sound but the clack and shuffle of his walking. He could hear the movements of others who were now stirring about the school. He hurried through the empty halls, hoping with all his heart to make it back to his chamber without seeing anyone. He could not face his classmates and make idle conversation, or worse yet, have them notice that he had been crying and demand to know why. He let out a relieved breath as he reached his door.

He stood in his room, his back against the closed door, trying to shut out the rest of the world. He looked down at the scroll in his curled left hand. He was sure it was his official dismissal from the school. He winced at the memory of shouting at the master, pouring out a torrent of self-pity and earning himself a richly deserved expulsion.

He sighed. It would not help to put it off any longer. He unrolled the paper, and much to his surprise, it contained but three words. He read them in a whisper, just the way the children had spoken them.

Asmund, help us.

CHAPTER THREE

The craftsman opened his eyes and blinked at the cloudy gray sky that hung above him. There was a diffused light filtering through the clouds, letting him know it was daytime, but the sky was careful to reveal no clues as to what time of day it might be. He sat up and took in the rest of his surroundings.

Many of the trees were leaning over, uprooted entirely, or just broken and splintered high up their trunks. The great dust cloud he had observed in Idunn's waters was gone – or rather, it was no longer airborne, but now lay coating the ground and trees and stones all about him. That meant that some time had passed since the event he had witnessed, but not overly long, judging by the silence that still hung heavily in the forest. He listened, straining his keen ears to pick up one note of bird song, or even the scuttle of an insect across one fallen leaf, but there was nothing. It was as if the whole of the forest were holding its breath.

He rose and stretched himself like a barn cat. With one glance he could see that all the trees were toppled in the same direction, making it plain from which direction the force had come. His course so determined, he set off.

He came to a rise in the ground which afforded him a better view of the sky. He dipped into his purse and found his navigator's stone. The stone was not magic – or perhaps it was, but merely one of those natural magics built into the world, like a tree bark that, when chewed, eases pain, or the wind which can be harnessed to push a ship. He held it up, twitching it back and forth slightly as he gazed through it toward the clouds. The stone flashed the colors of the rainbow as it passed over the hidden timekeeper in the sky. It was still slung low on the eastern horizon. He considered what this new evidence might suggest. The vision of the falling rock had been at night – so this must then be the following morning. He stowed the crystal stone and descended the hill.

After walking for a time, he could sense that he was getting close to the thing he sought. He crossed a small meadow and arrived at a narrow brook. He stopped and listened to it babbling across the stones. It was nice to hear any sound in the stricken forest. A good-sized tree that had been thrown down provided a handy foot bridge. He traversed it nimbly. Alighting on the far side, he froze. The muddy bank upon which he now stood was crisscrossed with footprints. They were made by several distinct pairs of feet, which had clearly been coming here every day for some time. People lived nearby. He moved ahead cautiously. He could see plainly that he followed a foot trail, even though it was now strewn with fallen trunks and branches. He navigated around them as well as he could, taking care to avoid any dry leaves or sticks whose cracking might announce his presence.

As he moved along the path, he caught scent of

the ghosts of old cookfires and heard movement up ahead. He stayed low and crept forward until he could see more clearly. The scene he encountered was heartbreaking. It was what remained of a cluster of huts. The dwellings were all turned to rubble, as were the remnants of what had once been fenced-in garden plots. There had clearly been pens housing animals – these were decimated as well. He saw a few chickens and a goat still alive. Many more lay dead.

He turned his attention to the people. He counted seven – all women. One was noticeably older than the rest. Her long silver hair hung loose about her shoulders. She was wearing trousers and a tunic much like those typically worn by men. He saw her giving instructions to two women in their middle age. Both wore bandages, one on her upper arm and the other on the side of her neck.

The women nodded, then went to one of the ruined animal pens and began making efforts to restore it. Another woman was stirring a pot on the fire. Yet another limped over to the fire, bearing a basket of vegetables salvaged from a ruined garden. The last two were visible by the side of the fire, one applying a bandage to the other's hand. The wounded woman was obviously trying not to cry, but she was failing. Her quiet sobs floated to the craftsman's ears as he stood hidden among the broken trees.

Had all the men left the village and gone for help? No, that wasn't it. Was this even a village? He tried to visualize all the trees and huts still standing as they had been a day before. These people had built their dwellings and pens and plantings around the trees. The clearing had actually been a natural gap in the forest. The foot trail beside which he now hid led to the brook. There seemed to be no other paths leading to or from this place. No, it was not a village, he realized. It was a hideout – and these women were its only residents.

As he observed their plight, he did not realize that a sad frown had formed upon his face. These women were in need. Most of them were no longer young, and some were injured. They had lost nearly everything because a stone had fallen from the sky nearby. That was unfair. They did not even have their shelters, and the night was promising to be cold and wet. He wanted to stride out into the clearing and offer them his aid. But if he understood what he was seeing, his arrival would only bring them terror, not relief. He decided to test this theory.

He selected two dry sticks from the ground nearby. Then he did what he had been careful not to do earlier. He broke one in half deliberately, its crisp cracking sound shattering the stillness of the afflicted forest. Each of the women froze in place, as he had suspected they would. As they all stood holding their breaths, straining their ears to listen, he provided the very thing they were dreading most. He broke the second stick.

At the sound of it, he watched the silver-haired woman wave her hands frantically at the others, three of whom ran to a spot by one of the toppled huts where there appeared to be a collection of blankets, clothing, crockery, and tools – items they had managed to salvage from beneath the ruins of their homes. Two of the women stepped away from the pile bearing bows. As they nocked their arrows, their movements were practiced and sure. He knew that hunting must be a component of their survival here. The third woman brandished a small axe. Her movements were not as sure as her companions', but her face held fierce determination.

He had his answer; precisely the one he had expected. This was not a place you lived hoping for visitors. This was a place you lived when you feared them. He did not wish to cause them more pain on a day such as this. Besides, as Idunn had said, time was his enemy. He must claim the stone and complete his task. Much depended upon it.

Regretfully, he melted back into the forest without a sound. When he came to the brook, he followed it for a time before turning again into the damaged forest. Now he would pass by the hideaway unnoticed, beyond the sight or hearing of its residents. They would never know he had been there at all.

He traveled at a good pace in spite of the destruction. Here he hopped over a downed tree and there he ducked beneath another. He proceeded in this fashion for some time, until finally he rounded a hillock, and there he stopped, for the direction of the fallen trees had changed. They now fell sideways to the left. He changed course and began making his way toward his prize.

After a short walk, he knew he must now be very close indeed, as the devastation had become more complete. He continued to walk until there was no vegetation to speak of. It had all been stripped away. A bit further and the very ground was scorched and blackened. Just ahead of him he saw what appeared to be a strange hill rising from the ground. Its sides were adorned here and there by strange glass jewels, the result of intense fire touching bits of sand.

Scanning the wasteland about himself, he saw two other holes where pieces of rock had struck, but he knew that the heart of it would lie in this hill. He climbed up the side and peered down. There below him lay the rock. He shook his head. This was it, this was the thing he so desperately needed. The thing that had fallen from the sky and stricken the earth with the force of... of a... Comparisons failed here. He did not think anything else could ever strike with such devastating force. He climbed down into the crater and stood next to the rock. He touched it tentatively. He had seen it burning as it descended and half expected it to still be hot to the touch. But it was cool. It also did not hum with the magic of the gods. It was just an ordinary rock, except that it also contained metal, and it was flecked throughout with beautiful deposits of some color which seemed to shift and change as he looked at it.

The craftsman reached into his purse and took out the apple his sister had given him. He stretched out upon the ground and wrapped his arm around the rock. As instructed, he bent his thoughts toward the Great Hall. He brought the apple to his lips and then... he lowered it again. He squeezed his eyes tightly closed, focused intently on conjuring a mental image of the Great Hall. He tightened his grip on the rock and lifted the apple to his lips once more. But try as he might to see the Great Hall, another place insistently occupied his mind's eye. He stood up and put the apple back in his purse. He lifted the heavy rock in both arms, holding it against his chest. He struggled up and over the crest of the crater with his burden and trudged back through

the forest

Asmund stepped into the courtyard, ready for his quest. He was greeted by the master, the house mother, and his three classmates. A cart hitched to a small brown pony stood at the ready.

The house mother wrapped her arms around him and hugged him so tightly, he half feared she would crush him. "I have packed you food and blankets in the cart," she said, finally releasing him. "Remember me and all that I have told you. Being different brings you strength, not weakness."

"I remember," he said. He felt as though he missed her already.

People from everywhere could be seen in the big port city. He had grown up seeing the Bulgars with hair like black silk, or Arabs in their long robes. But only rarely did one see women like Aida, southwomen with deep brown skin and hair almost like black sheep's wool. Long ago, she had fallen in love with a northman trader, and when his ship had left, she was on it at his side. Once her own children were grown, she had come to the school and acted as a mother to the students who lived there. For Asmund, she had been more of a mother than his own had ever been. She had taught him a great deal about life. He felt sadness welling up at the thought of leaving, and he hugged her again.

He stepped up to tiny Ama and she hugged him. She was the youngest student here at only twelve winters, but her spark was the strongest. So strong were her magic abilities that they had begun to manifest from early childhood; and children knowing nothing of guile or discretion, she used her burgeoning gifts unfettered. Everyone in her village, her family included, had been afraid of her, and she knew that they had been happy when she came to live at the school. "I have read what could be seen," she said. "Success dances on a sword's edge. Your wits and courage will decide the outcome. Look for your salvation under golden hair."

"Thank you, I think," he replied uncertainly.

Gert was next. She was a big, strongly-built young woman, a couple of years older than Asmund. She never smiled or shared in their youthful jests. She worked hard at her studies, which seemed not to come easy to her. But once she learned a magic, she commanded it with precision and authority. He knew nothing of her life before the school, as she never discussed herself with her fellow students. She handed him a small metal flask.

"Is this what I think it is?" he asked in surprise.

"It is a healing potion. It will not do much. But when life and death hang in the balance, it could make the difference."

He was shocked and deeply touched. A potion such as this was born as a product of her personal suffering. The magic that was captured in this process was far less than that which was expended. That was why you rarely saw them. The healing they could produce was hardly worth the making. But on the chance that it might help him, she had endured the pain and produced it nonetheless.

He was speechless. Of his three classmates, he had always had the least in common with her. He did not even think she cared for him. Almost as if she could read his thoughts, she said, "You know, I've never really liked you. I came from such poverty, and you... Well, when the master said that you were going on this quest, he said he told you that no one would think less of you if you would not go. He told us how you told him that you must use your gifts to help others, not sit and cry only for yourself."

Asmund looked down at his feet and said, "That might not be exactly what I said... word for word."

"Well, whatever words you used, it does not matter. What does is that it made me feel ashamed of myself, made me realize that there was much that I needed to just let go of and move forward."

"Well, I am very grateful to you," he said, putting the flask in his purse. "I will try my best not to let you down."

She shook her head earnestly. "You could not. Your bravery inspires us," she said, beginning to turn away. Then she turned back and quickly hugged him.

The last of his three classmates, the stout and sturdy Thorfinn, embraced him then. Thorfinn was brave and bold. Had he not been born with the spark, he would have been a warrior. More than anyone Asmund had ever met, Thorfinn embodied the type of carefree, open confidence that was so alien to himself. Asmund suspected that he might have harbored a deep and bitter envy were it not overpowered by Thorfinn's warm, openhearted affection for him. "I'm the one training for battle magic. I won't lie, I wish it were me instead of you going on this quest."

"I won't lie. I also wish it were you and not me," agreed Asmund with a laugh.

"I have something for you as well," Thorfinn said. "Let me see your staff." Asmund handed it over, and

Thorfinn drove a plain-looking nail into its end with a small hammer, speaking a simple incantation between each of the three blows required to complete the task. He left the square head of the nail protruding just a little. "I know you keep the spell for flame," he said.

"Yes, but I can only make a candle flame ignite from my hand. I cannot throw a fireball like you can."

"Take out your book and read the spell, but here," he said, handing him a scrap of parchment, "add this word to the end and direct your staff out into the open courtyard."

Asmund did as directed. He could guess what he was to expect, but he was doubtful. He held out his staff and said the spell with the added word. In spite of his doubts, a fireball the size of a good cabbage leaped from the nail head and shot a short way across the courtyard. He spun back to face the group. Everyone was smiling. Everyone save Thorfinn, who said, "I apologize, Asmund, I thought it would be bigger and fly farther."

"Nonsense," Asmund said with a smile. "With a nail and a word, you have turned me from someone who could scarcely conjure the flicker of a candle on one finger to someone who has the means of defending himself. I am eternally grateful." Thorfinn brightened at this and clapped Asmund on the shoulder.

At last he came to Rangvald, who was holding a basket under his arm, and said quietly, "Master, I really must apologize for my-"

Rangvald raised his hand for silence and shook his head. "Place your staff and satchel in the cart, Asmund. I have prepared a new robe for you. I have placed a charm upon it, but I do not want you to be deceived. If the charm were placed on armor, it would be of great value indeed. But placing it on cloth is not ideal. If a blade or an arrow does not hit true and square, this will tend to make it glance. But if the weapon strikes true, the best it will do is make it go a little less deep. It may save you, but I beg that you do not count on it. As for bumps and tumbles, brambles and thorns, even fists and fire, it will ward them as best it can. Now turn around and strip off the old, so I can put on the new." Asmund did as he was told and Rangvald slipped the charmed robe over his head.

Asmund looked down, running his hand across the gray fabric. "Gray?" He turned to look at Rangvald. "There must have been a mistake!"

"No mistake, Wizard Asmund."

"I'm no wizard. I'm the worst apprentice here! I can't be a wizard. I can only keep a handful of spells in my mind at once. Look at my spell book; I've only mastered a small amount of magic. It will be years yet until anyone can call me wizard."

"Well, once again, it is not for you to decide. You are a wizard. Now go out there and learn that for yourself," Rangvald said, laying a fatherly hand on his shoulder.

Asmund nodded once, not trusting himself to speak. He affixed his gear over his new gray robes, embraced Aida one last time, and then struggled up to the seat of the cart. He looked forward at the gate, and once again, he was at the bottom of a well, feeling the walls closing in. Could he do it? Could he really ride out alone for the first time in his life? He looked over at his classmates and was struck by the look on Gert's face. She looked at him as if she saw a hero riding into battle. He smiled at them and took hold of the reins. "Farewell," he called.

"Wait!" said Rangvald, looking pleased. "One more thing." He turned and called out, "Captain Sten." A moment later, the old soldier appeared in the doorway of the guardhouse.

"Yes, Master Rangvald," the captain called back.

"You have done as I have asked?"

"Yes, My Lord, he stands by at your command."

"Have him ride forth."

The old captain whistled. A tall black horse walked out from the stables. Its rider was a big, broad-shouldered warrior with long golden braids emanating from under his helmet. He wore sword and armor, and shield and axe were slung from his saddle.

"You've selected your bravest man, as I instructed?" asked the master.

"Yes, My Lord. This is Brandt the Bloody. He has steel in his eye and gravel in his belly. He has gone viking many times and fought in more lands than most men know exist."

"Very good, Captain. He is to go on a glorious quest with the wizard Asmund. He must swear to defend him with his life."

"I swear by all the gods. I will defend the wizard to my last drop of blood!" Brandt boomed like mighty Thor himself.

Rangvald watched Asmund's face while the oath was spoken, seeming to enjoy the look of profound relief he saw there. "Farewell! Luck in your quest!" he called. He watched as they passed through the gates and turned left onto the main road. He was still smiling as they disappeared from view.

◆ ◆ ◆

The craftsman did not make a sound while he waited for the right moment. It came as the stew was dished out and the women sat around the fire together and began to eat. Seizing his opportunity, he silently stepped over to stand in front of the pile of salvaged items, where the bows and axe were once again lying. He considered what to say. After a few moments, he dropped the rock to the ground with a loud thud, and said, "This is what caused all this."

The women jumped to their feet instantly, some of them crying out in fear. One took a step in his direction, her hand already reaching out for her bow. She stopped, realizing that the way was blocked. He saw the group preparing to scatter and run. "Wait!" he said. "Do not flee! I mean you no harm." He saw at once that his words were futile. He had terrified them, just as he had known he would.

To his surprise, the elder woman with the long silver hair held up her hands and called out, "No, my sisters, have no fear! Do not run! He will not harm you!" One by one the women stopped in their flight and turned confused faces toward her. "He is not one of them. He is not of this place.".

The woman who had tried for her bow scrutinized his appearance. Then, nodding in agreement, she said, "He is dressed as a northman and he is very short."

The elder woman said, "Yes, child, he is from the north, but he is no man, and he is short because he is a dwarf."

This did nothing to allay their confusion. "There are no such things as dwarfs," a woman who was cowering behind the silver haired woman said earnestly. She added, "Come away from him before he hurts you,

Cwenhild."

"No, he does not wish to hurt us," answered Cwenhild. "He wears a sword and moves in silence. If he wished to do us harm, he would have done it already."

"Is he really a dwarf, like in the old children's stories?" the one with the bandaged neck asked the old woman.

"Yes, child. Everyone, stop your crying. This is a great honor. Last night the sky caught fire, the earth shook; and today a Vaettir visits us. This was once the way of things long, long ago. I did not think to see such days again." She stepped forward and bowed deeply. "I am Lagertha, once a shield maiden to King Ragnar. We welcome you."

He returned her bow and said, "I am the last son of Ivaldi, called Asger of the Great Hall. I accept your welcome."

"Come, sisters, make a place for him by the fire and give him stew," Lagertha said.

The craftsman took a place in the circle by the fire. Cwenhild brought him a bowl of stew. "Thank you. Sit everyone, eat, you need your strength," he said.

"Sit. Eat," the old woman echoed, waving the women back to the fire.

They were slow to comply. He could tell they did not wish to. They were clearly afraid, but they were also hungry. Lagertha and Cwenhild sat close to him on either side, and they took note that he had not yet devoured either one of them. So one by one, they drifted back to the fire and resumed their interrupted meal.

Once everyone was seated and eating, Lagertha spoke again. "Let me introduce everyone. Our bravest protector who sits to your other side is Cwenhild. Next to her with the bandage on her neck is Eawynn. The one you see there with the injured arm is Mildritha. These are Sigeburg and Tate, who made the lovely stew we are enjoying. Lastly, the young one with the bandaged hand is Sweterun."

"I am glad to know you all, and I thank you for your hospitality," he said.

"Did you say that small boulder caused all this?" asked Cwenhild, talking around a chunk of carrot.

"Yes, it was much larger, but it cracked into pieces," explained the craftsman.

"Was it sent by God as a punishment for our sins?" Sweterun asked miserably.

"No. Why do you ask that? Do you believe that you have angered one of the gods?" asked the craftsman. "Is that why you hide here in the forest?"

The women did not answer. They just ate their stew sullenly. The craftsman looked to Lagertha, the silver-haired woman, and tilted his head, silently asking her to explain.

"There is only one god in these lands," she answered, "and yes, he is very angry."

Cwenhild turned to the dwarf and said, "Lagertha tells us that in the lands to the north where she was born, people can live as they please. She says a woman can run a business, buy property, be a warrior..." She paused and then added, "and love who they want. Is this so?"

"Of course it is. Is it not so here?" he asked. In answer the women were silent again. "So you do hide here from an angry god," the craftsman said, beginning to understand.

Cwenhild swallowed another bite of stew and

asked, "What is the boulder really? Why did it come?"

"It is the world stone," the craftsman answered. "Another such thing lies at the center of the earth. A thousand dwarfs working for a thousand years could never dig to it – so the great beyond has sent this one to me, that I may make what must be made. An ancient evil has risen from its tomb and is tearing babies from their beds at night. I need this to stop him. It is merely bad luck that it toppled your houses and left you injured. Which leads me to why I have come to you."

"Yes, My Lord, tell us why you've come. Whatever we can do for you, you have only to ask," said Lagertha sincerely.

"You can let me help you," said the craftsman, holding up his hand to forestall protest. "I know you will tell me you need no help, and I know you would manage. But you have been struck by misfortune. This rock has left you hurt and without shelter. I am a dwarfen craftsman of the Great Hall. I can build in a day what would take an army of workers a week."

Lagertha could not speak. Cwenhild did so for her. "You humble us, My Lord. We are grateful. But we cannot keep you from your quest to save those children."

"Many depend upon me – and yes, time is short. But what must be made cannot be built on suffering that I could relieve. I will work quickly and leave you a good, strong shelter. And just think, I will work faster since all the timbers have been chopped already." He smiled and then stood. He tilted the bowl to his lips three times and his stew was devoured. Food and fellowship was done, it was time for work.

◆ ◆ ◆

Cwenhild had not been very injured when the hut had collapsed the night before. She had only been slightly bruised by the falling ceiling. So she swore that she would help the craftsman every step of the way. He started by asking her to lay out every tool they owned. He said the tools would inform what could be built. Once she had completed this task, he looked the tools over quickly and said, "Now to gather timbers."

Cwenhild was strongly built with square set shoulders and lean, muscular arms and legs. "I am strong – I can help you carry." she told him.

"Very good. We will need all of these,' he replied, waving his hand to indicate a big stand of broken trees.

She lifted the nearest one and began dragging it. The craftsman passed her again and again, easily dragging trees that a team of oxen would not have been able to shift. She found she could not stop laughing at this. Her heart was full of the joy of working side-by-side with a dwarf. She could see up ahead that he had selected a new spot not far from the old one. It was nestled between some trees and brush that were still standing and would shield the new structure from view. She dragged her log the last few feet and dropped it next to one of the piles of trees he had brought. "Come on, master dwarf, do at least try to keep up with me."

He stopped and looked at her, then threw his head back and burst out with deep, booming laughter. She joined his with her own. He stopped abruptly and said. "Oh, dear. I had not figured in laughter. Now we are thirty seconds behind schedule. Quick! Fetch the small axe and the spade."

She was still laughing, but she ran and grabbed the tools. When she returned he had set out four long logs into the shape of a square. He took the spade and dug the earth out from the inside, piling it against the outside of the square, sloping it down and away from the logs. With the small axe, he sharpened the ends of some smaller logs. He worked with astounding speed and precision. "Please go and build up the cook fire. Get it nice and high," he said.

She had just finished stoking it to a fine blaze when he arrived, bearing the sharpened logs. They were all cut to length and shaved of bark. He set the points into the flames, turning them around and around. When the first ones were done, he instructed her to continue blackening the remaining points. He began taking away the finished stakes and bringing new ones for her to complete. Finally, he dropped off a few more and declared, "This is the last of them." When she had finished blackening the stakes, she hurried back to the craftsman with them. As soon as she arrived he took them and drove them into the ground, just as he had been doing with the others.

Once again taking up the small axe, he shaped the ends of yet more logs into squared pegs. He worked quickly, completing several at once. He took up several others and cut matching slots. Cwenhild was familiar with how building worked. *This is all wrong,* she thought. She knew each joint would be slightly unique – each would need to be custom fitted to its partner, especially cutting them with a hand axe like this. Also, she had not seen him lay anything out or use a rod or a rope to measure. There was no way the joints would fit. No way each log would reach where it needed to reach. It would be at least a bit off in a hundred different places, and that would mean nothing would fit together in the end.

Then, as she watched, the shell became a finished house in mere minutes. The dwarf tapped each joint firmly together. Every groove mated with its partner – everything tight, everything precise. The next moment, he was working with the hand axe to carve logs into planks and boring holes into them. He rapidly whittled points onto sticks and hacked them to length. She watched, feeling almost lightheaded as he, once again without having laid anything out or measured anything, pegged the boards together and lifted up a flawless door. He repeated the process in miniature, making two contraptions that turned out to be windows. He set their wooden loops onto their matching pegs in the frames and opened and closed them. Again, all was impossibly tight and precise. Each of these features could be barred from inside for security.

The craftsman stepped back and grunted what might have been approval. Standing before them was a strong wooden home. It was larger than all the previous huts put together had been. "Cwenhild, if you will help the others bring their belongings in here and make their beds, this will keep them safe and dry tonight."

"Will you rest now, My Lord?" she asked him.

"No, there are some hours of daylight yet and more to be built."

Cwenhild went back to the group and called out, "Come, sisters, help me carry our things to the new house."

"Is there really a new shelter built for the night already?" Sweterun asked hopefully.

"There is a little something that might suffice. It may at least keep the weather off of us." Cwenhild replied with a grin.

The group came through the trees and stood speechless before the newly built house. Cwenhild laughed delightedly at their reaction.

The craftsman emerged from the woods to their left, dragging a giant uprooted tree. He dropped it next to the other ones he had gathered and looked at the wide-eyed women. "Hurry, my sisters," he called. "Move your things into the house, for it promises to rain soon."

The women worked quickly to move into the new house. Cwenhild transferred the cooking gear and fire inside. The fireplace was in the center of the large room and they built their beds around it so they would stay warm through the night. A few drops of rain made their way down through the chimney above and sizzled as they hit the fire. "Oh, Lagertha. I meant to be by his side for as long as he worked." Cwenhild repined.

"It is all right, child. You helped him well."

"Will he come in now that it is raining?" Cwenhild asked, listening to another drip as it sizzled in the fire.

"I do not think he will," answered Lagertha.

She was right. The craftsman worked all through the night.

As dawn broke, the craftsman set aside his tools and rested. The rain had long since subsided, and his clothes were dry.

The women awoke to the smell of roasting meat and emerged from the house. Nestled among the trees in the misty morning were seven A-framed cottages, and off to one side they saw the dwarf lounging in a new kitchen area. It consisted of a pitched roof which protected a fire pit, a worktable, and a massive log carved out into a water cistern. Smaller logs had been carved into buckets for bringing water from the brook. He was roasting one of the goats that had died when the rock fell. He had buried the others. The surviving animals were in their repaired pens nearby.

He felt satisfied that he had done what he could in the time he had. The women wandered around speechless, taking it all in. Lagertha approached the dwarf and, falling to a knee, she bowed deeply, her long silver hair reflecting the early morning sunlight. "We do not deserve this, My Lord!"

The craftsman took her by the hand and rose her to her feet. "No, I think this life has given you much you did not deserve, but this is not among them. A kindness was long overdue."

They passed the morning joyously, eating, talking, and singing, their injuries almost forgotten. Their cares were but distant memories.

After breakfast the women explored the cottages, deciding who would live where. Lagertha and the craftsman walked together, watching and enjoying everyone's excitement. "You built too many houses, My Lord. We needed only four."

"Perhaps," said the dwarf. "But you have good and generous hearts – if others need sanctuary, I wanted you to have room to grow."

They walked back to the gap where the ruins of the old houses still remained, and he picked up the rock.

"So you must be on your way," she said sadly.

"Yes. I must make my farewells and go. There is much yet for me to do."

"I wish there were some way to repay you."

"There is. This rock is my payment," he said.

"Nonsense. The rock is yours. You could have taken it and gone without helping us. I wish I had something precious to give you," she said.

"But I need nothing. Knowing that you are warm and dry through the night is all I need."

"You do not understand," she said. "I know I could never have something you needed. I just mean I wish I had something so precious to me, that the sacrifice of it would say what I wished to say."

He opened his mouth to make reply, but a scream from ahead silenced him. Neither one of them hesitated; they at once broke into a run. When they reached the spot where the new houses stood, they stopped and crouched, hiding behind some brush and a tree that was still standing, and peered out at the scene taking place.

Cwenhild lay in the dirt with a bloodied lip. The other five women were crying and cowering. Four soldiers surrounded them. A fifth soldier emerged from the big house followed by a fat, bald man in a brown robe.

The craftsman suddenly felt very stupid. The fire falling from the sky would have been clearly visible from the city of Jorvic. This was how long it would have taken for them to journey here from there. Of course they would search this area, because all the fallen trees would have told them that whatever had fallen would be close by.

The bald man and the soldier had finished their search of the cottages. They stormed over to the frightened women. "Where are they?" demanded the fat man.

"Who?" asked Mildritha.

"Do not play dumb, woman! The others!"

The craftsman's eyebrows rose in surprise. Did the man know about him and Lagertha? Had someone spied on them and counted their number, perhaps as they breakfasted? He felt stupid again. They had let their guard down in their celebrations.

"I know there are more of you. There must be men. All of these houses have been freshly built. Where are they?"

"There is no one else. Just us," Eawynn said.

He stepped forward without a word and punched her squarely in the nose. She fell on her back, blood rushing down her face. "You think you can lie to a man of God, you bitch? There must be men living here!"

"I do not believe there are, Father Cuthbert," said the soldier who had been searching with him.

"What do you mean, Captain?" snapped the fat man, spinning around. "Do you mean to tell me these women built this themselves?"

The captain was looking at the women with thought creasing his brow. "Perhaps, Your Grace. I recognize one of these women. The one you struck was a midwife accused of some... well, crimes, shall we say. I think some of these others must have been her associates. She was rumored to have fled the city and gone into hiding before I could arrest her."

"Crimes? Father Cuthbert echoed. "What crimes? Robbery, blasphemy, murder? Speak plainly, man!"

The captain appeared to grow self-conscious, glancing around himself as if afraid someone would hear his thoughts. Then he leaned over and whispered in the priest's ear.

A look of shock played across the fat man's face. He traced a cross on the front of his brown robes and hissed, "Sodomites!" He reeled back around to face the frightened women. "Is that it? And what, do you try to take on the mantle of your masters yourselves? Doing your own hunting and carpentry, pretending to be your betters? Testify! How do you answer for your sins?"

"We do not answer to you," Cwenhild slurred from her broken lips as she sat up in the dirt. Without warning, a soldier kicked her in the side of the head, driving her back down.

Father Cuthbert gave the soldier a nod of approval, then, looking at the other women, continued. "Does anyone else have anything to say? Come now, it is not too late to repent: confess your sins and beg for mercy."

"If we do, you will leave us in peace?" Sweterun asked with a touch of hope creeping into her voice.

The man's face twisted in disgust. "That just goes to show how degenerate you truly are," he spat. "I offer you a chance to confess, in the hopes of saving your souls, and instead you seek to trade lies for undeserved salvation. This is your last chance, fall to your knees and beg His forgiveness!"

The women understood their situation completely now. They clung to each other, crying, but not one spoke.

"Very well then, I pass your sentence. You will be burned in this place as the abominations you are, that you may taste of the eternal hellfire of damnation that awaits you! Now, Captain, have your men carry out the sentence."

The captain stepped forward, saying, "Alwin, take charge. Bind them to the timbers of this house. We will burn it and them with it."

"Yes, Captain," replied a skinny soldier with a pitted, weaselly face. "Someone find some rope." The other three soldiers glanced around, shrugging their shoulders.

"Just tear their clothing and use it to bind them," said the captain.

"Very good, sir. You heard him, men. Carry on," Alwin ordered. The men herded the women toward the new house, tearing at their clothing with excited zeal and leering at the pale flesh it revealed.

Behind the bushes, the craftsman moved to draw his sword and stand. Lagertha placed her hand on his shoulder. She whispered into his ear and he nodded. She stepped through the bushes and into the open. In a loud voice she commanded, "Leave this place at once – this is your only warning." All eyes turned and focused on her. She stood defiantly, her fists planted on her hips.

The fat man looked at her in shock for a moment, and then he exclaimed, "There! Look how proudly she stands, wearing the clothes of a man! Pretending to be more than she is!" His eyes lit upon the silver hammer pendant that hung from a cord around her neck. "Aha!" he exclaimed. "And there it is! She does not know her place because she is a pagan! She is a follower of false gods!"

"Yours is the false god."

Father Cuthbert shook with rage, his face turning red. "How dare you?" he demanded, flecks of spittle coating his thick lips.

"Very good! Then it shall be a test," she proclaimed.

"What?"

"You say my gods are false, and I say yours is. So we shall put it to a test. We shall both call upon our gods. The true ones will come down and answer us, or they will send us their messengers to ask what we wish of them."

The fat man laughed. "Oh, I see, you wish to distract and delay us from doing the *true* God's will. Enough of these foolish games!"

"So you do not call on your god then?" she asked. "What's the matter? Afraid he is not there?"

"There is no need for such a test," sneered the man. "He has already sent His messengers to do His will. It is us. We will teach you to know His power and not mock Him with your willful sin. Now it is time for you to die!" He drew a small knife from his belt and stepped toward her. "I shall send you to Him myself, pagan."

"Then you are admitting defeat?"

"What?" he said again, stopping in his tracks.

"The test is not complete. I have not called upon my gods to send a more powerful messenger."

"Oh, of course," he chortled. "By all means, ask your false gods to send you a champion who can slay five warriors and a holy man. I'm sure they will not hesitate."

"Thank you. I will do just that." She raised her hands up to the sky and called out, "Oh Freya, oh Odin. True and powerful gods – I call on you to hear me from upon your thrones and defend us now from the servants of the false god."

"Well, we're waiting," said the man, looking back over his shoulder and sharing a greasy smile with the soldiers. He looked back toward her just as the craftsman hurtled down from the sky and landed in front of her.

The craftsman bowed to her and said, "Lagertha, shield maiden to the king. I am Asger, the spear of Odin, dwarf of the Great Hall. How can I be of service?"

The little man stood frozen. Nothing moved except for the stream of urine running down the inside of his leg.

Lagertha spoke loudly for all to hear. "My Lord, mighty dwarf of the gods, drive these men from this place and order them to never return."

The craftsman turned and faced the men, saying, "You have heard her words; you are not wanted here. I command you to leave this place and never return."

The fat man with the soggy robes stumbled backwards, desperate to be gone. Then the captain stepped forward. "Wait! We aren't going anywhere."

The holy man turned to him and began to babble incoherently in protest.

The captain ignored him. "There are no dwarfs! Just inferior-blooded runts born too small for honest work. They take up as performers and acrobats and play little tricks. Sometimes they will even climb a tree. Trees like that one there, for instance," he said, pointing to the nearby trunk. "The one our little acrobat jumped from. We will be going nowhere."

"A person's worth has nothing to do with what size they are born, and only a fool would think that performing is not honest work," said the craftsman. "However, you are mistaken. I am a dwarf. You have been given the opportunity to leave in peace. If you do not, there will be bloodshed. Now go."

"Oh yes, there will be bloodshed," said the captain. "Now that you are here, there will be a little more." He paused, then added mockingly, "But just a *little* more. Kill him!" His men advanced, swords in hand.

The craftsman drew his own sword and ran to meet them. The four soldiers stood shoulder to shoulder. When the ones on the right or left of the line tried to spread out and flank him, he would attack them fiercely and force them back into line. Otherwise, he was passive. He parried their attacks and gave ground. This made the soldiers grow bolder. As he retreated, they advanced, attacking confidently.

At last they gave him what he had been waiting for: three of the sword blades followed the same arc, attacking him in unison. He launched a beating parry and with his dwarfen strength, the blades were knocked aside and the soldiers thrown off balance.

The craftsman launched himself past the soldier on the right flank and delivered a backhanded slash. A moment later, the soldier's head completed its flight, plunking down into the newly carved cistern in the kitchen across the gap. It had already bobbed up to the surface of the water when the soldier's body fell to its knees and then crumpled forward. The other three soldiers regained their balance and spun to face the craftsman. He gave them a moment to see their comrade and to understand.

Things had suddenly changed. They had rushed forward to slaughter what the captain had said was a man born too weak and small for honest work, but now one of their number lay dead at their feet. A sickly fear showed on their faces.

The craftsman charged, swinging his sword in a

large arc that threatened them all at once. All three clamored back, batting away at his blade defensively. This was just as he had expected. These were no northmen. These ones only fought with certainty when they were assured of an easy victory. Now that they knew they could die, their spirits were broken. He tested the one on the left, jabbing the point of his sword toward him, not really an attack – just a question in steel. The soldier's answer was to squeak and shrink back. He did not even offer a halfhearted parry. The craftsman lunged then with a full attack and emptied his guts onto the dirt.

The tinkle of a mail shirt and a clash of steel sounded behind the craftsman. He swept sideways, turning to see what was there. Standing behind him was the captain. His sword had been on its way toward the dwarfs back, but it had been stopped mid-swing by the sword of the first soldier that the craftsman had killed. The sword that Lagertha had picked up as soon as it had dropped.

The captain's face was a mask of confusion. When Lagertha had blocked his blow, it had taken everything she had. She knew that the strength for battle no longer lived in her. Flowers of pain bloomed in all of her joints. Her hands felt weak. When this moment of surprise had passed he would knock the sword from her hands and kill her with ease. But at least she had saved the dwarf, and he would save her sisters.

Wait, she thought to herself. *Why wait for the moment of surprise to be gone?* She removed her right hand from the hilt of the sword and reached up into his surprised face, thrusting her thumb into his eye socket with every ounce of force she could muster. His howl of pain echoed through the forest. He fell to the ground and tried to scoot away, holding his ruined eye with one hand, while pointing his sword toward her to keep her at bay.

She knew she must press the advantage. If he was still defending himself, he was still dangerous. He would shake this off and rise more enraged than ever. She advanced, staying out of the reach of his sword, and slashed downward, severing the toes of his left foot. He howled again and dropped his sword, reaching for the bloody ruin that had been his foot. He never got that far. She thrust the sword into his face, killing him instantly. She fell to her hands and knees beside him, her heart nearly bursting in her chest. The clash and ring of steel told her that the dwarf was still fighting the remaining soldiers. She sat back on her haunches and watched.

The craftsman launched a slashing blow straight down at the head of one of the soldiers. He held his sword up squarely to ward the blow instead of creating an angle to make it glance. So the dwarf swung the same attack again, this time with force. It broke through the guard easily and clove the soldiers head in two. The final soldier turned to glance at his comrade as he was falling. The craftsman saw the brief moment of distraction. Using it, he swung with blinding speed and took his head.

The craftsman walked over and helped Lagertha to her feet. She reached down and pulled, dislodging her sword from the captain's face.

"That's it! No one move!" cried the holy man.

They turned and saw him, red-faced, crying, snot dribbling from his nose. He was holding Sweterun by the back of her hair and pointing his belt knife to her throat. "I'm leaving here and no one can stop me! You two, drop your swords or I will kill her! I'm leaving!"

Lagertha stepped forward and pointed her sword at him. "No! You had your chance to leave. You had your chance to do what was right, but you would not. Now you can go roast with your god." Then she nodded her head as a signal.

He gasped and dropped the knife. Sweterun broke away, crying. As the priest spun around, they saw the arrow protruding from his back. He faced Cwenhild, who once again slurred through bloodied lips, "We do not answer to you," and put an arrow through his heart.

The craftsman hung the spade back on its peg and brushed the dirt from his hands. There now remained no trace of their unwelcome visitors in the hideaway. It was late afternoon, and time weighed heavily upon him.

He exited the house, and the women were gathered there waiting for him. Each of them wore a sad face. "I shall carry your strength with me always," he said.

To his surprise, the timid Sweterun came forward and hugged him. "We are not strong. We are weak. We need you to protect us."

"You are stronger than you know," he told her.

"Never let anyone convince you otherwise."

Cwenhild smiled at him through her bruised face and hugged him tightly. He whispered to her. "Keep your bow close, and watch over them."

Lagertha was the only one who was absent. He turned looking for her and saw her emerge from one of the cottages and stride towards them. She wore her sword belted on her hip, and he imagined that she would continue to do so from now on. He heard the women around him gasp collectively – then he saw why. She knelt before him and tied the long silver braid to his sword belt. "It's not that you have need of it. Its that it is precious to me, and I sacrifice it. Besides, who knows, maybe it will carry a touch of the wisdom of old women." She stood back, and the sun glinted off her short silver hair.

They all hugged him once again and he settled down on the ground, holding the rock that had fallen from the sky. He could see his home, the Great Hall, clearly now. He took a bite of the apple and was gone.

Brandt the Bloody rode ahead on his huge black charger, and Asmund followed behind – sometimes very far behind. Well, maybe that was not so strange. The warhorse did have a very long gait and Asmund's little pony had to pull his cart over the bumpy dirt road.

Asmund had been relieved when he had learned he would have a warrior as an escort. A huge warrior who had sworn an oath to protect him with his very life. When they had first set out, he had remembered Ama's words; she had read the signs and saw that his savior would have golden hair. Now he kept looking at mighty Brandt's golden braids, and they made him feel much more confident.

He looked ahead, hoping for another glimpse of the braids, but when he tried to spot Brandt, he found that he had lost sight of him yet again. That had been happening more and more. He still felt confident, but he had to admit he would feel more so if Brandt would actually stay with him. A thought occurred to him. He wondered how long it would take the warrior to notice and to come back and find him if he simply stopped the cart on the side of the road. He knew he was being silly. This was a safe part of the road. They were still only a few hours out from the city; he did not need to have his hand held just riding down a public road. Still, if Brandt did not keep with him when they traveled in the wilder lands, he would have to have a word with him.

Asmund rounded a bend in the road and saw Brandt in the distance. He felt relieved at the sight of him and hurried the pony, trying to catch up. They traveled thus for another hour, passing one or two other travelers along the way. At last, Asmund glimpsed Brandt sitting at the top of a distant hill. He appeared to be waiting for him. When at last he reached him, Brandt said, "There is a town in the valley below. We will stop there to take food and drink."

"This first town is too soon for stopping," said Asmund. "We have food and drink aplenty here in the cart. We can travel a couple more hours before we stop." Brandt said nothing and the bored look on his stony face did not change. He turned his horse and continued down the hill. Asmund flicked the reins and followed after.

Why did he not reply? He could have said something. Actually, the oath he had spoken in the courtyard and his suggestion of stopping for food and drink were the only words Asmund had so far heard him utter. He was beginning to think they were going to have a long, quiet journey together. He watched as the little dot that was Brandt disappeared around another bend in the road. *That is, if you could call this together,* he amended mentally.

A short time later, Asmund could see the outskirts of the town ahead. He passed a train of wagons laden with timbers going on their way toward Einarshofn.

He could see no sign of Brandt as he entered the town. The main road was lined on both sides with businesses of every type. People were everywhere, going about their busy days. No one paid him any special attention as he passed by. He was just one more busy person with somewhere to be. He felt lighthearted. For all of his fears about coming out on this quest, he thought it was not going badly at all. He had studied the map Master Rangvald had given him, and at this rate, if luck held out, they could reach the village of Kalbaek in a week. Maybe he would learn that the village was plagued by a rash of toothaches or sluggish crops, and he would return a hero.

Stop daydreaming, Asmund, he told himself. *No time for that now.* He had to hurry through the town and catch up with Brandt, or at least catch a site of him and his black horse. His distinctive black horse. Just like the one standing ahead on the left side of the road. The one tied next to three other horses in front of the tavern. The one with Brandt's shield and axe slung from the saddle.

"Gods curse it!" he swore, stopping his cart behind Brandt's horse. So much for making a couple more hours before stopping for food and drink. Who was in charge of this quest, anyway? "It's my quest, not his, after all!" he spat, and then paused.

That is true, he thought. *I was chosen for this quest. I agreed to do this before I knew there would be a brave warrior to protect me. I can't fail to do what I was called to do simply because Brandt isn't protecting me every step of the way. Could this be a test of my resolve planned by Master Rangvald? No. I don't believe so. But that does not mean it isn't a test, and I mean to pass it. I must continue alone.*

He picked up the reins, ready to proceed. Ahead, he saw a rough-looking man in front of the blacksmith's shop eyeing him. *What could that grim character want with me?* he thought. *Why is he staring at me like that?* He considered for a few moments longer, then rolled around and parked his cart to the side of the tavern. *It would be wrong of me to abandon Brandt after just one misunderstanding. I will go in and talk to him so we can learn to communicate and find compromise.*

Brandt was quaffing a large pot of ale when Asmund entered. The woman sitting on his lap was tilting the bottom of the vessel more and more, causing ale to slosh into Brandt's face and gulping mouth. Hitting his limit, Brandt choked and coughed, spraying ale all over the stained blouse that was trying, and failing, to cover the woman's ample chest. She broke out in drunken giggles. Brandt emptied the rest of the pot and laughed along with her.

Asmund approached the table. Brandt looked up. "Oh no, not you again."

"What do you mean by that?" Asmund asked.

"Oh, nothing. Sit, drink!" Brandt barked at him.

Asmund sat uncertainly, looking with distaste at the filthy surroundings. "How can I drink? I don't have a cup."

Brandt regarded him with a look of mild disgust, then reached over to a nearby table and took the cup from in front of a man who was slumped over and snoring. He dumped the stale ale onto the floor and plonked the cup in front of Asmund, barking again, "Drink!"

Asmund looked into the cup to make sure nothing was growing in it, then lifted the pitcher of ale. He held his withered left hand at the bottom of the pitcher to help him tilt and pour, which was his normal way of accomplishing the task. The expression on Brandt's face grew slightly more disgusted. The woman on his lap whispered something sloppily into his ear and they both looked at Asmund and laughed.

Asmund took a long pull from the cup and collected himself. "I thought that you understood that I did not wish to stop until we had traveled at least a couple more hours."

"Why?" said Brandt, pouring himself another ale.

"Why?" repeated Asmund, growing vexed. "Because we are on a quest, and we have far to travel! We have to make it to the village of Kalbaek! If we travel sensibly we can make it there in a week."

"We don't have to go that far," said Brandt, then took another gulp of ale.

"What in all Midgard are you talking about?" Asmund said, losing his patience.

"We don't have to travel all that way. We can stay here for two weeks. There is plenty of ale, plenty of women," he said, grabbing a handful of the drunken woman's chest and shaking it as punctuation. "Then we can go back to your school and both tell the same story of your glorious quest. I get paid. You get a passing grade or whatever you're after, and everyone is happy."

"You are forgetting something, aren't you?" Asmund asked. Now it was his turn to wear a disgusted face.

"I can't wait to hear what that could be," monotoned Brandt.

"Who will accomplish the quest?"

"Oh, who cares," Brandt said mid-sip, letting beer run down his chin.

"I care!" Asmund shouted, garnering drunken leers from some of the other patrons. "And you should care, too, since you swore an oath to protect me on this quest!"

"Right, who will accomplish the quest?" Brandt said, rolling his eyes. "And what must you do on your quest? Pick an apple from an upside-down tree at midnight? Or find mushrooms growing between the toes of a magistrate? What load of horse dung are they calling your mighty quest?"

"What are you talking about?" growled Asmund, truly angry now. "I must go to the village of Kalbaek and fight an evil demon made of smoke, so I can save seven children who are in danger!"

Brandt set his pot of ale down and looked at Asmund. "Oh my gods! Wait! You're serious, aren't you? Is that really what they told you? And you believed it? Of course you did. Here you are, traveling all the way across the land like an imbecile, and thinking I will come with you."

"No one told me anything! This isn't some assignment or test from the school. I was called, in my dreams. I must go. I will face the demon and save the children! With or without your help."

"Without," said Brandt, resuming his look of bored disgust.

"Very well, but upon my return to the school, I will be reporting your actions to the captain and master Rangvald. I should not expect to retain my employment if I were you."

"Oh no! Not my employment!" mocked the big warrior. "Listen, places like that school need the appearance of being guarded. So they hire a tired old man-at-arms who in turn hires two or three bored drunks to haunt the place and act official. I'm not above taking the money to stand some watches there. But that is not my employment. I'm not one of those washed-up drunks. I am a true warrior!"

"So you won't be coming with me?" Asmund asked.

"Now you're catching on." Brandt smirked.

"And your 'true warrior's oath' to do so?" Asmund asked, smirking back. Brandt looked at him with death in his eyes. "So this is farewell then." Asmund stood.

"Don't forget to pay for the ale you drank," Brandt said, still looking as if he were contemplating murder.

"Of course. Allow me to pay for yours as well. You probably don't have the means, since you have no *true* employment." Asmund dug into his purse and withdrew his money pouch. He dug his fingers in, withdrew a hank of silver, and tossed it onto the table. When he looked up, he saw the woman on Brandt's lap smiling attentively at him. She winked both of her eyes and pursed her lips in a kiss. He put the big pouch of silver back hastily and turned to go.

"You know, boy," Brandt said before Asmund could take a step, "if what you say is true, and the idiots at that school sent you off to travel across the whole land and face a monster, then they are not really your friends. They probably just saw a chance to rid themselves of a sad little freak and took it. I am the only friend you really have. I am the only one who will tell you to your face that you are pathetic and you will never survive this. You should just stay here."

Asmund did not turn around. He walked straight out of the tavern, boarded the cart, and started down the road without hesitation. When he passed the blacksmith's shop, the rough-looking fellow in front of it was eyeing him maliciously once again. Asmund turned his face toward him angrily, and the man dropped his eyes, shrinking from the bold confrontation. Asmund grunted and rode on.

He put as many leagues behind him as he could. Every so often, he would pass another traveler who would give him a wave or a smile. It was at these times he became aware that he was riding down the road frowning deeply and muttering to himself.

In mid-afternoon, he came upon a small river spanned by a wooden bridge. Two rough-looking men were watering their horses beside it. Asmund, reminding himself to be civil, nodded to them as he passed and they returned the gesture.

It dawned on him that he had now come many leagues without feeling afraid. He had completely forgotten to feel any self-pity for some hours now. In fact, he had been traveling along feeling more determined to prove himself than he ever had before.

As night was approaching, Asmund pulled off the road and made his camp in a little copse of trees next to a stream. It looked like a nice spot to him. He was reassured by his discovery of a ring of old charred stones, suggesting previous travelers had thought so too.

He fed and watered the pony, then gathered kindling and firewood as the shadows grew long. He had never built a campfire before, but thanks to his fire spell, he had one going just before full dark. He ate some dried fish and washed it down with the last of the water in his waxed leather bottle.

The forest around him was quiet. There was no cricket song here and the stream was too small and slow moving to add any music to the stillness. He began to hear the occasional movements of some nocturnal animals arising from their slumbers and coming out to find their breakfast. He sat clutching his staff, straining his ears at every new sound. With each rustle of leaf or snapping of twig, he tried to imagine what might be making it and how close to him it was. He had never slept outside before. The thought that he ever would had never crossed his mind. In fact, he had only slept in two places his entire life: his parents' home and the school. A soft bed and a roof over his head were two things he had always taken for granted.

The pony flicked its tail and shifted its weight nearby, causing Asmund to jump in fright. If something came for him, would he be able to defend himself? If something dragged him into the darkness would anyone even know what had become of him? He felt his cheeks flush with anger. He could imagine Brandt seeing him like this and looking at him with that air of disgust. He heard his arrogant voice calling him pathetic.

He propped some more wood into the fire and then said angrily to the dark, "Here I am, come get me." Then he jerked the blanket over himself and slept.

Asmund found himself walking across an uneven farm field. He knew he must try to reach the battle, though he didn't know why. He found himself looking down into the darkness, the children's ghostly faces peering up at him. "Asmund, help us."

He sat up. All was dark and quiet. He was shivering. He had never felt so cold in all his life. The fire had died out, and he and all his surroundings were damp. He hugged his knees to his chest, wrapping the moist blanket around himself as best he could. He sat thus, rocking back and forth, teeth chattering, too cold to even cry. Why was he doing this to himself? What was he doing here? He tried to use the same device which had chased his self-pity away the evening before. He closed his eyes, attempting to conjure the image of Brandt's disgusted face to fuel himself with some sustaining defiance, some warming sense of spite, but it no longer worked.

After what felt like an eternity, the sky began to lighten. He rose and tried to build a fire. But even a magical flame emanating from a wizard's shaking fingertip was no match for wet kindling, hastily gathered and poorly arranged. He tried to re-roll his bedding as it had been the day before. Tasks such as this required him to develop a method over time that would work for him. Since he had never touched a bedroll before in his life, he ended up just cramming it into a bundle in the cart. He refilled his bottle and drew a bucket for the pony from the stream, wincing as his hand touched the frigid waters. He fed the pony and forced himself to eat two small barley cakes, even though he had no appetite. This proved a good decision, as he felt a bit better as soon as he had eaten.

He set about the daunting task of hitching the cart to the pony, struggling for several minutes with the harness until he finally got it secure. By this time, something was flying around invisibly, its sole point of existence seeming to be the stinging of his face and hands. At last, he struggled up and mounted the cart. He set back out onto the road, ready for the day's long journey. He had never felt so exhausted in his life.

The morning passed slowly as he rode miserably past the same never-ending scenery of trees and more trees. The big highlight of the morning was when a rider on horseback passed him going in the same direction. Following along behind the faster rider reminded him of the day before. Even though Brandt had proven to be a scoundrel and no fit companion, the leagues had seemed to pass a little more easily when he had not thought himself utterly alone. As if to complete the comparison, he lost sight of the man for good, the faster mount easily outstripping him and his cart.

At about midday he pulled over to rest the pony. They ate and drank, relaxing for a little over an hour. The sun had brought him warmth, and with it, a lightening of his spirits. He consulted the map and saw that they would reach no villages by nightfall. He thought for a few moments and walked to the trees. Using his belt knife, he shaved some sticks and gathered some dry leaves and bark, making himself what seemed to him might be good tinder. He placed the bundle in his purse, nodding with satisfaction.

He walked back to the cart and saw the bedroll he had crumpled up and shoved under the plank that served as the cart's seat. That would not do. It should be properly rolled. He pulled it out. It was unpleasantly soggy to the touch. *No, not rolled up,* he thought. He spread it out in the back of the cart so the air and sunshine could dry it through the day.

He walked to the front of the cart and prepared to mount, then paused, remembering one last thing. He withdrew his spell book and studied a recently-added page. Then reached back into his purse and brought out a small wooden disk, slightly larger than the palm of a man's hand. He twisted and separated it into halves, revealing a finely polished mirror on the inside. Holding it in his right hand, he gazed for a moment at his narrow, but not un-handsomely featured face. Then he held the mirror toward the sky and spoke the words he had just memorized, feeling a tingle of magic. He closed the mirror and placed it and his book back into the purse. He climbed aboard and was off once again.

The next hours were mostly uneventful. A merchant's wagon passed him going the opposite direction. The driver and Asmund exchanged a friendly wave. Other than that, he saw no one. He simply rode, trying to put as many leagues behind him as possible.

The afternoon passed by and evening had just set in when he heard hoofbeats from behind him. Another traveler, no doubt, coming up to pass him. Well, at least he would have the view of someone's back to keep him company for a time.

"Asmund, wait," called a voice from behind.

Asmund was startled at the sound of his name. He was even more startled when he saw the big black charger trot up beside him, carrying Brandt the Bloody.

"Asmund, please wait," Brandt called out again.

"What do you want?" Asmund replied, not stopping his pony. "Do you know what? I don't care! Just go away!"

"Please stop, Wizard Asmund. I want to..." Brandt paused, and then finished sheepishly, "apologize."

Asmund heard the soft tone of the warrior's voice and observed how he had addressed him respectfully as Wizard Asmund. In spite of himself, he felt moved. He stopped the cart and turned to look at the warrior.

"Thank you for stopping, My Lord. I have ridden very hard to catch up with you."

Asmund began to soften, but then frowned, remembering all he had said at the tavern the day before. "Wait! I don't know why I stopped! I have nothing to say to you! I don't ever want to see you again!" Asmund lifted the reins and urged the pony to begin walking again. Brandt stepped his charger in front of the cart, blocking the road.

"That is fair, My Lord. I deserve that, only I beg of you let me speak what I have to say, and then, if you wish, I will leave and never trouble you again."

Asmund felt his anger boiling. He thought about grasping his staff and unleashing a fireball into Brandt's face. No sooner had the thought crossed his mind then he felt sickened by it. That was not who he was, or what he stood for. To turn to violence when he was angry was unforgivable. He felt deeply ashamed.

"Speak," he said softly. "I will listen."

Brandt looked relieved. "When I awoke in the tavern, sick from the drink, and in the company of those who were only company while I had money to pay, I could see myself clearly. I did not like who I saw. I remembered all the terrible things I said to you when I was drunk. How I told you that I was a true warrior and how you pointed out that I was not, because I had made a warrior's oath falsely. I had sworn an oath for show, with no real intention of honoring it. I am in disgrace. When you said it, I thought I hated you for it. But now I know it was not you I hated, it was myself. You are the one who acts with honor, not me. You are willing to go on this quest in spite of..." He stopped speaking, then finished awkwardly, "Well, in spite of everything. As I promised, if you do not wish my help, I will leave and trouble you no more. But I am lost and without honor, and I beg you to let me fulfill my oath of protecting you. If you do, I promise I will not let any harm befall you. You have my true oath this time." He placed his fist over his heart and looked at Asmund pleadingly.

Asmund could not deny that he was much moved by Brandt's speech. He also could not deny how much relief he felt at the prospect of Brandt's protection. He hesitated, remembering the deep well of hatred he had felt just minutes ago. No. He would not be ruled by anger. He knew how proud Brandt was. Coming to him like this and humbling himself could not have been easy. One of the great failings of people was that they lacked empathy and understanding. If Brandt had lost his way and was looking for a second chance, then Asmund was not going to be the one to turn him away.

"If I accept you back and you tie your destiny to mine, you must understand that the quest is the only thing that matters. We must put our wants and our comforts aside to reach the village and face the beast."

"By all the gods, I swear it," said Brandt. "And this

time I mean it, with all my heart."

CHAPTER FOUR

*T*he raven flew high above the notice of mortal things. Even the keenest eye turned skyward would have seen only a speck among the clouds to denote its passage.

He had flown many leagues, following a vague memory of where to go, and now the dwarf was growing impatient. That was the strangest part of this day. For the last three hundred and seventy-five years, when he would visit, the dwarf had always been working on that same small golden box. The box looked finished, but he insisted it just was not perfect enough. The dwarf's patience was at the level of madness. Any more mad and he could be a prophet. And yet today...

The Raven looked down far below and saw the dwarf staring up at him with an almost pained expectation. That made his wings feel heavy. Curse it, I know it's close. It's right around here somewhe...

"Cawww!" His brother's voice broke through the sunny afternoon skies. He was a speck far ahead and to the east. And he was circling. Relief flooded the raven's heart. They had found it, just as they'd promised. Down below, he saw the line of dust as the dwarf's mount thundered toward the circling black dot.

The massive boar charged through the last of the trees and into the meadow. Ahead, the strange rocky hill jutted from the earth like a jagged tooth. This felt good! The ground beneath her hooves, the cool wind that she snuffed into her snout, fueling her powerful body, the straps of the saddle tight and secure, the weight of her friend upon her back. He was once again alive with purpose, and she loved it. She opened and closed her jaws four times as she galloped nearer to the rocks, rubbing her upper and lower tusks together to ensure that they would be razor-sharp for anything awaiting them.

They slowed to a walk, entering the semicircle of boulders and outcroppings of mossy stone which formed a natural courtyard at the foot of the rocky hill. In its center was a ring of small stones and charred wood. It appeared campfires had been built and rebuilt here many times, but now the stones were scattered about and weeds grew up through the charred remnants of wood. No fire had burned here for some time.

The craftsman dismounted and walked over to the boulder upon which perched the two ravens. He fell to one knee and bowed his head. "Tell him that with this last coin, his account is paid in full."

The ravens spoke in one voice. "He says to you, 'Praise a weapon when it is tried. It has been tried, and I praise the hand that made it.'"

The craftsman was struck speechless. The ravens rose from the stone as if to take their leave. But instead, in a flutter of black feathers, they perched one on each of the craftsman's shoulders, in the same way that they sit on the shoulders of Odin. They sat for the twinkling of an eye, then beat their ebony wings and rocketed into the sky. As they flew they both wept, for they knew they would never see him again. Down below, the craftsman was weeping too.

The craftsman knelt for a few moments longer, then looked up at the sun setting low in the sky. He rose quickly and went to his saddlebags. "Not much time and much to do, Trufflesbane," he said to his trusty mount. He retrieved what he needed from the saddlebags and set to work. He drove a stake far into the earth. He made sure each link of the iron chain was strong and true, then covered it over with his blanket. He rebuilt the fire pit and quickly set about gathering firewood. Darkness had just begun to set in as his cooking pot began to simmer. He threw the last of the stew's ingredients into the pot and settled down on his blanket. There would still be hours yet to wait. Hours when he would be watched. He set about playing the weary traveler: he drank from his little cask of ale, stirred his pot, and sang a cheerful tune.

He was just finishing the five hundred and seventh verse of his song –

> *Oh, I am a wily Hroovitnir*
> *And I live from paw to maw*
> *And if I can't dig or catch it*
> *Then I'll never eat at all.*

– when he heard the quiet footsteps In the dark. He was careful not to show that he had heard. Instead he launched into the chorus:

The land it is sacred where the giants fell
And gods and elves together forever and forever
Will in Thruthheim's endless glories dwell

He was about to start the nine hundred and twenty-seventh verse when a figure approached from the darkness. It had just stepped up to the edge of the firelight when the craftsman drew the sword from beneath his cloak and set about sharpening it with a stone.

He looked up. "Ho, there, traveler, I did not see you approach. Will you not sit down? Eat, rest. My fire will be the warmer and my stew the heartier with the added fellowship." The figure sat down across from him still just outside the glow of the fire. "I hope you don't mind if I sharpen my sword. I used it to chop the firewood and it has grown dull."

"Not at all," the figure said from across the fire. "It looks to be a fine sword. I did not know you were a warrior when first I approached."

"A warrior!" exclaimed the craftsman. "I am no warrior. Forgive me; I failed to introduce myself. My name is Sven. I am but a humble wanderer. A teller of tales, a singer of songs."

"But... that sword."

"I found it," said the craftsman. "I passed a field where long ago a mighty battle raged, and in the center of the field a rosebush had grown up from the earth. Twined in its thorny fingers was this sword. I thought that I would not be doing wrong to take it. I use it now as I told you to chop my firewood and dig my latrines."

"You use that sword to dig your privy holes?" screeched the figure. "*That* sword?"

"Yes," replied the craftsman, and then the figure laughed. The laugh was the scraping of a closing coffin lid, or the creak of a gallows rope when it bears a weight.

"My apologies, friend," said the craftsman. "I've been doing all the talking. I have not even given you the chance to introduce yourself. What is your name?"

"My name?" repeated the figure. There was a long pause. "I am Vard the Hermit. I come here sometimes, for the shelter of the rocks makes it an excellent place for a fire. I was surprised to find you here, Sven the Wanderer."

"I'm sorry to have intruded," said the craftsman, running the stone down the edge of the bright blade once again. "At least I have saved you the time of building a fire, and have made a nice stew to share with you. But I just noticed, you've had no stew. Please eat your fill, there is plenty and it is quite good."

"Thank you," said the figure from across the flames. "Soon I will eat my fill. For now simply let me rest by the fire."

"As you wish. I am glad for your company, Vard the Hermit, and I will repay it with a song." The Craftsman glanced at the sky. He judged that a mere three hundred verses would be enough. He launched into song before anything else could be said. As he sang, he slowly and methodically sharpened the sword. After the forty-seventh verse he heard the figure heave a great sigh. After the hundred and thirty-second verse, the figure broke in.

"I thank you for the song, but you have traveled far – you must be weary. Lie down and rest."

The craftsman looked up at the sky. *Not yet,* he

thought. "You are too kind, Vard the Hermit. But I'm not tired and we are almost to the best part." He launched with even more gusto into the hundred and thirty-third verse.

After the two hundred and seventy-seventh verse the figure groaned loudly. "I pray you, Sven, please rest your voice. The night is almost spent and we have not slept. Let us rest while the sun still slumbers. I see even now the start of a glow faint on the horizon."

"Quite right you are, Vard, I forgot myself and got lost in song. We must lie down and rest. But first, I have finished sharpening this sword – now let me tie it in these oilskins, and return it to my saddle to keep it safe and dry." He saw the shadowy figure lean forward and watch anxiously as he carefully tied the oilskins around the sword; he felt the eyes watching him intently as he walked over and strapped the sword to his saddle.

He returned to his place at the fire and sat back upon his blanket. As he did, there was a quiet *tink* of iron against iron. "Sleep well, my friend," he said, a bit too loudly, as if he could conceal a sound which had already happened. He saw the figure cock his head, as if listening. A long silence passed, during which neither spoke. Then the sliding coffin lid and creaking gallows rope of laughter split the night again.

"Silly little man," said the figure. "I had begun to think that fate really did protect fools when I saw you holding that sword – the sword of Alver The Just, who passed it to Voll Ironfist, who lost it to Halder Helmbreaker in battle. The sword named Scattersoul, which was forged by the dwarfs of the Great Hall of legend. Now, as promised, I will eat my fill. But first you will know my true name, for I am known as the moon of the dwelling Hrungnir; wealth sucker; child of the storm; beloved of the seer; guardian of the corpse fjord; swallower of the wheel of heaven. For what is a troll if not that?"

Thus saying, the figure leaped over the fire and was upon the craftsman, gnarled hands twisting around his neck. Drool dripped from the troll's slavering jaws with anticipation. He slammed the dwarf's head against the ground again and again. This did not actually aid in the strangulation process, but it always seemed to increase his victims' terror, which was, truth be told, his favorite part.

He heard a snort and felt a tiny pinch on his right foot. Who dared distract him from his murderous ecstasy, especially after he had patiently waited all night and suffered through this man's interminable singing? He looked down, and to his astonishment, the boar the man used as a mount was trying to sink its tusks into his ankle. The beast was huge. In all his years, he could only remember ever having seen two that were larger.

"Ha! My dessert!" he crowed. "Wait your turn!" With that he gave a kick that sent the meddlesome pig tumbling from the circle of stone and out into the darkness.

Now where was he? Oh, yes. Time to squeeze the little man's head right off. He was going to start by eating the eyeballs first. He loved the eyeballs. He could almost feel sorry for the fool. Usually they would fight back – grasp at his hands, strike at his bony face. But this one made no attempt – he did not even raise his hands.

Or perhaps he is drawing a belt knife to plunge it into me. Good – let him. No peasant's blade, nameless and uncharmed, will injure me. Then, just as the man's face was turning that final shade of purple, the troll discovered what his hands had been doing.

He felt the weight of the iron collar as it was clamped around his neck. He heard, smelled, and felt his skin searing all at once. He clawed at the collar, but to no avail. He screeched and cursed and jerked at the hateful thing. He rolled over, writhing in agony, and saw the man standing now above him, gasping in great gulps of air.

The terror of his situation struck him all at once. He had not lived through all these many ages just to die here, at the hands of Sven the Singer of Boring Songs. He rose and dashed toward his hidden cave. Just a score of steps and he would be safe. All at once, he found himself lying flat on his back, looking up at the sky as it paled with the hint of morning.

He felt an excruciating tugging at his neck as the little man dragged him hand over hand across the ground. He scrabbled at passing stones until he found ones he could grip – something to stop him from being pulled back. He held on with all of his might, but the burning iron was sapping his power, leaving no strength in his limbs. The man hauled him slowly back.

"No!" he shouted. He grabbed the chain and yanked at its heavy links. But they held fast, burning the palms of his hands. Who? Who could even forge such a chain?

He was dragged back to a stake that he could now see had been hidden beneath the man's blanket. He rose up and tried to strike a blow, a blow that would have felled an oak tree. The man stepped aside from it and caught his wrist in a loop of chain.

He kicked out at the man, a kick that would have toppled a house. The man nimbly stepped aside once again, looping yet more chain around his ankle. The little man then dealt him a blow on the brow with his open hand, driving him to the ground.

This could not be! He had been struck as if he were an errant child instead of the devourer of kings! He had outlived empires! The craftsman wrapped loop after loop of chain around his body, causing him to sizzle and writhe.

"Sven! Sven!" he begged. "I have treasure in my cave, all you could ever want. I will give it to you. Just set me free!"

"Yes, you will be free," said the craftsman grimly. "But first I will tell you my true name. I am called the child of iron and stone. The last of the sons of Ivaldi. Dwarf of the Great Hall. I am called Asger, the spear of God. For 'twas I who forged Gungnir the weapon of the Allfather. And *you* shall call me Dawnbreaker!" His voice now rumbling like a crushing avalanche. "But you will call me it only once."

He thrust the chain-bound troll up to stand before the morning sun. "*DAWNBREAKER!*" screamed the troll, and then was silent – as all stone is silent.

The craftsman walked around the new stone pillar which was shot throughout with streaks of iron. He was tired from his toils. It had taken twelve days and nights to make the stake, chain, and collar from the rock that had fallen from the heavens; forged by his own hand and quenched in his own blood.

He was bone weary, and yet he could not rest. There was still much to be done. He glanced around. Where was...?

He hadn't time to finish this thought when Trufflesbane trotted back into the courtyard, covered with dust and seemingly none the worse for the blow she had endured. He retrieved his hammer and chisel from the saddlebag and regarded the pillar, studying each curve and contour, judging where to begin. As the morning sun rose ever higher in the sky, he began to hew the ironstone into shape.

Asmund felt optimistic that things had taken a turn for the better. This time, Brandt stayed with him and did not ride far ahead. Occasionally, they would pass another traveler. He greeted each one with a wave and an easy smile.

As the sun began sinking lower in the sky, Brandt said, "May I suggest we make our camp soon while we still have some light?"

Asmund thought back to the night before, when he had scarcely had time to make fire before it was dark. "Good thinking, Brandt."

They were coming down a gentle slope in the road that rounded the bend of a hill. Leveling off on the other side, they saw three wagons pulled a short way off the road. Their drivers were making camp for the night.

Asmund stopped his pony and called a good evening to them, which they all returned cheerfully. An older man with a gray beard scrutinized them for a moment, casting a doubtful gaze on Brandt. Then he regarded Asmund and smiled. "If you are looking to make camp, this is the spot for it. There is a natural spring in the rocks over there," he said, gesturing toward an outcropping at the foot of the hill they had just rounded. "We make this journey to and from the city every month, and we always make camp here."

"We wouldn't be intruding?" asked Asmund.

"You would be welcome. This place does not belong to us, and you and your animals will be glad of the fresh water."

"We thank you," said Asmund heartily, and he lifted his reins to move.

"My Lord," said Brandt. "I think we should find a place further along the road."

"Why, Brandt?" asked Asmund.

"It's just that we do not know them."

"Do you think we have reason to fear them?" Asmund asked cautiously. He looked at the six drivers and saw no weapons. The men all tended to the older side. "They seem harmless to me. Besides, the spring will be useful." Brandt simply nodded.

The drivers were now building a fire, and Asmund and Brandt made camp nearby. This time, Asmund had enough daylight to feed and water the pony and arrange his bed and a shelter cloth. He covertly watched the drivers make their beds so he could copy them. The biggest help was learning to lay down some spruce branches first. This would add greatly to the comfort, and he now recalled being told to be wary of the ground more than the air as a thief of the body's warmth. He felt tonight's bed would be much kinder to sleep in.

When he had finished, there was just a little daylight left. He longed to sit at the fire and eat his salted fish, but instead, he walked into the trees and gathered some good-sized sticks. He brought them to the fire and added them to the fuel pile. The drivers had gathered more than enough, he was sure, but the contribution seemed to him a good gesture.

At last he sat next to Brandt and ate. When he was finished, he sought to make some polite conversation with their hosts. "What is it that you carry in your wagons?" he asked.

"Bundled wool for the traders' ships in Einarshofn," answered the old man, setting down his porridge and berries. "You are a wizard from the city, are you not?" Asmund nodded. "I thought so. I was born there and I am familiar with the wizards and their schools. What magic is your specialty?"

"I am mostly trained in the healing magics," answered Asmund, "but I would hesitate to call it my specialty."

One of the other drivers began laughing. "You would have to excuse me if I didn't trust your magic, looking like you do! If you were a real healing wizard, wouldn't you heal your twisted little body? Just a boy in a robe, says I."

There was a blur of movement, and suddenly Brandt was standing over the man with his sword at his throat. All mockery had fled from the man's terrified face. "I should take your filthy tongue for speaking that way to the wizard Asmund, you dog!" growled Brandt the Bloody.

"I apologize for Aver, My Lord!" said the old man pleadingly. "He is a fool, just a country drover – he does not know what he says!"

"Stay your hand, Brandt!" Asmund said, fearing for the man's life. "We are guests at these men's fire. We will not spill their blood."

"As you wish, My Lord," said Brandt. He sheathed his sword and sat back beside Asmund.

Well, Brandt really is taking his oath seriously this time, thought Asmund. *But I really must have a talk with him about constraining himself to my physical safety alone, and leaving my hurt feelings to me.*

An awkward silence hung over the assembly now. At last Asmund spoke. "We have a long journey ahead of us tomorrow."

"As do we," said the leader of the drivers, on cue.

"Well then, good night," said Asmund. "Thank you again for the hospitality of your fire."

"Asmund, help us!"

He sat up with a start, the voices of the children still echoing in his head. In the faint gray light of morning, he saw Brandt sitting up as well, his sword half drawn from its sheath. Asmund held up his hand and shook his head, signaling all was well. Brandt nodded and slid his sword back in its place.

Asmund rose and did his necessaries and washed up at the spring. The spruce limbs had made a huge difference to his warmth and comfort, but he happened to see a tick as his morning-blurred eyes passed over his bare legs. A careful search located two more. *For everything, a price,* he mused as he disposed of them.

When he returned, the drivers were up and breaking camp. Asmund stowed his bedding and ate some barley cakes. Upon finishing, he went to care for the pony. He found that Brandt had already done so. Now he was hitching it to the cart.

"Oh, thank you, Brandt."

"Of course, My Lord."

"Have you eaten?" Asmund asked.

"No need, My Lord. I eat in the saddle." As if to illustrate his words, he mounted his black charger and took a bite of an apple he had retrieved from his saddle-bag along with a piece of flatbread.

Asmund pulled himself up into the cart, a task at which he was improving with practice. He called to the leader of the drivers. "Farewell, and thank you again for your hospitality."

"Farewell to you as well, wizard," replied the man. "Be careful as you travel toward the land of Brekka. There are sometimes bandits that waylay travelers. Although you may not have any troubles with that," he added, eyeing Brandt, who was wearing his customary stony face and chewing his apple.

Asmund set off down the road, and Brandt took up his close and watchful position, just as he had done the evening before. He certainly appeared eager to redeem himself. His swift defense of Asmund when the wagon driver had ridiculed him had gone a long way toward banishing any lingering doubts about the warrior. Asmund looked at the golden braids gently swaying with each step of the big horse and felt the same level of confidence he had when they had first set out. Surely with Brandt protecting him, he would reach Kalbaek in one piece. Once he got there? *Well, that may prove to be a different matter altogether,* he thought.

After a few hours' travel, they passed a sign which informed them that they were only ten leagues to Brekka. They were making excellent progress. "We should stop now and rest," Brandt said, breaking the silence. He might be keeping with Asmund now and protecting him, but he certainly had not provided any conversation to pass the time. Now that he did speak, it made no sense, and Asmund told him so.

"We will be in Brekka a little after midday, and we need to stop for provisions anyway. We will rest the horses and treat ourselves to a hot meal in town."

Brandt's only reply was a half shrug, and the silence resumed. Another two hours passed and Asmund began to feel excited to reach the town. The monotony of the journey was wearing on him. He would be happy to see some civilization and forget about the road for a short while.

This is what Asmund was thinking when he heard Brandt's charger whinny and saw Brandt draw his sword in a flash of polished steel. He halted his pony and looked ahead at the three men who had stepped onto the road. One carried shield and axe, one shield and sword, and the last held a bow with an arrow nocked and ready.

The one in the center rested his axe on his shoulder casually and smiled. "Hello, gentlemen," he said cordially. "I'm afraid I'm going to have to ask you to give us all your possessions. If you do not, we will be forced to kill you and take them anyway. So I really suggest you do as I say."

Asmund looked at Brandt and saw his eyes narrow. He could see the muscles in his jaw clench. He watched as Brandt kicked the sides of the charger, causing it to spring forward. Then he wrenched hard on the reins, spinning the horse around, and galloped back up the road the way they had come.

The three bandits stood smiling at Asmund, saying nothing. Asmund listened to the hoofbeats of the galloping charger grow faint in the distance. When they could no longer be heard, the three smiling men strolled over to Asmund, their weapons lowered harmlessly at their sides. The leader continued. "So, as I was saying, if you would be so kind as to leave everything you have in the cart and climb down, we will be on our way."

"Please." Asmund said. "If you must rob me, at least leave me the cart and the things I need for my quest."

"Quest?" repeated the leader, sharing a bemused look with his friends. "What kind of quest would a bent little goblin like you be on?"

"I am a wizard," replied Asmund. "I go to fight a creature and save seven children."

The men looked at him a moment, mouths gaping. Then all three burst into laughter. At last, when the man could regain his composure, he wiped the corner of his eye and said, "Oh my, thank you, little goblin. In all my days I have never heard such a creative lie, and I have heard some good ones. 'Please, mister bandit, don't rob me!'" he recited in a high-pitched whine. "'I have a sick mother at home, and twelve starving children!' Those are classics. But I've never heard, 'I have to slay a monster and save seven kiddies!' That one wins hands-down for creativity." His voice lost all its mirth abruptly. "This is your final chance. Get down from the cart, and you can walk to town. If you are too bent to walk, someone will take pity on you and give you a ride if you beg them. By the look of you, I'm sure you've had to do some begging before."

"I need my cart. Here, I have silver," Asmund said, taking a pouch from his belt and opening the top. The three men leaned forward to see, and without warning, he flung the contents across all three of the men. They were shocked for a moment, then laughter came again. The leader reached down and plucked something from his tunic. "Did you just throw seeds at us?" he asked, still laughing.

"Yes," answered Asmund.

"Oh, wait. Let me guess. They are supposed to be magic seeds, aren't they?"

"No. They are just normal seeds," said Asmund. "I provide the magic." Then his lips moved and he waved his hand toward them. Instantly their feet and legs were entangled in dark green vines. The surprised men started to rip at them. "Stop!" shouted Asmund in a booming voice, straining to deepen his tone and sound commanding. "If you tear at the vines they will rise up in an instant and choke you to death." The vines all crawled a couple of inches higher as if to illustrate this potential fate.

"Quickly, shoot him and put an end to his magic," said the leader to the archer.

Before he could raise the bow Asmund shouted. "You fools! Only my magic is preventing the vines from strangling you! Throw your weapons away at once!" The bow and the sword were instantly flung away, but the leader looked at his axe then back at Asmund, his face taking on a skeptical grin. "How do we know you aren't just trying to deceive us with a simple magic trick? We threatened to kill you. If you were a mighty wizard with powerful magic, you would have simply killed us. I think maybe these vines can't choke any-one."

Asmund was regretting the deepened voice and shouting. He knew he was seeming too desperate to convince them, and the smart one was beginning to see through it, but there was no choice now but to continue and try to drive it home. "You stupid man," Asmund said, looking deep into his eyes. I could have killed you the moment I saw you, but I am a wizard of light and I do not take a life if it is not needful."

The man lifted his right foot, tearing some of the vines. "I don't believe-"

"Stand still and be silent! Or I will turn you into a pile of ashes!" Asmund thundered. He lifted his staff straight into the air and unleashed a fireball the size of a man's head. It flew into the air and burst, leaving a black smear of smoke hanging on the breeze. The pony whin-nied at the sound of it. The man's axe clattered to the road and he began to blubber for mercy.

"Did I not order you to be silent?" Asmund's throat was beginning to feel scratchy from the forced baritone. "I have taken pains to not kill you, but you have tried the very last of my patience! Utter one word more and I will unleash the vines and they will smother you and drag you down into the ground where any memory of you will be forgotten forever!"

The three men were now quaking in fear and avoiding his eyes. "I will now continue on my way. When I have gotten some distance down the road I will cease my enchantment upon the vines. Then you will be able to break free without them killing you. I sug-gest you use the time to contemplate a different line of work."

Asmund continued down the road without looking back. He had done it! He had fooled the brigands with the simple grow spell he used to help farmers. That and a fireball, thanks to Thorfinn. He wished Thorfinn could have seen the fireball. This time, he had believed more strongly in it, and it had been larger and more impressive.

The one person to whom he certainly did not owe any thanks was that faithless dog, Brandt. Why had he ever trusted him again? The absolute gall of the man! And what a loathsome coward! He fumed at the thought. Still, the episode had proven that he did not need him and he never had. Asmund calmed himself and shook his head. It did not matter now anyway. That was one person he would never have to see again.

When a good distance had passed between himself and where he had left the bandits, he pulled to the side of the road and stopped. He knew he must be close to the town of Brekka by now, and he wanted to be prepared. There was only himself to count on, and he may need to defend himself again. He had thought that he understood how treacherous the world could be, but he had led a very sheltered life until now. These last couple of days, his real education on the subject had begun in earnest. He prepared some spells and then withdrew the small mirror from his purse. He repeated the same process as the day before, holding it toward the sky and speaking the words.

He was putting the mirror away and preparing to ride on when he heard a clatter of hooves from behind. Fearful that the bandits had finally seen through his bluff and were giving chase, he turned around on the seat. He watched in disbelief as Brandt galloped up, slowed to a stop, and then dismounted and approached the cart.

"You must be insane if you think I would believe a single thing you have to say this time!" Asmund started. "I suppose you want another chance to fulfill your oath. Provided you don't actually have to do anything dangerous."

"No," said Brandt, wearing his usual blank, bored face. "I'm here to finish what I started and kill you."

"I don't want to hear it!" snapped Asmund. Then Brandt's words registered. "Did you say you were here to kill me?"

"Yes," confirmed Brandt, his bored face unchanged.

"Why?" Asmund asked, stunned.

"You really are unbelievably stupid. The first reason, and the most practical, is for that big pouch of silver you so brazenly displayed in the tavern back in town."

"Here, take it," said Asmund, his voice slow and deliberate. "My big pouch of silver." He reached into his satchel. "Here, you can have my big pouch of silver."

Brandt's face finally showed some life as he saw the heavy pouch jingling with treasure.

"Here it is, it's yours, catch." Asmund tossed it to him. He saw the big man wince as the heavy bag hit his palm, stinging it. "There, take it, and then you never have to see me again."

"Stupid boy. I could've taken this whenever I wanted. But that was only half the plan. The best part was going to be when I got you off the road behind the trees, where I could take my time and kill you the way I prefer, nice and slow." Saying this made Brandt finally smile and his eyes took on a far-away gaze, as if he were imagining the torture.

"When I caught up to you last night, everything was perfect," Brandt continued. "You believed my ridiculous story about wanting to redeem myself, and you rode along with me without a care in the world. But when it was time to camp, you ruined everything by taking up with those wagon drivers. Today I tried to get you to stop where all was quiet. But no, you wanted to go on to the town. For a moment I thought everything was lost when we were caught by the bandits. Afterward when I came creeping back I expected this to be gone." He gave the pouch a shake, listening to it jingle. It made him wince again; his hand still stung from catching it.

"But I figured that at least you would be on foot after the robbery and even easier to drag off without a trace. Imagine my surprise when I saw that you had tricked them. I watched from concealment as they stood there afraid. I almost began to believe that you had performed real magic on them. But then they finally figured it out. They weren't really trapped. They could just step out of the vines with ease. What fools they were! After that, they picked up their weapons and ran into the forest. I was delighted at the prospect of getting to kill you and still take the silver." Brandt stepped forward.

"I don't understand!" Asmund protested.

"You don't need to understand. You just need to die." Brandt replied. "Unfortunately, it's not going to be slow like I wanted, but I can't take any more chances."

Asmund held up his hand, stopping him again. "Wait!" he pleaded. "You want the money. That I understand. You want to kill me. Okay, I got that. What I don't know is why."

"Because I hate you."

"Why? Just because of our argument at the tavern?"

"No. Because you are disgusting and pathetic. You should not exist," Brandt said with true loathing in his voice.

"What do I do that makes me disgusting and pathetic?" asked Asmund.

"It's not what you do. It's what you are!" Brandt snarled.

"What, a wizard?"

"No. Don't play stupid, boy. You know what makes you pathetic. How you were born!" Brandt spat.

"That's what you hate me for?" Asmund asked. "I didn't do that! I'm not responsible for how my body is formed! Is this really how you go through life? Hating everyone who is different from you?"

Brandt opened his mouth to reply, but shut it again as his stomach threatened to empty its contents. He must be very angry, he thought, because even his vision was blurred, and he had to blink to try to clear it. In fact, he realized he felt sick with rage now. He wanted very much to go lie down and rest. This was taking more time then was necessary, anyway. What was all this talking for? "You have been trying to stall for time, hoping some travelers will appear and interrupt us. But your luck has run out, you putrid little vermin."

"Oh, in that case, there is just one last thing," Asmund said, smiling at Brandt, who was sweating profusely, his face now white as snow. "You are familiar with the hoggorm, correct? Some call it adder or viper. It's the only venomous serpent that lives in the north-lands. Its bite is not often fatal to a big, strong man. Usually, it will just make him very sick."

"Why are you telling me this?" Brandt croaked, his throat feeling as though it were packed with sand.

"Because I want you to imagine what might happen to that same big, strong man, if he stood holding a hoggorm, letting it bite him again and again and again, and did not do anything to stop it. If, for instance, this man were very stupid, and a wizard had created a glamour to cloud his tiny mind, making him think that the poisonous serpent were something harmless instead, something he wanted very much. Something like, say, a big pouch of silver."

Brandt held up the pouch and its fangs struck him in the face, injecting the last drops of venom into his now-bleeding chin. Brandt screamed in high-pitched terror, grabbing what he could now see was a brown and tan colored snake. He twisted it in his bloodied hands and threw it to the ground at his feet. He looked at Asmund and tried to draw his sword, but managed only to expose three inches of blade before letting go of it and abandoning the attempt. He felt death's embrace coming very close now, and he whimpered to Asmund with watery eyes, pleading in a voice that was little more than a whisper, "Help me, please."

Asmund reached out with the bottom of his staff and gave him a tiny shove, toppling the big warrior. He sat silently for a time, thinking about all that had just happened. Then he gasped. "Oh no! What have I done?" He climbed down as quickly as he could, came around the cart and knelt by the body. He was relieved to see some life still flickered there. He reached into his purse and grabbed the healing flask Gert had made for him. If this did not work, he would never be able to live with himself. He opened the slack mouth and poured the elixir in, whispering to himself, "Come on, work! Please work!" He did not have long to wait, and a massive feeling of guilt released its grip on his heart and tears rolled down his cheeks.

A few minutes later, he started the cart toward the town of Brekka. The very last image that Brandt's dying eyes beheld was that of Asmund leaving on the cart, the snake curled on his lap with the healing potion still working inside of it, bringing it back to health.

CHAPTER FIVE

*T*he whale grew quickly accustomed to its harness *and pulled the longship swiftly across the sea. The ship looked big and heavy, from its mighty rudder the size of a castle door to the carven figure at its prow, the size and shape of a real dragon's head. But to the whale, the burden felt as a mere toy. Thus, traveling far more fleetly than by sail or oar, the voyage of days became one of hours.*

The craftsman stood upon the deck, watching the distant shore looming ever larger on the horizon. The day was cool and clear, and his heart felt light and strong with adventure. Seabirds flew out to greet the ship, signaling to the craftsman that it was time to make ready. He covered over the dragon's head at the front of the ship so as to not frighten the spirits of this land. He saddled Trufflesbane, checking to make sure that they had all the provisions they would need in the saddlebag.

Lastly, he secured to the rear of her right flank the big, rectangular hammerhead he had fashioned from the Ironstone. It was yet unhafted, but he had bored a hole down its center where the haft would soon go. Its surface was deeply carved with the runes of the old tongue: on one side it bore the symbols of life, and on the other, death. The striking face of the hammer was blank. He had yet to carve and inlay the name that would be needed, for those who lived in death had not yet told it to him.

When at last they reached the land, he unharnessed the whale. "And now to your payment," he said, "just as promised." He leaned down again and fastened the long, straight horn that came to a needle point onto the whale's head. "The Kraki is old. His skin has grown thick and hard, but this weapon will pierce it.　　　·

"When the sons of Bor made the world from the body of the giant Yamir, some animals were given weapons of horn and antler, tooth and claw. Others were not. Two of these weapons did we, the sons of Ivaldi, forge in the Great Hall: one for the steed who would fight the lion, and one for the whale who would fight the beast in the depths. The steed's weapon would eventually be discarded; yours you shall wield until the riders of Muspell come again." Thus saying, he mounted Trufflesbane. They leaped from the ship onto the land and galloped into the east.

They traveled many leagues. Always, the path would turn aside and lead the wrong way, but the craftsman would not be deceived. He knew the way in his very bones and took not one misstep, avoiding rockslides and trees falling in the road, leaping over yawning chasms and fording raging rivers. They would not be turned from their path. Finally, ahead, he saw the entrance he sought. His heart leaped and they directed their steps toward it.

For a brief moment, he glimpsed from the corner of his eye a man in golden armor passing behind the trees alongside them. The craftsman turned his head to regard the man, but another gap in the trees showed he had been mistaken, for instead of a man, he saw a large tawny stag with a mighty rack of antlers crowning its head. It was walking parallel to them, but did not seem to see them. He lost sight of it again behind the trees.

There was a clearing just ahead which they would have to cross before reaching the entrance to the place they sought. If the stag continued pacing them, he would be able to see it clearly from there. They proceeded forward, passing the last copse of trees. An old man came into view, standing in the clearing, gray and bent with age. He wrung his hands, looking quite miserable. Of the stag there was no sign.

"What ails you, old man?" asked the craftsman.

"Oh, grim day," cried the man. "We came here to mine the old pits. My back has long since given way and I cannot mine. But it is my job to stay on the surface and watch the rope as the others go below. It must be watched, for there are Vettir here who delight in only mischief and pain. I chase them away by keeping a hazel pole driven into the ground – I rebuke them and throw salt at them and they leave us alone. But today I wish I had never been born. Curse me for an old fool!" The man spat and hid his face in his hands.

"What happened today? Tell me," said the craftsman quietly.

"I'm very old and tired," replied the man, "wearied from my many years of labor. I have of late forgotten the art of sleeping through the night. So it is that come afternoon times I drowse and doze. Today my head grew heavy and I rested my eyes for but a moment. I opened them to the sound of laughter and saw that someone had reached up and moved the sun in the sky. I looked to the pit and saw that the rope had been untied and thrown down. I begged the Vettir for mercy. I told them the men would surely die. They laughed and replied that maggots and worms must eat just like everyone else."

The dwarf nodded. "Show me to the mine." The man led him to a large hole leading straight down into the earth. Its sides were completely smooth. He could hear the men calling for help from far, far below. "Have you another rope?" he asked, turning to the old man.

"That is my other sorrow!" answered the man in an anguished voice. "Come, see what I would show you." The man led him to a rough-hewn hut with a grass roof. Inside, all the materials and tools for the making of rope had been set out, and with them was a short length which had just begun to be twisted. "This is the final cruelty," moaned the man. "I have the knowledge and materials to make a new rope, but alas, these are my hands now."

He held them up before the dwarf's face. They were gnarled and spotted with age. The short length of rope he had managed to braid must have been agonizing. The elderly man lowered his shaking hands with shame. "It would take a master craftsman who could work at the speed of falling water to make a rope so long it could reach the men before they starved."

The craftsman instantly sat and fell to plaiting the strands. He worked with the swiftness and precision of a son of Ivaldi; and no rope braided before or since could compare to the one taking shape in his nimble hands.

The elderly man stared in amazement. "Surely some Aesir has sent you here this day."

The dwarf paused in his work for a brief moment, then nodded his head and began braiding again. He had been leery of this distraction, because it turned him from his path, and time was growing short. But when the man said that a god had sent him here for a purpose, he knew that it was true.

The old man, now seeing hope where before there had only been despair, launched into action. "The cauldron is already boiling. I will keep preparing the materials on one end and coiling and measuring on the other. You make rope in the middle. In that way will we see the men back home to their wives and children."

Trufflesbane awoke in the clearing on the third morning. She yawned and stretched. The air was sweet and crisp. She looked at her friend. He was still where he had been before: hunched forward, eyes firmly fixed on his work as his nimble fingers moved with blinding speed. She turned her eyes to the entrance just past the clearing -- the place they had come so far to find. She sighed, then trotted off to break her fast in the meadow she had found by a nearby stream. A bit later, she ate an apple from a nearby tree for dessert. She made sure to reach up and pluck one from the low branches. She did not eat any of the ones that had fallen. She needed to keep a clear mind; she had begun to worry, and she had some thinking to do.

She came back to the clearing. Her friend was still there, still in the same pose as she had last seen him. Usually she did not bother much with thinking. Life was easy to live and enjoy. Thinking too much about things always seem to spoil that. But something was wrong, and she had determined, perhaps against her better judgment, that she must think about it.

Where to begin? They had been just about to arrive at their destination when a stag had started watching them from the forest. Then they had come to the opening in the trees. Her friend had dismounted and started saying words to the stag. After a while, the two of them had stepped over to a rock that was lying on the ground. They had bent and stared at it for a long while, and the dwarf had said more words.

Then they had rushed over to this spot, looked around at nothing, and her friend had sat down on the tree stump and begun twiddling his fingers in the air before himself, repeating the same pattern over and over again, eyes fixed to his fingers, so as to get the twiddling just right. And there he continued to sit, engrossed in this activity; night and day, day and night, without end.

As she concluded her review, the answer presented itself. Funny, this thinking stuff was not as difficult as everyone made it out to be. If everything worked out, she might start doing it on a regular basis.

In their long acquaintance, her friend had only ever asked one thing of her, and that was to never disturb him when he was working. She never had. But now that she thought back, there had always been the 'things'. This time the 'things' were missing. The 'things' were the stuff that he made objects from, and the 'things' were also tools, tools he used to shape the stuff into other 'things'. All of that was missing. Thus, she concluded, he could not be working, and she would not be disturbing him.

This was some top-notch thinking, even if she did say so herself. She would simply walk right over and put an end to his sitting and staring and finger twiddling, and make him come drink water from the stream and eat fruit from the trees.

She had this last thought while already striding forward toward the stump. But before she could reach it, there was a thunder of hoofs and the stag appeared before her. It stood towering above her. The air grew colder as its shadow engulfed her. She noted that the sun still lingered behind her and that this shadow should not be cast her direction. On some level she understood that the stag wished it to be and so it was. She tried to walk around, but again her path was blocked.

And where do you think you are going? said a voice in her head. Well, voices in her head? This was certainly something new, she reflected.

I am going to see my friend, she thought back in reply.

Friend! the voice echoed, then seemed to laugh. *You are no one's friend! You are a walking garbage bin wearing a saddle. Not a friend.*

Nevertheless, I am going to see him.

No you are not! thundered the voice, and the stag snorted steamy breath from its flaring nostrils. *I am much stronger than you, and if you try, I will slay you!*

But why? she thought at him.

Because, the voice answered.

She waited, but then realized there was no more. *Because? Because why? For what reason?* she asked.

Why? Why? Why? shouted the stag in her mind

and stamped a massive hoof. *Who are you to ask me why? Why do you want to see to him?*

Because he wishes to go to the tree and to finish the hammer and to save the children of the two rivers. But now he sits as one entranced, and I would go to him and wake him.

No!

But why no?

Because I do not will it! Because I am a god that revels in mischief and never forgets a slight! And I know his true name and the one bait with which to trap him: he will not turn away those in need. He will always aid the suffering, and thus is he undone.

But why trap someone such as that? she cried. *Why punish the just?*

He has aided those I've injured and spoiled my games.

And for that you trap him in a dream?

Yes.

Forever?

No, not forever. For, as you see, he does not eat or drink. He does not rest nor seek warmth, and so soon enough, he shall die.

Die! she cried out. *You will let him die?*

What of it? Everybody dies.

With that, she hung her head and quitted the clearing. Returning to the stream, she lay down and set her mind once again to thinking. Time passed swiftly while she considered. When the time came at last that she knew what she would do, she looked up to the sun and found that it was well past midday.

She took a cool drink from the stream and then walked back through the meadow, retracing her steps until she came once again to the apple tree. This time she sniffed at the apples that had fallen to the ground, selecting five of the proper type and eating them very quickly. In a short while, she began to feel warm and a bit numb. She opened and closed her jaws four times just so.

She returned to the small clearing, and once again the huge stag appeared to bar her path to her friend. *I have thought much about all you have said,* she called out with her mind.

And? came the voice of the stag.

If I do not wake my friend, he will starve or freeze or give out from thirst.

And do you remember what I told you would happen should you try?

Yes. You said you would slay me.

Very good. So you understand, said the stag.

Yes, said Trufflesbane. *But you said one other thing as well.*

And what is that? asked the god.

You said – she paused and locked eyes with him – *what of it? Everybody dies.* Just as the words were leaving her mind, she struck – struck with the speed of lightning kissing iron, her razor tusks tearing the chest of the astounded stag from one shoulder to the other. His bloody flesh hung in tatters. She sought to press her advantage and strike again, but the moment of surprise had already passed. As her tusks sought out flesh again, the stag reared.

With a deafening bellow, he crashed his hooves down upon Trufflesbane's back, driving her into the dirt. The saddle acted as armor and kept her back from being torn open. In the next instant, the stag lashed out again, striking her in the chest with lowered antlers, goring deeply, spraying her blood across the ground. With a toss of his mighty head, he flung her end over end like a child's rag doll.

He watched her flight as she sailed over the tree-tops. Judging from the arc she followed, he estimated that she would be falling in a heap at least a quarter of a league away. He made to leave, but just then, his ears pricked at the sound of far-off thunder. He had just espied a line of dust beyond the trees when Truffles-bane appeared, bursting through the brush in a shower of sticks and leaves, breathing steam, eyes aglow, blood covering her torn chest. She struck a fraction of an instant later. Now it was his turn to fly, hurtling like a comet.

Trufflesbane looked, but did not see any sign of him. A swath of forest was cleared of trees as far as she could see. She did not move. She waited motionless, searching with all her senses, but he was gone. She started slowly toward the dwarf. She must shake him and...

The hoof came down, shattering the left side of her face. She staggered, tried to scream in pain, but did not have the chance before the hooves rained down again and again. She tried to dodge, to retreat, anything! The voice of the enraged god screamed in her mind as he delivered one smashing blow after another. She felt the antlers pierce her side and her ribs being staved in. He flung her aside and she came to rest against the foot of a tree.

Well, garbage bin, said the stag, his rage spent. *You did earn one victory. Now the dwarf will not waste away and die slowly. Because of you, I will simply kill him so I can retreat and escape this wounded body.*

Trufflesbane tried to look at him, but saw only blackness. She realized that her left eye no longer worked. She shifted painfully until she could regard him with her right eye. He looked almost as bloody and battered as she. He was walking toward the craftsman, who was still sitting, silently twiddling, surrounded by the gouged and plowed earth and broken and splintered trees from the battle. He would die, never knowing how or why, and all because he had tried to help.

The stag reached the craftsman and prepared to strike. *Goodbye, Dvalinn, last of the sons of Ivaldi, maker of the mightiest of weapons.* The stag stopped talking all at once, then threw his head back and laughed until his antlers shook. *Oh, and that's the best part!* he said joyfully. *The irony was delicious! Maker of the mightiest of weapons,* he repeated. *If only you had forged a magical weapon that a pig could wield, she would surely have saved you.*

Trufflesbane's voice sounded in his head. *I've learned one peculiar thing about this thinking business. Sometimes the answer comes from the unlikeliest of places.*

The golden stag turned as he heard her struggling to her feet. He could not believe she was standing. She was an utter ruin, broken and bleeding. Her breathing came wet and rasping, but she met his gaze defiantly.

I had meant for you to watch him die first, and then finish you. But if you insist-

You will finish no one, she interrupted. *I will not allow it.*

He started to sneer, then stopped. The sound of her voice, the look in her remaining eye. A cold feeling danced down his spine. Beneath it all, he knew he was a coward. He only fought when he knew he could win. He was suddenly aware she was everything he could never be. Thus, when she began her final charge, he hesitated. Then he lowered his antlers and he charged as well. As their impact became imminent, he knew. In a head to head charge, he would win. He knew. Yet still, he doubted.

At the final moment just before they clashed, Trufflesbane leaped into the air and spun her body, striking with her right rear flank. Striking with the magical Ironstone weapon still securely fastened to her. Striking and slaying a god.

Some time later, Trufflesbane opened her eye. She tried to rise, but found that she could not. She had to reach him. But he was so far away. She stopped. Maybe if she just rested, perhaps slept. *No!* She had to reach him and she had to do it now. Inch by inch she dragged herself. This would all mean nothing if she couldn't...

There, almost there.

One more...

Trufflesbane dragged herself one more inch. Her head fell against the craftsman's leg, and then she died.

The craftsman took no notice.

Brekka was bustling at this hour of the afternoon. Asmund found a stable that would see to the feeding and watering of the pony and set off toward the tavern to give himself the same treatment.

A group of grubby boys ran past him in the street. They were chasing a smaller boy, shouting jeers at him as they went. Asmund turned to watch and observed them overtake the small boy in his flight, knocking him into the dirt. They encircled him and began kicking his crumpled little form, calling out all manner of unsavory assertions in regards to his parentage.

Without a second thought, Asmund called out, "Hey, you boys, leave him alone! That is quite enough of that!"

The boys stopped and turned to see what authority figure was spoiling their fun this time. They looked at Asmund with somewhat confused expressions on their grubby faces, then they all looked expectantly at their leader. It was obvious with one glance that he alone was singly qualified for the role of leader, because frankly, he was huge. He must be at least a few years Asmund's junior, but he was nearly as tall and twice as thick. He stepped forward, cracking his filthy knuckles. "Look boys, it's a little troll. It looks like he needs to be taught that he does not belong in town where proper people live."

Asmund saw with some small satisfaction that once the ruffians had turned their attention on him, the little boy who had been the original target of their abuse was able to slip away, limping and bruised. But now the town of Brekka's youth welcoming committee was fanning out into a semicircle around him. What was he to do? He actually felt woefully over-prepared for this level of threat. Something told him that fireballs and venomous snakes deployed against the neighborhood children might not make him too popular here. He thought quickly. A little theatrics and minor magic should do the trick, he decided.

He never got a chance to try, however, for no sooner had he devised his plan than the barrage began. The boys pelted him with clods of dirt and stones and whatever else they could dislodge from the ground around their feet. *This is quite enough of this,* Asmund was thinking, when suddenly the lead boy wound up and hurled a huge clod that struck Asmund in the chest, providing him an excellent view of the sky from flat on his back. This garnered a huge cheer from the gaggle of little monsters, who danced around him, chanting, "Troll! Troll! Troll!"

He caught sight of two adults, a man and a woman, passing by. They were being very careful to pretend not to see what was happening. "How do you like that?" he said to himself as he struggled to a sitting position.

"No one said you were allowed to sit up, troll!" snapped the leader, then kicked Asmund in the chest, driving him back down. Asmund saw bright spots of pain before his eyes and could not catch his breath. If the charmed robe had helped at all, he was sure he couldn't tell. His vision still was not clear, but he made out the form of the huge youth looming above him. He was lifting his boot to stomp Asmund's face, but as it began to descend the boy flew back out of view. Asmund saw another figure appear, the one who had shoved his attacker, sending him sprawling. He had a vague sense that the newcomer looked familiar. Then his dazzled eyes caught sight of the golden braids. *So that was the answer,* his confused mind told him. *To get Brandt to finally protect me, I simply had to kill him.*

"You'll pay for that, Kolga!" shouted the angry youth.

"Here I am, make me pay!" replied a girl's voice.

Asmund's vision cleared and he briefly forgot the pain that was splitting in his chest. He lifted his head and surveyed the scene. The big youth stood with his fists clenched, surrounded by his little henchmen. Standing between them and Asmund was his defender. It was a girl about his own age. She wore the short cloak of a woodsman as well as trousers and leg wraps. Her rough tunic was belted at the waist, where a short axe was hanging.

The leader of the pack charged her with a growl. He jabbed with a right followed instantly by a round-house left that caught her on the chin. She was already rolling with it when it landed, and in a heartbeat she had spun around, delivering a clubbing right which sounded like a snapping tree limb. The youth staggered back, catching his heel in a divot he himself had created digging out missiles to hurl at Asmund. He planted on his seat with an "Umpf!" and instantly began crying, blood streaming from his broken nose.

"Get out of here!" she shouted, taking a step forward. He scrambled to his feet and ran, pausing only to kick at his younger minions, who were fleeing as well.

"Let me help you up," she said, rushing over to where Asmund still lay. She steadied him as he struggled into a somewhat upright position. Finding it difficult to stand straight, he doubled over, grasping his staff for support. Drawing a deep breath was impossible. When at last he could stand up a bit straighter, he faced her. "Thank you," he said in a shaky voice.

"You're filthy," she said, brushing lightly at his

sleeve.

"I have a horsehair brush in my cart. It's right here at the stables." He pointed his chin in that direction, not wanting to chance loosening his grip on the staff.

"Here, let me help you," she said, supporting him as he walked.

He reflexively opened his mouth to refuse, then closed it again. He had a great aversion to being helped. It often made him feel guilty for being angry about it, as he knew people meant well. He just hated the insinuation that he was not capable. But this time was different. She was helping him because he had been attacked, and honestly, without her help, he did not think he could make it to the stables.

When at last they had reached their destination, she helped him to sit down on the back of his cart. He was certain that at least one of his ribs had been broken by the blow. He reviewed his options. For a healer to use healing magic on himself, he must give the hurt to another living thing. This was a deed he refused to do. It was one thing for an animal to meet a swift end to be eaten, but the thought of willfully causing it torture was one thing he would never do. He could lay in vegetation and use the magic, but even if he turned an entire meadow brown, the amount of healing he would gain would still be very little.

His best bet was thanks in part to how small a snake's stomach was. The flask of healing potion Gert had made for him was more then he could give the snake, so there was still a swallow left. He had thought to save it for a life-or-death moment, but this injury would take at least several weeks before it began to mend, and the quest would not allow for such a delay.

He dipped into his purse and drew out the flask. Even this small effort was excruciating.

When Kolga saw the flask, she said, "Good thinking, have something to dim the pain."

"I'm hoping it will do more than that," Asmund said, and then drained the last sip, leaving the flask upended in his mouth, hoping to capture every drop within. When it was finally drained, he inhaled deeply and put the flask away. It dawned on him that this deep inhalation had been impossible but a moment before. He experimented with another big breath and was pleased to find no pain. At last he could regard the state of his appearance. She had been right; he was covered with filth. He reached over to his larger pack and found his clothing brush. He rose and began preparing to clean his robe when he caught sight of her standing frozen, staring at him. "What?" he asked.

"What was in that flask?" she asked, astonished.

"Oh, that," he said, smiling impishly.

"You had cracked ribs. I didn't want to say anything and worry you, but you definitely shouldn't be moving like you are."

"It was the last of a healing potion that I had."

She folded her arms across her chest and squinted dubiously at him. "Right," she said. "If there is such a thing as a healing potion, then maybe a king or a wizard might have one, but not you."

"Well, I am a wizard!" he protested.

"I highly doubt that."

"Wait! Why is that?" he asked, offended.

"Well, for starters, when I first met you, you were lying in the dirt while children threw rocks at you."

He opened his mouth to reply, then closed it

again. Then he smiled and said, "Well, it's hard to argue with that." He set about ridding himself of the dirt and grime. She helped cheerfully, brushing the back of his robe for him, while he wet a cloth and wiped his face and hands.

Once they had finished she said, "There, not bad. Almost as if you were a real wizard."

He turned to face her and saw that the fist-shaped bruise covering her cheek and chin was turning an angry purple. "I just thought of a way to prove I am a wizard, and to properly thank you for coming to my aid." He stepped forward and took her cheek gently in his hand.

In response, she grabbed him by the collar and flung him back, sending him sprawling into the back of his cart. "You have some nerve trying to kiss me!" she shouted.

"No, I-"

"Not only do you have the delusion that you are some kind of wizard," she thundered on, "but to also have the delusion that after knowing you for less than half an hour I would ever welcome your sloppy advances!"

"No! No that wasn't it at all!" he stammered. "It was wrong of me to touch you like that without explaining. I'm sorry. Here, look." He pulled the wooden disk from his purse, then opened it and held up the mirror. "Look at your face, the bruise. I know it must hurt. You got that saving me. I can cure it with magic."

She shook her head and pushed the mirror away. "Whatever. You're not a real wizard, and I'm leaving." She turned around and headed toward the stable door.

"Were my ribs cracked or not?"

She stopped at the door and stood with her back still to him. Finally, she let out a groan and turned back around. "I don't know why I'm doing this," she said, more to herself than to him.

"All right then," he began. "I'm sorry again about before. This time with your permission, I would like to lay my hand on your face."

She managed a response that was eye roll, shoulder shrug, and a "just hurry it up" hand gesture all rolled into one.

Asmund placed his hand on her bruise tentatively, half expecting to go hurtling back again. He spoke the spell and felt the punch burning in his own face. He kept his eyes closed and repeated the words for dissolving the hurt away. When he opened his eyes, she was looking in the mirror and poking experimentally at her face. "If you are a wizard, then why..." She finished the thought by simply tilting her head a few times toward the street.

"Why what? Why did I not incinerate a pack of ten-year-olds with a fireball?"

"Oh, yeah," she said, rubbing her now bruise-free chin. "That could be frowned upon, couldn't it?"

They both broke into giggles at this. At last he said, "I'm starving. Let's go to the tavern."

"Are you paying?" she asked, still giggling.

"Sure! Provided you can get me there without being waylaid by packs of angry toddlers, then I'm paying."

In the tavern, Asmund tasted his first hot food since he had left the school. He closed his eyes, savoring the first bite. The prospect of facing danger had been paramount in his concerns, and he had not even considered how the long journey would deprive him of all the small comforts he had always taken for granted. When he returned from this quest, he would remember to be thankful for every bed, every bowl of stew, every loaf of bread fresh from the oven.

"How does one become a wizard?" asked Kolga. She was talking with her mouth full, elbows propped on the table, hunching over her food in a predatory manner. She seemed absolutely devoid of anything one might call traditional femininity. She moved and talked and ate like a rough woodsman. He made these observations without questioning them. He had rarely met anyone so confidently themselves, so completely without airs or conceits. It did not occur to him to question it.

"Well, one must have what is called 'the spark.' It is a natural affinity some people are born with."

"So you're born with the ability to do magic?" she asked, chewing a chunk of meat.

"With the potential. A good way to think about it is; to make fire you must first have a spark."

"How do you know if you have it?" she pressed, seeming truly fascinated.

"Well in my case, I was tested and a spark was in me, hidden and probably quite content to never be found. But some people have strong and hungry sparks not easily hidden. People know something is special when their child is predicting births and deaths, or speaking to animals and having them perform favors."

"Can you do those things?" she asked excitedly.

"The foretelling, no. I do not seem to have that

gift. I can, well not really talk to, but share thoughts with animals, and if they want to, they can do me favors. But I don't control them, I only ask."

She seemed amazed at his words. He felt a sense of pride wash over him and he sat up straighter. He wondered what else he could brag about. He wanted to tell her anything that would make her keep looking at him like this. It felt wonderful!

Then an odd sensation of being watched came over him. He glanced around the room and caught a man and woman looking at him. They seemed familiar. He considered for a moment, then realized where he had seen them before. He remembered watching them pass from flat on his back in the dirt being vanquished by a pack of children. They saw him looking and treated him to a repeat performance of awkwardly pretending they didn't see him.

He no longer felt like bragging. "How does one become a woodcutter?" he asked instead.

She sat back, noticeably disappointed to have the subject change from him to herself. "Well, there's nothing to tell, really. I live in the forest just south of here. My mother died; I never knew her. I was raised there by my father with my two older brothers. So that means I can fight and hunt and chop wood, but not much else. And I know what you're thinking."

"And what am I thinking?" he asked.

"That I should put on a dress and act like a woman."

"I wasn't thinking that," he said. "In fact, this whole time I've been thinking that I had rarely met anyone who was more comfortably themselves."

"You say that to be kind. But everyone thinks the

same thing. I should just be what I am meant to be and act the way they want me to act."

"Is that the way you think I feel?" he said seriously. "Look at me and then tell me if you think I feel like you should just be what other people expect you to be."

She seemed to consider this for a few moments and then smiled, taking a bite of bread. "What was it you said, comfortably myself? I like that. Besides, I would be awful at wearing a dress and trying to find a husband. I have bad manners, and my face isn't pretty. The only thing I have is these, I guess." She said cupping and lifting the breasts that were pressing against her tunic.

Asmund laughed. The action might have been lewd or sexual if someone else had done it, but Kolga did it innocently, just like a worker showing someone a tool or something they had made. His laughter was contagious and she started laughing as well.

After the laughter had mostly subsided, he asked, "Are you a good woodcutter?"

"Yes. It's what I've done all my life."

"Are you the best woodcutter in your family?"

She thought for a moment and then said, "No. Both of my older brothers are bigger and stronger and more experienced."

"But you are still good at it?" he asked. She nodded. "It would be the same if you ever wanted to wear a dress and find a man. Other girls would be better at it and know tricks to acting and looking feminine, but you would be good at it as well. We do ourselves a great disservice when we compare ourselves to others all the time."

"You're wise for someone the same age as me," she said. "It must be from studying to be a wizard."

"No, If I have any wisdom, it was taught to me by Aida, the woman who was like a mother to me. Without her, I don't know what I would have done, or who I would have become."

Kolga dropped her eyes, looking sad. Asmund observed this and asked, "Have I said something wrong? Something to upset you?"

"No. No, of course not," she reassured him. "It just made me a little sad for the mother I never knew."

Asmund nodded, then said, "She would have been proud of you."

"Ha, right," she said sarcastically. "I'm everything a mother could have dreamed of."

"But you are!" he insisted as she rolled her eyes at him. "I'm being serious. Do you see those people sitting over there?"

She looked at the man and woman he was now pointing at and said, "Yes, what about them?"

"They passed by me while I was lying in the dirt being attacked. They pretended not to see and walked right by. Do you know who didn't? You! You put yourself in danger for someone you had never met, simply because it was the right thing to do. I'm not even condemning those people for not going for help; for saying, 'That's not my problem, I'm not getting involved.' I'm just saying that the people who don't hesitate to do what's right, who are brave and step forward when others need help – those people are special, and their mothers would be very proud of them."

Kolga looked like she was about to cry, which was something Asmund suspected she never did – at least not where anyone could see her. She clenched her jaw and took a few deep breaths. "Are you also that kind of person?" she asked.

"I don't know," he said. "I would like to say I am. I'm on a quest right now, going far away from home to fight a monster and rescue children from harm."

"How can you possibly think that you are not one of the special people, then?"

"Well, because, to be perfectly honest with you, I wanted to pass by and say, 'That's someone else's problem,' just like those people over there did. I had to be convinced, to be shamed into coming. I'm always angry when people treat me like I'm useless or 'less than' because of how I was born. But when I was finally asked to prove myself capable, I argued. I insisted I was not as good as everyone else and should not be expected to do this task." Asmund paused, looking down at the table, reliving his meeting with Rangvald. "Then my master did the most painful thing I have ever experienced. He agreed with me. He told me I could go hide and not do anything. That no one would blame me, because life had treated me so unfairly."

"So then you decided to come on the quest?"

"No, I was relieved. I was going to give up trying to do anything. I was going to just hide away and start a career as a drunkard."

"So what changed your mind, then?"

"He reminded me that the children, the ones I told you about, needed my help. If I refused them, turned my back on them, then no hole I could ever climb into, be it ever so dark, no drink, be it ever so strong, would ever bring me peace. So I came. I will stop at nothing now. I must try to help them if I am able."

They were silent for a long while. Then Kolga spoke. "It is you who are the special one, not me."

"What? Did you not listen to anything I just said? I didn't want to come! I was scared! I had to be shamed into it. I've been scared the whole time I've been on this quest!"

"Precisely! Don't you see? I wasn't afraid when I saved you. I've beaten Olaf before. Chasing those little goblins away is no great act of courage for me. You were terrified to come and do what you knew was the right thing, and you did it anyway. That is true courage, Asmund."

Asmund had to admit that that did make a lot of sense when she said it that way, but he still hung on to a feeling of guilt for trying to refuse this quest. "What about you?"

"What about me?" she replied.

"Is there anything you are truly afraid of? Something you would do if you could only find the courage?"

She looked away and was quiet. Finally, she said, "Maybe, but it's not important."

"What is it?" he pressed.

"It's nothing. I said it wasn't important."

"That's fine. I just thought-"

"I've never been anywhere!" she said in a rush. "I've never done anything. I dream each and every day of leaving, even just visiting somewhere, seeing something new, but I'm afraid."

"Well, that's not so strange. You are afraid of leaving what is known for the unknown."

"Yes, but what scares me about it is also what excites me about it."

A thought struck Asmund, but he hesitated. She

saw the change in his face and asked, "What?"

"You know, I could use some company on my journey. I'm camping outdoors each night. Having someone experienced with the forest would be a great asset." He was pleased to see her getting excited. "I could pay you, since you would be away from your work of woodcutting."

"Are you in earnest, Asmund?" she asked, smiling broadly.

"Yes, I think it's a wonderful idea!"

"When do you intend on leaving?"

"Soon," he said, sitting up and draining his cup. "I need to buy provisions, settle up at the stables, and then get back on the road. This stop has already gone on longer than I had intended."

"If I run home to grab my things and tell my father, will you wait for me?"

"Yes," Asmund answered, retrieving money from his pouch for the meal. "Here, give him this, so he can see that you have been hired." He handed her a cut of silver.

"No! You mustn't pay me so much. I want to go," she protested.

"Nonsense! That is just to ensure that your family doesn't miss your axe too dearly. I shall pay you more than that for accompanying me. Silver I have aplenty. A helper and companion is what I lack. Now go, we must hurry!"

The craftsman worked quickly, his nimble fingers braiding the strands into rope. About an hour into the work, he felt something press against his left leg.

Perhaps the finished rope was piling up against his leg. Yes, that must be it. The old man was supposed to be coiling it neatly, but perhaps he'd fallen asleep again. He would spare a glance as soon as he was able.

I'll just finish one more foot, he thought. He hated to lose his stride. The lives of the miners depended on him now. He paused and glanced down, but the finished rope was neatly coiled, and there was nothing touching his leg. He kept working as quickly as he could, plaiting and twisting the strands just so. Inch after inch, foot after foot, moving into the second hour. Good, coming along now. But...

There is something there. He could feel it still touching his leg. He glanced down again. No, nothing there. He kept braiding. On and on. On and on. Perhaps his leg had fallen asleep. He had heard of that happening, though he'd never experienced the phenomenon for himself. Could that really happen after scarcely one hour of work?

He decided to ignore it. On and on he worked. On and on. The miners were depending on him. Yet more time passed. The pressure against his leg was becoming a distraction – what was it?

Okay, so he could not see it. Well, maybe he would be able to feel it. He stopped working for a moment and reached down, feeling all around. His hand felt nothing. There was nothing there! He continued his braiding and twisting.

He saw with a shock that there was blood on the rope he was making. Where had that come from? Had a blister formed and burst from the work? That was another thing he had heard of, but never experienced himself. What in all the world could give a dwarf's hands a blister? *I mean, what is this rope made of?* he thought with a chuckle.

Then he froze. Slowly, he repeated, *What is this rope made of?* He began working again, but his fingers seemed to hesitate. He continued working. On and on. Inch by inch. But he could not stop asking himself the same question: What was the rope made of?

The sons of Ivaldi had been given a gift: they could divine the ingredients of any object. He could even see the place they were from and the person who made them. It was his magical birthright, to know what anything is made of. So once more he repeated to himself, *What is this rope made of?* He could touch it, see it, he could even smell it. And yet he could not feel what it was made of. It was as if it were made of nothing.

That was it – it was made of nothing. He stopped working once again, and reaching behind him, placed his hand on the back of his chair. It felt good, strong; it was even warm from his body heat against it. But it was made of nothing. Like the rope, it was as if it were not there at all.

He reached down and touched the seat of the chair and felt a surge of relief: the power was not gone from him. He felt oak, strong and true. He knew what family of trees this came from. They grew near the entrance he had sought, right outside this hut. If he concentrated, he would see the face of the worker who had made the chair.

That's strange. He could see the face of the woodsman who felled it, but not the carver and joiner who fashioned it. *What else?* The little coil of finished rope to his side. There was not much of it, as he had only been working for about an hour. He reached out and touched it. No – just as if it did not exist. *What else?*

He thought for a moment. Then he reached down and touched the spot where he felt the pressure against his leg. He felt something. Something was there, but he was confused. He knew this thing. He knew it well. The ingredients? Confusing. The face of the maker? Nothing. What was this made of? He squeezed his eyes shut and concentrated. Concentrated on the one main thing it was made of. Then he had it.

Love. That was it. It was made of love. He opened his eyes. He was sitting all alone on a tree stump in a clearing. He was stroking Trufflesbane's head, though she could not feel it anymore.

CHAPTER SIX

The craftsman's eyes were now fully open and he saw and knew all that had transpired. He removed Trufflesbane's saddle. He felt faint with hunger and thirst. He open the saddlebags and ate and drank from his provisions. He packed some of the remaining food into a smaller purse.

He donned his shirt of coppery scales, banding it at the waist with a wide leather belt. From the belt he hung Scattersoul in its scabbard. He took out his helmet, which was darkened with rust and covered in dents. He set about plaiting his hair into two braids so as to wear his helm, but try as he may, his fingers could not remember how to twist and braid the strands. They would never have that knowing again.

His uncertain hands picked up the helmet once more, and he felt the luck go out of it. He left it on the pedestal of the tree stump. Finally, he strapped the carved Ironstone hammerhead to his back and took a few steps. Then, hesitating, he turned back. He took hold of the imaginary rope that he had made. He now knew that he had toiled upon it for days, so it was indeed the very longest rope that had ever never-existed.

He coiled it across his shoulder and he knew it

would not weigh him down or encumber him, since it did not exist. As he placed his hands upon it now, his gift of knowing worked very clearly. Its main ingredient was *belief*. He was now ready for all that would need to be done. He stooped and gently lifted Trufflesbane in his arms. On this, their last ride, he would carry her.

The craftsman strode into the entrance. It was a great hallway formed of ancient elm trees, their branches coming together and forming an arch overhead. The craftsman carried the body of his friend silently down the path. In all of history, Trufflesbane was the third largest of her race to ever live. But for all her weight, the craftsman bore her as though she were a feather. A part of him wished he could carry her down this hallway forever. But the hallway was not endless, and at last he carried her into the circle of the dead before the white door.

He looked all around. They stood in a grassy yard encircled by pale stone walls. He found a space on the turf between two armored skeletons and set her down. "If we can go no further, then this is a good place to rest, and I will rest beside you, and now and then the horn will sound for us and we will be whole again, if only for an hour at a time."

He stood and drew Scattersoul, scanning the circle of the dead. He saw movement to the right of the white door. One of the dead was being reborn, muscle and sinew returning, blood and flesh forming anew. The shirt of rings that had lain inside the bones rose and took shape. The skeletal hand gripped its sword in its scabbard and then became whole. The warrior rose to his feet and regarded the dwarf.

"Who seeks the tree?" asked the warrior in a deep,

commanding voice. He was now tall and thick of wrist and ankle, fair-skinned and stormy-eyed, with a golden crown atop his long brown hair.

"I am the craftsman of the Great Hall, oh Fjolnir, King of the First Dawn."

"You know me, dwarf?" asked the king in surprise.

"Stories are still sung of your glory, oh King. Your wisdom is legendary, your skill with the sword unsurpassed. I knew you by your crown, forged by my grandfather in the western caves before the building of the Great Hall."

"Ah, yes," said the king, placing his fist over his heart. "I knew your grandfather, and I know you now by your voice and bearing." The king drew his sword. "You are well met, master dwarf. I wish you luck in battle this day." With that, he struck, and cut off part of the craftsman's ear.

The craftsman struck back, but the king spun away with the speed of thought, leaving him lurching clumsily. He regained his guard and circled, blood flowing down from his ear and dyeing his beard crimson.

The king attacked again. The dwarf congratulated himself on catching the stroke with the flat of his blade, but then found himself staggering first one way and then the other as the king's second and third strokes fell. His coat of coppery scale held true, and his flesh was not cut, but the landing of the blows was so hard and heavy that he felt fiery pain as some of the bones in his chest cracked.

The warrior who had risen to meet him on this day was the greatest swordsman of legend – the fastest and strongest who had ever lived. The craftsman had relied on fate when setting out on this quest. He had planned to face each trial as it met him and find his way through – but now he was face-to-face with the truth. He knew now that he would die here, and no one would save the children of the Village of the Two Rivers.

The king, seeing the dwarf's armor holding true, renewed his attack. He made a feint and the dwarf fell for it, swinging his sword to ward off the blow and finding only empty air. Then the true attack struck home. This time, he avoided the armor and slashed the thigh of the dwarf, cleaving to the bone. The craftsman's body spun with the force of the blow and he slashed out at the king as he passed. The king parried his attack with ease and responded with a backhanded strike that opened the dwarf's left arm below the elbow.

The craftsman retreated, his sword up in defense. Each step he took was accompanied by a sloshing sound. His right boot had become a bucket of blood, catching the torrent as it ran down his leg. The king looked at him from across the circle. The dwarf looked back. The circle was too small. There was no cover to seek, no way to turn it into a running battle. It was a slaughterhouse, and he was being butchered bit by bit.

The king was coming. The dwarf took the initiative away. He leaped forward and attacked first, launching a feint at the king's head. At the last moment, he changed the direction of the slash, aiming it at the king's forward thigh.

The king watched with a sense of almost sad admiration. It was good for the noble dwarf to die this way. On the attack; trying to win. The dwarfs feint came at his face, but its true intentions were written all over it in a bold hand. The king did not even pretend to take the bait. He simply awaited the true strike. It came for his leg, slow and unbalanced. He turned the blade aside with ease and struck his final blow.

The craftsman lay on the ground in the growing pool of his own blood. King Fjolnir's final blow, which had been intended to remove his head, instead only sunk into his neck. The neck of a dwarf as compared to that of a man's is like a tree to a sapling. It was not a difference that would save him. He would very shortly die. In truth, he had already sustained more wounds than a man ever could. Every part of a dwarf was thick and tough. But it did not matter.

The King's speed and precision were unmatched, his training and experience unparalleled, and in such a small space, there was no way to avoid his attacks. The craftsman did not fear his end, though he was unhappy that he would not finish his work of building the hammer and saving the children. It was frustrating to have set about the work, to posses the ingredients, and then not finish the making. To have the materials and not put them together was galling.

Then, all at once, it occurred to him. *You fool!* he thought. *You were given the ingredients here as well, and you failed to put them together to build what was needed. First, a dwarf can sustain far more wounds than a man. Second, this circle is small; there is nowhere to hide, no way to avoid your opponent. There! Build what is needed.*

The dwarf began rocking violently on the ground. Breathing in huge gulps of air, he lifted his forearm to his mouth and bit the flesh deeply, tasting his own blood. He began moaning, then his moans became growls. His growls became screams. Lurching to his feet he bellowed, "For Odin!"

He locked his inhuman eyes on the king. His face purple and distorted, he screamed a berserker scream and charged. The king fought as brilliantly as ever, striking out quickly and strongly, wounding the dwarf again and again. But it did not matter. None of it mattered. The dwarf did not slow his advance for one moment.

The king sought to evade, but there was nowhere to go. The dwarf's powerful body drove him up against the wall. The king lifted his sword to strike again, but the dwarf grabbed the blade with his naked hand, ripped it from his grasp, and tossed it aside. The dwarf screamed again, and Scattersoul clove the great swordsman in half from top to bottom, leaving a great scar in the wall behind him. He sheathed Scattersoul, reached down into the ruin of Fjolnir, and claimed his heart. The body of the king became a skeleton once more.

The craftsman returned to Trufflesbane, bore her up upon his shoulder, and strode forward, kicking in the white door and entering into the presence of the Great Tree.

Asmund had finished obtaining provisions, making sure to get enough for two, and returned to the stables. He had paid the stablemaster as the groom prepared the cart and pony for departure. Now he sat waiting in front of the stable.

He looked at the sky, gauging the position of the sun. There were still plenty of hours left to travel, even with the delay. He looked at the place in the road where the ground had been potholed by dirty little hands seeking ammunition. He regarded the spot he had fallen and thought for a few moments. Then a small smile came to his lips. He fetched his spellbook and opened it to his healing arts spells. He had been working this entire quest to adapt otherwise harmless magic into an arsenal of weapons. It was to this end that he studied a particular healer's spell. He had just finished and closed the book when he saw Kolga approaching. "Oh good, you're here," he said with a smile.

She did not return his smile. She was dragging her feet and her shoulders were slumped. "I can't go, Asmund," she said glumly.

He climbed down from the cart and asked, "What's wrong, would your father not let you go?"

"No. It's not that," she said.

"Then what?"

"Asmund, I just can't!" she said in a pained voice.

"Oh," he said. "I understand."

"It's not that I don't want to. It's just that this is the place I know, this is where I belong."

"I'm not going to say anything to try to convince you, Kolga. I don't know what will happen on this journey. If you come, it has to be your own decision."

"I can't," she said, almost in tears.

"I understand," he said again.

"I'm sorry I held you up. I'm sorry, here." She held out the cut of silver.

"Don't be sorry. You saved me from being beaten to a pulp. Your mother would still be proud of you for caring about a stranger. You made my midday meal a delight. Don't feel bad because of not going. You are young, you have plenty of time to go and see what's out there."

Then she did something that was likely very out of the ordinary for her. She reached out and hugged him tightly. Asmund hugged her back and closed his eyes. She smelled like pine needles and sawdust. He realized that in spite of his words, he was deeply disappointed that she would not be coming. He very much wanted to talk her into it and tell himself he was doing it for her own good. But it would not be true and he knew it. Finally they parted and she said, "I'm still holding you up."

"I'm going," he said, mounting the cart rather smoothly this time. "Wish me luck."

"Luck," she said with a wave as the cart pulled away. Asmund pretended not to see her tears.

Back on the main road, he had traveled for only a few minutes when he reached the wooden bridge that traversed Brekka's main river. A wagon with a broken wheel was blocking the center of the bridge. Two men were trying to make repairs. Asmund's shoulders slumped and he sighed. *Great,* he thought to himself. He was still trying to process the disappointment of Kolga not accompanying him, and now, instead of launching into his journey and making progress, he was halted and going nowhere.

Realizing he was going to be here for a while, he surveyed his surroundings. His eyes followed the river to his right as it ran into the town he was trying to leave behind. Looking up the river to his left, he saw a millhouse surrounded by farm fields. The side road that went past the mill continued into the hills and would eventually make its way to Lundvar. Straight ahead, he could see the open road stretching out before him. He fidgeted in his seat, longing to be upon it.

Through the trees ahead and to his right, he could see a fortress overlooking the town, perched on a hill. He had seen it clearly from in front of the tavern. It was dark and squat with a traditional wall of pointed timbers. *Right now,* thought Asmund, *whoever calls himself king of this little chunk of land is holding court.* Perhaps this evening there would be feasting and entertainments. Asmund shifted restlessly on his seat. *I will probably still be waiting here by then,* he mused despondently.

Perhaps he could help these men mend their broken wagon somehow. He watched them working. They seemed to have it figured out, they just could not quite get it all to fit together. Asmund told himself to stop feeling anxious over that which could not be helped. He took a deep breath and forced himself to relax. Just then, he heard a distant horn from somewhere ahead. The men seem to get a handle on the broken wagon at precisely the same moment. They fit the wheel back in place and tapped the block that kept it all together snugly into its spot. They pulled the wagon to the other side of the bridge and moved it off the road.

"Is everything all right now?" Asmund asked as he pulled up beside them.

"Oh, yes, My Lord. We are going to check all the wheels on our tired old wagon and make sure it is fit for travel once again. We are sorry to have detained you for so long," the driver of the wagon said apologetically.

"Not at all. Farewell, then," Asmund replied, all impatience now forgotten. He urged the pony forward, happy to once again be moving.

He started to whistle along with the pony's clip-clopping tempo. He gave a little salute to the fortress as it loomed alongside. He had almost reached the side road that would lead to it when a troop of men emerged from the trees and blocked the road. The men were all armed and armored. Asmund glanced behind him, looking for an avenue of escape, and saw the two men in the now-mended wagon pulling up behind him. He opened his mouth to call out a warning, but then he saw the faces they wore and the weapons they now held.

"Hello again," said a familiar voice.

Asmund focused on the owner of the voice, which turned out to be the leader of the bandits he had last seen blubbering for mercy with dark green vines entwining his legs. "You!"

"My lord wizard, I beseech you, do not kill us until you hear me!"

Asmund's mind was racing. He had feared that the bandits had realized his bluff and were out for revenge. But the man's voice and words seemed to speak another tale.

The bandit pressed on. "My lord wizard, I serve the king, Calder the Bold. I come to you on his behalf. When we reported to him why we had failed to rob a stranger who was passing through the kingdom, we told him that you were a great wizard. He commanded us to invite you to meet with him. He has need of the services of a wizard. He will pay you most handsomely for your aid."

Asmund already knew everything he needed to know about this king. He was the kind of ruler who had his men act as bandits, robbing the defenseless as they passed through his realm. This practice was not considered odd or even particularly evil by most. Everyone knew that you either traveled with enough men to make attacking you too costly, or if you were in trade, you brought something extra to bribe your way along. But whether it was common or not did not matter much to Asmund. He hated those who took advantage of the weak. He also had no doubt that the people of the town he had just visited were very heavily taxed, and woe to those who could not pay. These were feelings that he knew would be best kept to himself. His refusal must be firm but respectful.

"You must give my regards to your noble king, but make my apologies. As you will recall, I told you I am on a quest, and thus have no time to stop," Asmund said. He saw a pained and apprehensive look play across the bandit's face. Some of the other warriors' faces were showing a different reaction. They had not seen Asmund's earlier performance and could see no reason for their spokesman's detestable weakness.

As if to confirm this, the driver of the wagon with whom he had exchanged friendly words earlier came striding up beside his cart, hissing, "This withered sapling is your great wizard, Holger? Enough talk! I will do what you are too weak to do." He reached for Asmund.

If he were going to have a chance, Asmund knew he must put on another convincing performance. He spoke loudly to the man so all could hear. "If you touch me, you will be very sorry."

The man grabbed Asmund by the front of his robes. Asmund whispered, "Sleep," in the forgotten tongue and tapped him on the head lightly with one finger. The man crumpled instantly. His knees buckled and he fell like a sack of rocks. Since he had been leaning forward to reach Asmund, his path to the ground was not clear. The man's body was completely slack; there was not a bit of muscle tension or resistance, and as his chin struck the edge of the cart, his head snapped back at an unnatural angle.

The second man from the wagon ran to his companion and examined him. Despite having seen his chin hit the cart on his way down, Asmund was shocked to hear him report, "He's dead!"

Asmund leaned over to look, and the second man scrabbled backwards with terror in his eyes, avoiding his gaze. The assembled warriors had not taken note of the man's neck-breaking collision with the cart. From their perspective, Asmund had simply touched the man on his head and he had fallen lifeless to the ground. They had no choice but to believe that he could kill with a thought. Only Asmund knew that it had been the healer's spell he had just prepared at the stable, the one he had been intending to use as a less lethal defense. Its typical use was for when extreme pain called for total sedation. He wanted very badly to show some emotion, to apologize. But looking into the terrorized faces of the assembled warriors, he knew that he must own the deed so they would let him go on his way.

"Did I not warn him?" he said in his most commanding voice. "Let he who would be next stand in my way. I have only to point one finger at you and you will follow this fool into the dark. Now give me the road!"

The warriors began to scramble out of the way. "Wait!" called Holger, holding up his hands to stop them. "My Lord, please forgive me, but will you not just come hear the king?"

Asmund held his index finger straight into the air. He began to ever so slowly lower it in front of him, making it apparent that when it came to rest, it would mean death for anyone still foolish enough to be standing in his way.

Holger signaled to the man standing next to him, who rose a horn to his lips and gave a short signal burst. Asmund felt a sense of dread. What was he signaling? He looked around and saw nothing at first, but then his attention was drawn to movement on the side road leading to the keep. He watched as two soldiers stepped into view, one of them pushing Kolga ahead of him with his knife pressed to her throat. Now he knew what had been happening while he was detained at the bridge. He looked back at Holger, wishing desperately that a point of his finger really could cause instant death.

"Our spy located you as you prepared to leave the stables and observed the fond embrace you shared with the woodsman's daughter. Now, I am most sorry to tell you, if you kill any more of us, or if you refuse to see the king, she will be slain without hesitation."

"What do I care for her? I can be observed embracing a girl in every village I pass through," bluffed Asmund.

Holger shook his head. "No, My Lord. I know you do not speak the truth. You forget that you told me that you are a wizard of light. You went to great pains to not kill us if you did not have to. You only killed Ivar when he put a violent hand upon you, and even then I saw the pain in your face from the deed. I know you would not let a young woman be put to death when you could prevent it simply by talking to the king."

Asmund did not feel up to this level of play. He had hoped he could use some simple deceptions and bluff his way through any of the obstacles that happened to fall in his path. He was learning that this had been wishful thinking on his part. Many of the people he encountered wanted to do him harm, and their ability to deceive and manipulate him seemed to be a much more powerful magic than he could ever wield.

"Very well, Holger, lead the way. You win," he said, then added with what he hoped was a little menace, "Enjoy your victory. You may live to regret it."

"I already do," replied Holger quietly.

The troop of warriors led Asmund up the hill to the dark fortress. Holger went ahead with Kolga and her two captors. Asmund wished he could speak to her, could tell her how sorry he was that she had gotten mixed up in this.

When at last he arrived in the courtyard, the clearly terrified soldiers directed him toward the throne room, keeping their distance from him and avoiding eye contact. They made use of awkward hand gestures and nods until they had led him to where he needed to be.

Asmund entered the room and was greeted by a well-fed, perfumed man, who leaned much too close to him and whispered, "What is your name, My Lord?" The warriors who had been on the road held their collective breaths as the fancy man did this. Asmund's only reply was to step away from the man and stare at him wordlessly. The man got the message and stepped back. "My Lord King, may I present to you," he paused for the space of a breath, "The Wizard!"

Asmund took in the scene. Holger had just finished whispering in the king's ear. Sitting on the floor at the king's feet was a girl a year or two younger than Asmund. She had a hint of dark circles forming beneath her hollow, distant eyes. He saw four small bruises on the left side of her throat. The man sitting over her had a fat paunch under his bright red tunic, which he was smoothing with his soft, small hands. Asmund was struck by the man's ugly mouth, whose lips seemed to be perpetually and deliberately pursed, as if the man thought this made him look handsome. Encircling the king's brow was a crown that was crammed with large jewels but held no aesthetic beauty. Finally, Asmund's gaze took in the top of the man's head, where poorly tinted hair from the sides was swept over the top in a vain attempt to conceal where he was balding.

Asmund knew he was meant to be impressed. Everything about the man was desperate to impress, from the child at his feet who would be beautiful if she did not look so broken to the brightly dyed fabrics of his garb and glittering jewels on the gaudy crown. Asmund looked at the girl and his blood boiled. He felt an urge to ask when a real king would arrive. He wanted to point out to the jackass sitting before him that his father's manservant had more wealth then he did. But he knew Kolga was somewhere close by with a blade held to her throat, and so he held his tongue.

For a time, no one said a word. He watched the ugly pursed lips go poutier and poutier. *What is going on?* he wondered, then he realized. He had come in, looked the little king up and down, his derision showing on his face, and then stood without making any sign of acknowledgment. He had made no bow, no sign of respect. Made no introduction. After all, Asmund had not asked to be here. He had nothing to say, and so he said nothing.

The king was not accustomed to this. Everyone in his life had one function, and that was to validate his delusions of greatness. Asmund was disrupting that, maybe to his and Kolga's peril. He hoped not. But now that he had begun, he would have to keep it going. Perhaps this would be a good play for power. He must still seem dangerous; someone not to be trifled with. They had forced him to come here, so the king could do the talking.

"They tell me you are a wizard," said the king, at last breaking the silence. Asmund's only reply was a single, tiny nod. This made the pouty frown deepen for a moment. Then the king pressed on. The tone of voice carried an affectation of command that would only be performed by someone who had no idea how ridiculous it sounded. Someone insulated from reality. "I have need of a wizard. You will serve me now and I will give you great wealth."

"No, thank you," Asmund replied calmly.

The king looked around, seemingly confused and looking for an explanation. The word 'no' was quite foreign to him. Before anyone else could speak, if they were so inclined, he continued. "We are not some small kingdom, if that's what you're thinking. We may not be as big as some other ones, but we have just as much wealth. I'm wealthy, you can count on that, believe me."

"It's not that," Asmund said, anxious for the king to shut up. "I am on a quest. I cannot stay."

"Yes, yes. Holger told me you were on a quest. Someone else can do that quest, and you can stay here."

"I can't."

"Holger!" the king shouted. "Where is the woodcutter's girl?"

"She is nearby, my king," he answered.

"Does she have a knife to her throat?"

"Yes. Just as you commanded."

"Very good. Then I will ask him nicely once again, and if he answers with anything but yes, I want them to slit her from ear to ear."

"If she dies, you die!" Asmund said, trying not to sound as desperate as he felt. He couldn't say that he was surprised by the direction this interview was taking, but he knew that Holger must have told the king about his seemingly lethal display on the road. He must be firm and threaten the king with death. Men like this were cowards, weren't they? Of course he would let them go if he feared for his life. He saw Holger, who was standing behind the throne where the king could not see him, wave his hand to get his attention. He looked into Asmund's eyes sadly then shook his head very deliberately. *No? What does he mean, no?* Surely this pompous little dimwit would not sacrifice his own life because he did not get his own way! It didn't make any sense! Asmund looked back into the king's face and ice gripped his heart. That was exactly what he would do. This was a level of narcissism, of ignorant certainty, that could not be reasoned with. Kolga was a hair's breadth away from dying. Dying because of him.

"For the last time," said the king. "Wizard, will you serve me?"

"Yes," said Asmund immediately.

The king's smug smile communicated to everyone that he had known he would win the entire time.

"With one compromise," Asmund added. "You will tell me what it is you most desire from a wizard, what is most important. I will serve you in this, and then you will release me and the girl so I may complete my quest."

Asmund saw the king's face scrunch up in disapproval and his mouth open to protest. Asmund headed him off, saying, "I know the king, in his great wisdom, will accept this arrangement. Why win his way brilliantly and get the service of a powerful wizard, only to then turn around and, for the life of one peasant girl, have the wizard strike him with a slow rotting disease, a burning pestilence that starts in his crotch and then eats its way through the rest of his body? Only a fool would do that, not a wise king who could outsmart a wizard."

He searched the king's face to see what effect his words had had. Had he laid it on too thickly? Too much burning crotches and false flattery?

"Very good," the king said. "Have my wizard taken to his chambers. I will consult with him in the morning."

Relief washed over Asmund. He considered demanding to see Kolga, which he very much wanted to do, but he did not think it would be wise to press his luck. Instead, he gave a small bow. The king's eyes darted around the room, checking that everyone had seen, and Asmund was led out of the chamber. The king immediately started telling everyone assembled the story of what had just happened in front of them, including revised dialogue and everything he and Asmund had been thinking. Asmund was still in earshot when it began.

"He is this great wizard. Maybe the greatest. They all said that. Everybody told me that. He won't work for you, they told me. Well, I said, bring him to me, I will..." Fortunately the ridiculous voice grew too faint to hear as Asmund was led down the hall.

They came to a bedchamber, and Asmund was locked inside. He walked calmly across the room, stood by the bed for a moment and then fell across it and hid his face in the blanket, silently weeping.

This was not fair. A couple of days ago he had been at school, studying magic. Now he was halfway across the land, imprisoned, pretending to know what he was doing. This day already seemed like a dream to him. Had he really killed people? Is that who he was now? He was weaving lie after lie, and he knew it was going to come falling down around his ears.

He may have bought himself one more night, but tomorrow morning, Calder the Brainless was going to demand that he wield some great magic. When they learned that he could not do great magic, they would also learn that he could not really kill them all with a thought, and then he would meet the end that had been inevitable this whole time.

I wonder if they'll let Kolga go and just kill me, he thought, looking for some sort of bright side. No, that was too much to hope for. *They'll probably keep her, and she'll end up the same as that poor girl sitting in the throne room.*

At that thought, Asmund sat up and dried his eyes. He clenched his jaw, remembering the abused girl. Anger flared in him. He must escape and find Kolga. She was only here because of him. He could not let her suffer. What if he could not escape? What then? Well, he had been doing pretty well bluffing his way along, making small magic seem big. He would find out what the king wanted and try to deceive him. *I wish I knew in advance what he might want, so I could prepare for it,* he thought.

A knock sounded at his chamber door. He stood, straightened his robes, and wiped his face, making sure there were no signs of tears left. A moment later the door opened and Holger stepped in.

"What do you want?" Asmund snapped.

"I came to tell you I'm sorry for all that has happened. You spared my life. I know that you are peaceful and good. I regret the part I have played in all of this."

"Then you will set Kolga and me free?" Asmund asked.

"I cannot. I would that I could, My Lord, but no."

"You mean you will not. Do not lie and tell me you would if you could."

"No, My Lord. Even if I were not afraid for myself, I couldn't. I have no power with those who guard the girl. They cannot be bought or intimidated. They follow him for neither money nor duty. They believe in him! They worship him! He tells them how majestic he is, and they gobble it up by the spoonful."

"Can you at least take me to see her?"

"Impossible," Holger replied, shaking his head.

"Then just go! Leave me!" said Asmund, irritated.

"As you wish, My Lord. Please be careful. You showed wisdom today. Make him think he is always getting his way. Threaten him with discomfort or embarrassment, but not death or defeat. He is not careful or rational. He can be manipulated, but not intimidated. If you give him what he wants, there is a chance he will honor the bargain. Good luck."

"Wait," Asmund said, halting him at the door. "Not that I trust a single thing you say to me, but if you would help, then tell me, what will he ask of me?"

"I have given that some thought. I cannot say for sure. I know he covets wealth. He is also distressed because his nephew, Elof, has become a threat. When Calder's brother died, the throne was passed to Elof, but Calder seized the throne and ordered his young nephew put to the sword. The soldiers that were to be his assassins took pity on him and sent him far away.

"Elof grew big and strong. He went to sea and raided everywhere he could sail. Unlike his would-be killers who showed pity, Elof shows none. He became famous for killing children and for roasting alive those whom he conquered. Now he is a greatly feared war chief. He has grown wealthy on plunder and is using that money and his rightful claim to the throne to gather men in Lundvar.

"This Calder greatly fears. So a larger army is also what he craves. But that brings me back to wealth. If the king has wealth then he can hire and equip and feed a large army." Holger stroked his chin and thought for a moment. "Yes, wealth is my guess."

Asmund was already considering what he might prepare.

"Goodnight, wizard, good luck tomorrow," said Holger, and went out, closing and bolting the door behind him.

Asmund sat down at the room's small table and began to plan until the shadows deepened on the chamber window. Another knock sounded on the door, and a young man entered with a serving platter.

Asmund forced himself to eat, though he was not hungry. While he did, he stared at the plate, lost in thought, trying to imagine a solution. The remaining carcass from the squab gave him an idea. Using his teeth and knife, he removed its bones. He cleaned and polished them with his napkin until he had a convincing pile. He might not actually have the seeing gift, but now, with a little acting, he could add some magical authority to his opinions.

Next, he cleared a space and set out the supplies he would need to try an illusion. These consisted of an apple from his dinner platter, a handkerchief from his purse, and a handful of silver from his pouch – enough silver to hire at least twenty warriors. Studying the apple closely Asmund prepared the glamour and cast it upon the pile of silver. Now there were two identical apples laying before him. He removed the real one and set it aside.

"Behold, my king! But an ordinary apple," he rehearsed. "Now lay this magic cloth that I give to you over it and say the words that I will tell you." Asmund paused, scratching his head. "Blah blah blah," he said when imagination failed him. He would need to come up with something before he used the trick. He whisked back the cloth and revealed the pile of silver. "Once a day, place the cloth over a piece of ordinary fruit and say the words. Day after day, a new pile of silver will be yours. Now do not forget, hang the magic cloth over a freshly cut yew branch between uses so it can soak up as much magic as possible. You see, it has not been hanging on a yew branch, else the pile would be three times this size." *Oh yes, that's a nice touch,* Asmund thought.

So Calder would ask him for wealth, and with a simple illusion, he would give him a handkerchief and a pile of silver. He would be at least a day away before the king realized that he did not have an unlimited supply of wealth, only a little piece of cloth. Not bad. Act it well and it might just do the trick.

Asmund yawned and stretched. He needed rest. He got into bed and closed his eyes, but sleep eluded him. When finally it arrived, it was a troubled sleep, haunted by his fears. At last his dreaming mind went where it always must. The children looked up at him and said, *"Asmund, help us."*

He awoke with almost a sense of relief.

The morning passed slowly as he sat in the chamber, waiting for his meeting with Calder. A breakfast platter came and went. He began to get nervous as he looked outside and saw the sun climbing in the sky. His mind began to wander from one doubt to another. He was starting to imagine the scene wherein someone was even now reporting to the king his very wizardly episode in the town, the one where he was lying in the dirt being terrorized by a group of tiny tots. Then he could see the king spending at least an hour telling the court how he had known the wizard was a fraud and how he had told them so all along. To which they all dutifully agreed, "Yes, that's right, he told us all so all along." Then he could see them all coming in here as one merry band to start sticking sharp things in him.

Asmund was clacking and shuffling from one end of the chamber to the other when a knock came from the door. A soldier poked his head in and said, "The king is awake now. He will see you."

Asmund shook his head. Nothing was wrong. Nothing had happened. It had not even been a power-play to make him stew, although it had had that effect. This was just the time of day that idle drunkards typically arose.

The soldier led Asmund through the fortress. As they passed doors and staircases and hallways, he wondered where Kolga was being held. When they arrived at the throne room, he paused, but the soldier said, "The king wants to speak to you alone, in his personal chambers."

When they arrived, the king was eating breakfast and quaffing ale. The soldier was directed to wait outside.

"Wizard," the king said happily, as if greeting an old friend. "Come, sit." He pointed to the chair across the table from himself. "Do you want some food? Have you eaten?"

"Yes, I ate some hours ago," Asmund replied.

"Did you try the eggs? We have the best eggs here in our land. Last year the king from Einarshofn was visiting, and he would not stop talking about the eggs! You have to try them! I shall ring for another plate."

"No, My Lord. I mean, I already had some," said Asmund, then added, "They were so good that I had a second plate."

This seemed to please the king. He showed his pleasure by sitting back and pursing his lips in that exaggerated way he thought to be handsome. Asmund marveled at how he constantly lied to impress anyone and everyone about the stupidest things, and now, just like everyone else here, he was going along with it and humoring him. Asmund was perfectly aware that there was no king in Einarshofn; there was a queen, and she certainly had not visited here, where the king's fortress was smaller than her stables, to rave about the eggs. But Asmund was depending on the king's good graces, and so was prepared to humor him in whatever fantasy he cared to concoct.

"Have you given thought to how I may serve you, Lord?"

The king became thoughtful, casting his eyes down and to the left. He picked at the wood on the chair's arm. Asmund realized that the king had not given it much thought, if any at all. That was obviously the king's way. Someone like him could act on the fly -- it did not much signify how things turned out, as he was going to retell it with himself having been brilliant anyway. And then everyone around him would confirm it to be true, just as he said it was. Asmund imagined that Holger was likely responsible for any of the thinking around here that was not spur-of-the-moment, while King Calder the Bold took credit for it.

At last, Calder stopped picking at the chair and looked up. "To be honest, I wanted you so I would be unstoppable in battle. You know – the fireballs and vines arising from the ground. Killing with the touch of a finger. That's why I really don't think this 'do one thing and then leave' is honestly going to work for me."

Asmund quickly steered the conversation away from that idea. "Well, the real way to be unstoppable would be to have the wealth to grow and maintain the biggest army. If I were to give you that wealth you could-"

"I hear you," interrupted Calder. "Of course, I already have the wealth to hire an army like you've never seen. But there just are not that many warriors around here to hire. I could get the men, the farmers, the craftsman, the shepherds. They love me! They are always asking me, what more can we do for you? They always ask me that! But you know, they are not real warriors and while I have them doing that, who runs the farms? Who runs the shops? No, I need magic to win battles! To strike fear into my enemies' hearts!"

Asmund was losing him. He was not interested in the gambit he had prepared. Calder had formed visions of a battle wizard hurling fireballs at his terrified enemies, and he was not letting go of them. He was like a dog with a bone – minus, of course, the loyalty and basic intelligence.

All at once, Asmund saw the solution. He knew what he could do. It would take a little longer than he had hoped, but in the end it would be true magic, the one type of enchantment he excelled at above all his peers. Now he just needed to tell it to Calder and convince him that it was his own idea.

"This is a grave matter," Asmund proclaimed loftily. "The fate of the kingdom hinges on your wisdom this day. And so I must counsel you with powerful magic." Asmund reached into his purse and drew forth the bones from the previous night's meal. "Ancient and most sacred bones! We seek your guidance." Thus saying, he cast them on the table in front of him. He hunched over, examining them intently, then gasped and raised his brows in mock surprise.

"What do you see?" Calder asked, leaning forward to look at the small white bones.

"There are two paths to victory in this. You will have to choose your course very wisely. But first I must warn you, Lord. Another seeks your crown. His name is Elof. Oh, I see it now, he is your nephew. He was thought to be dead, but he is not, and he seeks to take that which is yours." Asmund took a quick glance and was pleased to see Calder staring wide-eyed, his little hand clutching at his chest. Asmund continued. "Even now he gathers men."

"Yes, in Lundvar," the king added in a cautious whisper. "My spies tell me he does not yet have many, but he is gathering more all the time! That is why I need you, don't you see?"

"Yes, you are very wise, my king," Asmund said, garnering a nod from the rapt king.

"What must we do? Tell me!" entreated the king. "What are the two ways we can prevail?"

"Yes, I see." Asmund traced the tip of his finger along the length of one bone. "Yes, you were wise indeed. If I stay here and fight on your behalf, my magic sweeps Elof's men from the field! Everyone far and wide hears of this great victory. It reaches all the way to the ears of the king of Einarshofn!" This made Calder smile widely; that his old egg-loving friend should hear of his great victory warmed his heart.

"Oh, that is very nice," Asmund said, leaning close and examining a bone intently.

"What? What else do they say?" asked the king.

"Oh, it's not important. It's just something that is nice."

"What? Tell me!" pressed the king.

"Oh, it's just that after I wipe Elofs army out, the people sing songs about me for generations to come. Everyone knows the story of my greatness! Well, isn't that nice? Oh!" Asmund leaned extra close. "This is a wonderful testament to my devotion to you. Everyone says that you sit on the throne that I gave to you. Isn't that a sweet thing for everyone to say?" Asmund sat back, smiling, and looked at the king, who was now quiet and picking at the chair's arm once more. He let him sit for a little more and then said, "Shall I read the other path, or is it even necessary?"

"Oh, yes, tell me the other path," said the king, perking up.

"Very wise, My Lord. You must hear all options, that you may choose the correct path." Asmund leaned forward once again, looking closely at the bones. "Hmmm," he said, nodding his head, hoping to build the king's anticipation.

"What? What do they say?" Calder asked again, enraptured.

"In this path, I do not fight. Instead, I give you powerful battle magic. Magic that people do not even know I gave to you. It makes you invincible in battle. You defeat Elof, and the people sing songs about your greatness for generations." Asmund sat back in his chair. The king was silent but wore a little smile. *Time to drive it home,* thought Asmund. "It is you who must decide, but I favor the first course. I shall defeat Elof for you, My Lord, and secure your throne." As he was speaking, the king was already shaking his head.

"I know you would prefer that course," Calder said. "But you do not know how to see the whole picture like I do. The second course is what the bones are telling us. That's the perfect one, you give me the magic power, I defeat Elof. You will be gone; no one will know about you. Oh! You can go on your quest. That quest is very important. This whole time I've known I had to think of a way to save the kingdom and have you complete this quest. I said to myself, the quest is so important! I have to think of a way to kill Elof and still send the wizard on this important thing! And I did."

Asmund found himself slightly entranced as the

king's tiny hands made their constant gestures that seemed so disjointed from what he was saying. It was as if his hands were in a different conversation altogether. His speech itself was a series of circles going around and around. He was both saying what course he was taking and congratulating himself on taking it. He was bestowing and receiving awards for his own brilliance.

When a chance finally presented itself, Asmund broke in. "You are right, My Lord. I do not have the head for seeing all these factors as you do." He could sense that this was an invitation for the king to launch back into a speech about how good he was at thinking about lots of things all at once, so Asmund hurriedly added, "We must begin right away," and stood up from the table.

"What must we do?" asked Calder, rising as well.

"There is only one kind of magic powerful enough to accomplish what is needed. Bring me your sword."

"Wait. Do you mean a charmed sword?" the king asked doubtfully.

"Oh, no my king. A charmed sword would not suffice. I am talking about an enchanted sword. Yes, I will place charms upon it, rendering it unbreakable and ever-sharp, but the true magic will be that it can never leave its master's hand if he does not will it, and it responds not to his body, but to his thoughts alone. Those enchantments will render you invincible."

Calder stood looking at Asmund blankly. It was plain that he was not convinced.

"Let me explain, My Lord. When a warrior wishes to swing a sword, he must decide in his mind something like, 'I will swing it from my right to my left.'

His mind must then write a message to his body that is sent down until it reaches his hand. Once it obeys this message, how hard and strong he swings it is governed by his muscle and sinew. But not so with this enchantment. As soon as the master of the sword thinks it, the sword has completed the task, and it strikes with the force of thought, not muscle."

The king seemed to be understanding more, but was clearly not completely sold. Asmund continued. "This is a great magic. It will take me at least two days to complete. Then you can test it on your soldiers. Once you see how helpless they are against you in practice, you can send for Elof and challenge him to single combat. He is a Viking war chief. His position depends on the fear and respect of his men, so he will have to accept. Then, in front of all his warriors and yours, you will reach out with the speed and strength of a thought, striking him down instantly. You will be a legendary war chief. If you wish, Elof's men will follow you. If you choose, you can march on Lundvar and rule over all."

The king stood with his chest and lips puffed out. Asmund could tell that he was watching the dream that he had just set out for him in his mind's eye and liking what he saw very much.

"Wait here. I will get my sword," said the king, breaking away from the dream. He strode to the door of his bedchamber and threw it open excitedly. Asmund heard the king's voice scolding from the next room. "Don't drink all morning again! I don't like it!" He looked through the door and saw the girl who had been sitting at the foot of the throne. Now she sat naked on the rumpled bed, staring blankly at the wall while taking big sips from a cup of wine.

Asmund's thoughts turned black. He wondered if he could kill the king and bluff the soldier outside the door into taking him to the cell where Kolga was held. Once he got there and encountered the guards whom Holger said were fanatical in their love for the king, would he be able to fool them or slay them? The king closed the door as he reentered, and the sad girl disappeared from view.

"You promise that it will make me invincible?"

"Completely invincible, My Lord," Asmund assured him, not letting his murderous thoughts show on his face, "and the best part is, no one will know that the sword is the reason you are so mighty. You can say that I charmed the sword, making it strong, but no one will guess that there are enchantments as powerful as the ones I shall place on it. Even many wizards cannot perform these magics."

As Asmund said this, he realized it was, in fact, true. Master Rangvald had told him that he was the keenest student in this art that he had ever taught. Heretofore he had only been called upon to make simple items such as un-loseable keys for merchants, or glowing rods for miners, or directing stones for sailors. He had only performed the stronger enchantments in his training. He had begun to take for granted his abilities in this discipline of magic. Now he was hoping with all of his heart that it would save his and Kolga's life.

"I will need a place to work undisturbed for a couple of days. Also, I will need some items brought to me, and you can release the woodcutter girl. There is no need for her to be detained any longer."

The king handed the sword he had retrieved from

the bedchamber to Asmund, then called to the soldier outside the door. The warrior stepped in and bowed. "Take my wizard somewhere he can work undisturbed, and assign servants to assist him. They are to bring him whatever he requires. But first, take him to the wood-cutter's daughter. He may visit her, but she is not to be released."

Turning to Asmund, he said, "You will just have to trust that I still see the whole picture better than you. She will stay my guest a little longer, and you will be very motivated and do your work the best that you can."

"Very wise, as always, my king." Asmund smiled with a small bow.

Kolga was being held all the way across the fort-ress in chambers whose layout mirrored the king's. As-mund was led into the sitting room, where three guards sat at a table. They looked up as he and his escort entered. Asmund had to stifle a laugh. All three were emulating the king's habit of wearing a pursed, pouty mouth.

"What do you want?" one of them asked tersely.

"The king's wizard to see the prisoner," Asmund's escort said.

One of the guards got up and unbarred the door. "Knock when you're finished," he told Asmund as he entered. Once he was inside, the door was closed and barred behind him.

In a flash Asmund was caught in Kolga's tight em-brace. He felt hot tears against his cheek. At last she let go and stepped back, wiping her eyes on the back of her hand.

"I was actually afraid you would hate me," Asmund said sheepishly.

"I do. I was going to slap you, but that happened instead. Just consider it an angry hug."

He looked her over, catching his breath as he saw that she had a black eye. "Who did that to you?" he demanded, pointing at her face.

"I don't know which one. They grabbed me a little after you left. Two soldiers began dragging me away, so I knocked one out with the back of my axe and the other one punched me in the face."

"I'm so sorry about this. I never in a thousand years thought this would happen," he said.

"I had no idea it had anything to do with you at first. Not until they dragged me out so you could see me and I could see you. I just thought I was going to end up one of the poor girls that Calder the Bald singled out for his abuse."

Asmund began to laugh and she shoved him hard. "What in the world is so funny about that? Is it the rape that tickles you so? Or is it the ridiculous notion that I thought I was pretty enough to be one of the unfortunate ones? Answer me!"

"You called him Calder the Bald," Asmund said timidly. "I'm so sorry. The insult was funny, nothing else about this is funny. I swear I'm going to get you out of here."

"When?" she demanded.

"In a couple of days."

"What? I can't stay here a couple of days! I need out now!"

"Listen, I have a plan, but it will take some time. I have promised to make him a magic sword so he can defeat his nephew. Then he will let us go."

"Is that what he told you?" she asked. "Make one magic thing and then he won't want anything else? He'll just let us go?"

"Well, I haven't told you everything," he whispered, leaning closer in case anyone was listening in. "I tricked him. He thinks that us going away is part of the plan, and I made him think everything was his idea."

She looked at him doubtfully then whispered back. "Well, maybe so. I don't know about such things, only what I've been told. But are you sure he will still think the same way in a couple of days? Is he really someone you can trust?"

Asmund's certainty was quickly fleeing. Even were his plan successful, would the king honor their arrangement? Asmund believed he had convinced him that it was a plan for success and that everything had been chosen by himself, but what worried him was what version of the plan was the king telling himself. He had already noticed that the king had a habit of retelling events to himself in new and creative ways, and reminding him that things had ever been otherwise was fruitless. Kolga was right – the situation was still precarious. Asmund could not play this gambit and just hope for everything to turn out. He would have to delve a little deeper.

"You've given me much to think about. I promise I will get you out of here. Just be patient for a couple of days."

"You better get me out of here or I will never forgive you," she said miserably.

"I will. Now I have to go. I have a lot of work to do, but first come here," he said stretching out his hand to her. She wrapped her arms around him again and hugged him deeply. Asmund breathed in the pine scent of her hair.

At last, she stood back and said, "This isn't like me. I never hug anyone."

"It's very nice, it gives me courage," he said awkwardly. "But I was going to say, come here so I can heal your eye."

"Oh, I'm sorry. Of course," she stammered, embarrassed.

"Quite all right. Let me..." He placed his hand on her face, taking the pain and dissolving it into nothingness.

"Since I've known you, everybody wants to punch me in the face."

"Yes, being my friend just makes them so jealous of you," he jested.

"Yes that must be it," she said with a laugh.

"I must go. Wish me luck twice."

"Why twice?" she asked, cocking her head to the side quizzically.

"Once for the plan, and once to keep from accidentally calling him Calder the Bald to his face."

Her no longer bruised face split into a big smile. "Good luck, and good luck."

CHAPTER SEVEN

The woman of incomparable beauty turned toward the sound of approaching footsteps. She watched as the sacred white door was kicked open with a squish and a boom. The squish was the sound a boot filled with blood makes when it kicks a sacred white door, and the boom was the sound that door makes when it is kicked.

In strode a dwarf, covered head to toe in crimson gore. In one hand, he bore a dripping human heart, and over his shoulder was slung a giant dead pig. He walked up to her and wordlessly held out the heart. His face, covered in blood and missing most of one ear, was a mask of some strange, suspended insanity and rage. It was like a pot, just beginning to boil, being moved on and off the fire again and again, held in that moment of volatile limbo.

She looked at him closely, studying every minute detail, taking him in. She absolutely loved this! For thousands of years in the future, whenever she was at a gathering and the contest of "the strangest thing to ever happen" started up, she would tell this story and always win.

If pressed, she would have to admit that she immediately wanted this story to have a happy ending.

Thus, instead of doing what someone might expect her to do when a bloodied dwarf carrying dead livestock thrust a disembodied organ at her, she instead accepted it and called for Ratatoskr the Drill-Tooth.

The big red squirrel ran down the tree, bearing a seed pod of the old ash tree. She retrieved it from him and gave it to the dwarf. She swept her hand between the roots of the mighty tree, and a grave opened in the earth. Then, helping him to lie in it next to the big boar, she waited as he placed the seed pod into the hole in the hammerhead. His fingers were bleeding and trembling with rage. He lay back and she covered them over, then she spoke the words.

Yes, she helped them. Because it was a better story that way, and because she knew everything. She knew why the pig was dead. She knew that the lingering berserker's rage was the only thing keeping him from dropping dead at her feet. She knew why he was building the hammer. Also, once, long, long ago, he and his brothers had built her a ship, and she had always liked him.

The craftsman opened his eyes and saw darkness. He did not know where he was or how he had gotten there. He had to think. What could he remember? *Wait, that's it.* The last thing he could remember he was lying on the ground, waiting for death. His neck had been cut deeply. He reached up and felt for the wound. It was gone. He felt his ear. It was whole.

If his wounds were gone, he must be dead. He could vaguely remember the face of the goddess and being in a grave. Yes, now he was certain: he was dead.

At that moment, Trufflesbane licked his face. "Bluah!" he sputtered. "Trufflesbane, stop, or you'll drown me!" He reached up and hugged her about the neck. They were dead, but they still had each other.

His eyes slowly adjusted to the darkness. As he regained his sight, he saw that beside him on the ground lay the hammer – and hammer it now truly was, for where before it had been but a head, it was now fully formed, its wooden haft born of the seeds of Yggdrasil, the Tree of Life. He lifted it in his hands. Its power hummed through him. He strapped it on his back, and they set off through the darkness.

After traveling for a time, they heard the sounding of a battle horn. They began to see a faint light ahead. As they drew nearer, they saw the bridge of many colors, and in front of it, six strong women, noble of appearance and bearing, clad in bright silver armor.

A line of men were walking across the bridge toward a grand mead hall on the other side. The last of the men stopped before the women. One of the women placed her hand on his shoulder. "Leif," she said. "You were wounded early in the battle and might have retired from the field, but you stayed and were slain in a charge. You are worthy. Go and take your place in the hall of your fathers, where only the brave reside." The last man crossed the bridge, following the others.

As the craftsman and Trufflesbane approached, the women blocked the way to the bridge with their spears.

"This place holds nothing for you," said one of them, pointing her spear at him.

"Test us," said the craftsman. "We are worthy."

"You speak like a fool, dwarf. You are not dead.

Even now you lie at the foot of the tree, healed by Queen Frigg. This beast is dead, but it cannot cross the bridge. Beasts fight by instinct, for food or territory, never bravely. You make a mockery of that which is sacred."

Now he remembered – the goddess at the tree. Freya was helping him. He was not dead. He still must finish the hammer and face the wraith that took the children.

This changed things. He paused a moment, considering. How did he feel about this? Honestly, he felt tired. Just tired. They had worked so hard – finding the ingredients and putting them together, setting traps and being caught in traps, journeying and fighting.

He sat down on the ground and put his arm around Trufflesbane. She rested her head on his shoulder. Why did he feel this way? He had not failed his quest, not yet. So why this hollow feeling? He knew why. It was because he had actually been relieved. Relieved when he thought they were both dead and that they would be welcomed here. But now, he was supposed to go on with the quest. And Trufflesbane had given everything – sacrificed her life for love – and now, as thanks, she had been condemned to an eternity of wandering in the dark.

He was sick of this! One god tried to kill him, another god healed him, and all for what?

"Why do you sit on the ground? Are you waiting for the kitchen slop?" sneered the woman who had spoken before. "Would you still mock this sacred place? How dare you sit blocking the path to the bridge where heroes tread? A filthy pig and a simpering runt. Be gone, or I will crush you!"

"Test Trufflesbane!" shouted the craftsman, standing up. "She fought when she did not need to. She was wounded but did not retreat. She fought and died for the love of another."

"Impossible!" insisted the warrior woman.

One of the other silver-armored women spoke. "Test the beast. If it is not worthy, then cast them both down and be done with it. What does it harm?"

"What does it harm? What does it harm, Gondul?" spat the angry one, spinning on her. "The dignity of Asgard itself is what it harms!"

The craftsman had heard enough. He placed his hand upon his friend's head. "This is Trufflesbane, of the line of Hildisvini the Battleswine, who was friend to the goddess. She died in glorious battle this day, and I demand you test her!"

The woman spat in his face. No one spoke. All was silent as her insult hung in the air between them. Then, taking her spear in both hands, she moved to the side, away from the other women. "No one can say I did not give you a chance. "

The craftsman un-slung his magic warhammer and walked out to face her.

"Now, you vile runt!" crowed the woman, "I shall cast you down into the lowest pit. For I am Gunnr the Skullsmasher, horse maiden of the moon, Valkyrie of Odin, guardian of the Bifrost."

"And I am Dvalinn, last of the sons of Ivaldi, called Asger, the spear of God, the Dawnbreaker!" shouted the dwarf, lifting the hammer above his head as it began to glow.

Gunnr tightened her grip on her spear and looked into Dvalinn's eyes. He stared back without flinching and readied himself. The Valkyrie's eyes narrowed to slits and she launched forward. At that precise moment, Trufflesbane sent her hurtling down into the black mists in the chasm of the forgotten which runs below the rainbow bridge. Trufflesbane watched her as she fell, gave a short snort of approval, and trotted back to the craftsman's side.

The other woman who had spoken before came forward, her beautiful face smiling. "I am Gondul. I will test you, Trufflesbane." She knelt before the boar and placed a hand upon her shoulder. A moment later, her eyes widened in surprise. They remained wide as she watched the tale of the pig's deeds, and as it came to its end, a single tear formed in her amber eye and slowly rolled down her cheek. No Valkyrie had ever cried a tear, though they had watched the deeds of many.

The dwarf saw the tear on her perfect face and knew, even though he had lived so long and seen so many of the rarest treasures of the world, it was the most beautiful thing he would ever see. In that instant his heart was captured and he fell deeply in love with Gondul, though she would never know.

In a way, that pleased him, because pure love from afar and the love of animals were the only two kinds of love that ever stayed unchanged. Later, when he was killed fighting the wraith that took the children, it was of her perfect face bearing one of only two tears that a Valkyrie would ever cry, that he thought of as he died.

The Valkyrie reached the end of the boar's saga, and at last she spoke. "Behold, sisters: a hero! But her name is not Trufflesbane. Her name is Godslayer! Bane of Loki! Downcaster of the Valkyrie! Savior of the last son of the Great Hall of dwarfs!" The single tear rolled passed the corner of her soft mouth and dropped from her porcelain chin. It splashed off of Trufflesbane's pink tongue, and for a moment, Trufflesbane remembered the taste of fermenting apples.

Gondul turned and fixed her eyes on Dvalinn, for as she had lived the saga of Trufflesbane and had seen the many years of their life together, she saw the dwarf through the eyes of the boar's unchanging love. She saw his ways, both gentle and true. His compassion. His care for his fellow beings. She saw the goodness of him, and in that moment, she fell deeply in love with him, though he would never know it. And though she would never die, she never stopped loving him or thinking of the way his eyes had looked at her, just that once.

Trufflesbane understood all now, and thus she turned and spoke to the craftsman. "Our path together has ended, Dvalinn." He hugged her tightly. Then she spoke three words more and walked across the bridge.

The big white dog lay curled up just inside the gates of the underworld. Like all old dogs, sleeping occupied the majority of his day. People passed through the gates on a fairly regular basis. He paid them no heed. Never did someone who was not dead try to sneak into the underworld. Well, almost never.

Well, actually, come to think of it, there did tend to always be some hero or another sneaking in here, trying to rescue someone's immortal soul. Rescue from what? He was sure he did not know. Not like anyone was being tortured. At worst, someone might fall into the pit of darkness. More of an inconvenience than outright torture. Others came seeking lost information. He snorted at the thought. Why couldn't they have found someone in the village who knew how to write while Grandma was still alive? Then that recipe for rømmegrøt wouldn't have been lost forever.

He had nothing but time. It would yet be ages until his howl would be needed to call forth the wolf. So mostly he just slept. A large party of freshly slain warriors had just passed by, laughing and complementing one another on how well they had killed each other, when he sensed it: someone who did not belong here. Someone who was still alive. *Oh well.* he thought. *I guess someone really needs that recipe.* He stood and stretched. Then, sniffing the air, the huge, perpetually blood-soaked guardian of Hel trotted off to find his next meal.

He spied the party of warriors ahead, still laughing and slapping one another on the back. After a short way, roughly half of them turned off the great road Helvger, bidding the others merrily adieu. These headed through the mists toward the distant field of Fulkvang, the field of the fallen warriors. The remaining men cheered and waved and continued down the road.

The dog paused, sniffing the air again. No, not here. He walked on, following the remaining warriors. They passed the great ocean on the left-hand side. The shore was littered with the remnants of hundreds of wrecked warships. The dead warriors saluted Queen Ran as they passed. The dog sniffed the wet salt air and caught a hint of old, dead fish, but nothing living. He continued on. The warriors ahead were presenting themselves to the guardians of the Bifrost.

The realms they were passing, be they mists or

beaches or bridges, were reached through the under-world. But they were realms of Asgard, and those who dwelt therein would be called to fight once more after he howled on the last day. But the road and all that lay beyond, all the way to the inner wall of Helheim itself, was his to protect. So he would find whatever fool had come here, and when he did, he would feast.

He watched the last of the band of merry dead crossing the bridge and prepared to move on, when finally he located the scent. *There.* Strolling up to the women, with the spirit of a boar walking at his side, was a dwarf. He was not even trying to be sneaky about it. He was walking right up to them. Okay, so it looked as though he would not be feasting after all. But he was certain he was in for a show. The Valkyrie were without mercy. They would surely slaughter the dwarf for his foolishness.

He waited in the shadows, listening and watching and growing more and more – what was it called? It had been so long since he had felt it, he had forgotten the word for it. Astonished. That was it. He grew more and more astonished.

He watched the scene to its conclusion. The pig trotted over the bridge and the dwarf stood, watching her go. She stopped at the doors and turned back. He waved to her one last time, and she entered to the sound of cheers and singing. The dwarf started down the road. Gondul stood watching him go. Just as the pig had done, he stopped and turned before the road bent and looked back. Gondul waved to him one last time, and he slowly walked on and disappeared from view.

The dog stood still, and for a moment he half considered howling. *Now I've seen it all. What else could there be? I'll just howl and end it all. But no – it is not time. Not time for the end. Instead, it is time to feast.* And when he caught up with the dwarf, that is exactly what he did.

Asmund arranged his supplies on the table. He drew the king's sword and examined it. The hilt was as richly carved as any he had ever seen, but of course it would be. The overall weapon was very light, much lighter than this style of sword should be. He looked the blade over. This sword had seen no use. It was nothing but an ornament. He would definitely need the charm of strength to keep it from shattering. He would be able to skip the charm of eversharp, however. Most people thought swords were sharper than they actually were. In fact, they simply beveled to an edge that never needed to be honed as sharply as a kitchen knife or a woodman's axe. This was good, as it was already midday, and he had promised to be finished within two days.

Asmund buckled down and got to work. So focused was he on his task that he did not stop until hunger became a distraction. He stepped out and found the soldier who was attending him asleep in his chair. Asmund woke him and asked, "Has the evening meal begun?"

"Begun, My Lord? It has long since passed."

"Oh! My chamber has no window, and I was lost in my work."

"I can see what I can find," offered the soldier.

"Yes, please. A little bread and ale would be fine." The soldier left, but returned quickly with a plate of bread and cold pheasant. Asmund ate, finally quieting the growls in his belly. "How stands the hour?"

"It is almost the mid of night, My Lord."

Asmund yawned deeply. "I will take some sleep then. Please see that I do not sleep past dawn. I have much yet to do tomorrow." The soldier bowed, and Asmund closed the door.

Asmund, help us!

He gazed at the ceiling of his darkened chamber. "Don't let me sleep past dawn," he said, parroting his own words from the night before. He had forgotten that he had seven little voices ensuring that would never happen. They never took a night off. *Asmund, help us! Help us! Help us! Yes, yes, I'm coming as quickly as I can.* He struggled out of bed, still feeling tired.

He gave instructions that meals be brought to him in his workroom. This would keep him from getting too hungry and make him cognizant of the passage of time. The king came as the midday meal was brought.

"How goes it, my wizard?" asked the king, trying to look at everything at once.

Asmund held up his hand. "Please, My Lord, touch nothing. All is going perfectly to plan. The sword will be finished and ready to test in the morning."

"Excellent! That's excellent," the king said. "Elof will be here."

"Elof? Here?" Asmund asked in surprise.

"Yes. I've challenged him to single combat, just like I planned."

"What about testing the magic sword first? You were to test it in practice against your warriors, then once I left on my quest, you would challenge him."

"What's to test? You said the sword does it all and makes me invincible. Also, Elof has accepted the challenge, as I knew he would. But he will still bring his men. I want you there if anything goes wrong. If they do not accept my victory over Elof, then I have you there to wipe them out. See, I was looking at the bones at the same time as you, and I'm very magical myself. People say that all the time. Everyone says to me, you're very magical, and I caught something you didn't. It wasn't one path or the other. It was a combination of the two. That's what the bones were saying."

There was silence, and Asmund realized that the king was waiting for a reply. He smiled and said, "Very wise, as always, My Lord." This complicated matters. But he had to stay focused. "Well then, I must not delay. I want to make the sword the most powerful one there ever was."

It seemed that the king liked the sound of that. "Then I will leave you to it," he said, withdrawing with a spring in his step.

Asmund looked up as a servant entered the room to remove his dinner platter from hours earlier. "What time is it?"

"Just after ten, My Lord."

"Thank you," said Asmund. He waited until the servant left before turning and lifting the completed sword from the table. He was glad he had skipped the eversharp charm. The shortcut had allowed him to finish in under two days, and it left him time to rest before what promised to be a big day.

The sword's beauty was unchanged, but now it held a vast well of magic inside. Only a magical creature would be able to see the glowing energy within it. To everyone else, it was just a regular sword.

A magic sword must be given a name in the enchanting process. Asmund would tell Calder the Bald it was named Bonecutter. He would like that. But that was not its true name. He put it in its sheath and put it back down upon the table. He poured some water and washed the sweat from his face and hands. He lay down, hoping nervousness over the coming day would not make sleep elusive. He needn't have worried though; exhaustion took him swiftly into a deep sleep.

The children's voices woke him, and within moments, he was gripped with anxiety. So much could go wrong today. He squeezed his eyes closed, wishing he could go back to sleep.

He rose and dressed for the day. The room had no window to show him the time, but he knew it must still be very early. He was dreading the hours of anxiety between now and when the day's events would unfold.

A knock came on the door, followed by the king barging in, wearing his armor. Like the sword, it was beautifully chased with regal designs, and probably too light to be strong. "Oh, good! You're up," he said excitedly. "We must go."

"Already?" Asmund asked, surprised.

"Yes, my rider from Lundvar just arrived at a gallop. Elof and his men left before dawn. They are only an hour behind. They are hoping to catch us with the sleep still in our eyes. We will ride out past the mill fields and meet them on the road. Quick, where is the magic sword?"

Asmund brought the sword to the king and bowed as he presented it, adding a touch of pageantry to the moment. This is Bonecutter, My Lord." Asmund backed away and the king drew the sword slowly. He turned it this way and that. He had obviously been expecting to see or feel something magical. The fact that he did not was written in bold lines of disappointment across his face.

"Perhaps you should just use your magic to wipe out Elof and his men. You know, since we did not have time to test the sword."

Asmund felt a stab of panic, but was careful not to let it show on his face. "Of course, My Lord, if you think it best. It was, after all, one of the courses the bones foretold. As for testing the sword..." Without warning, Asmund grabbed an iron cauldron from the worktable and hurled it straight at the king with all of his might. There was a blur of streaking steel, and an instant later the cauldron slammed into the wall, the iron split in two by the sword. The king's eyes were like dinner platters; his mouth hung agape.

When at last he could speak, he said, "The sword moved so fast I could not even see it, and hit with such force I thought for sure it would fly from my hand."

"It strikes at the speed of its master's thought, and it cannot be dropped unless he wills it." Again with no warning, Asmund flung an iron ladle followed by a stone mortar. The sword flashed first one way and then the other in the blink of an eye, cleaving both missiles apart. "As promised, My King, a magic sword so powerful it makes its wielder invincible! And no one can tell it is the sword that makes him thus. To their eyes, he is the mightiest of warriors. Perhaps it will be useful to you one day. As for today, I will do as you ask and strike down Elof and his army and secure your throne for you."

"That is a terrible idea, wizard!"

"It is, My Lord?" Asmund said dimly.

"Yes!" scolded the king. "Everyone knows I issued a challenge to Elof to fight me man to man. If I listened to your counsel I would lose all honor! I must fight him and teach them once and for all who is the mightiest! You must only use your magic if there is a large force and if they do not respect the outcome of the chieftains' fight."

"You really do see everything, don't you, My Lord?"

"That is why I am king, wizard. Now, hurry up, your cart is ready for you. Come to the courtyard as quickly as possible."

Asmund gathered up his possessions hurriedly as the king sheathed his magic sword and swaggered out of the room. When he reached the courtyard, the king and all his warriors were on their horses, dressed for battle. He mounted his cart as the king stepped his horse forward and faced the assembled host.

"For far too long," he began in what he thought was a kingly voice, "Elof the pretender has coveted my throne. Now, even though he is no great threat to me, it is a wise king who sees that the oak trees of insurrection can grow from the acorn of treachery. So I have decided to deal with him once and for all. I will meet him in battle, one on one, and defeat him. But if his rabble are still hungry for the riches of our land, you must be ready to do battle." Some of the men shifted nervously. Asmund saw that the young man who had been bringing him his meals was wearing a shirt of ill-fitting armor, as was the groomsmen who had brought his pony and cart. So Calder was padding his numbers a bit with whoever could look the part. The king noticed the nervous faces and added, "My wizard shall also accompany us. He who can kill with just a point of his finger. They will be very sorry if they act with treachery this day. Now come, men, victory awaits!"

They made the short journey, stopping briefly at the mill to press four of the younger men working there into service. Each of them was given a leather helmet and a spear. This brought their number up to thirty-four. Asmund noted that Calder did not seem worried by this. Was that because his spies were telling him that Elof did not have more men than that? Or, more distressing to think, was it just because he thought his mighty wizard could kill an army of men, no matter its size?

They had all dismounted and begun shifting from foot to foot nervously when a column of warriors came into view, riding two and three abreast. They came trotting down a hill in the distance, allowing Asmund's keen eyes to take their number. He was relieved to see that they were not a vast army. There were only fifty-seven warriors. They did, however, appear to all be real warriors, led by a huge chieftain surrounded by a small corps of hardened Vikings, so his relief was small.

The band of warriors halted and dismounted. They approached with a casual demeanor. This spot was very open. One could see from the river to one side all the way across the fields to the forest on the other, and they feared no traps.

"You should have brought more men, Uncle,"

said the burly man with the sand-colored hair and red beard.

"Why, Nephew? We are the only ones fighting. They are just witnesses. That is, unless you are afraid to face me man to man."

"Now I know you have gone mad, old man," Elof sneered.

"He sounds afraid to me. What do you think, Holger?"

"He sounds terrified to me, My King," agreed Holger.

"Very well, Uncle. If today is the day you have chosen to die, then do not let me delay you any further," said Elof, drawing his big, well-used sword.

The men on both sides backed away, clearing a space for the fight. Asmund jumped when the king's herald began to shout next to him.

"All here stand witness to this challenge. King Calder the Bold versus Elof the Viking. Man against man, to the death. The winner takes the day."

The king drew his sword and stood ready. "Time to die, boy!"

"Today, I take back what is mine!" Elof roared. A lusty cheer rose among the ranks of his men. The cheering continued as he charged, bringing his sword down in a mighty arc toward Calder's face. The cheer died abruptly a moment later when in a flash the king struck the sword from Elof's hand and his head from his shoulders. The onlookers stood dumbstruck as Elof's tall body buckled at the knees and toppled at Calder's feet.

No one wore a more astonished look then the king himself. But it was replaced with a look of smug satisfaction when his men rose a wild cheer.

When the cheer at last subsided, Calder said cheerfully, "My nephew was very brave, but also very foolish. You men who followed him are free to go."

Elof's men turned as one to look at a young warrior who wore a crimson cloak slung on his back. The young man, seeing their expectant gaze, stepped forward and glared defiantly at Calder.

Asmund's panic began to rise. Why did the king not ask the warriors to join him? Probably because the wealth he bragged about did not exist and he could not pay them. Holger leaned over and whispered in the king's ear, who then turned and regarded the young crimson-cloaked warrior.

"Prince Oldrik," he hailed cheerfully. "So am I to take it that this is an official act of war from Lundvar on Brekka?"

"No, My Lord," aswered the youth. "My father does not know I am here. I came of my own accord to support the slain Elof. He was rightful heir to the throne."

"You cared not for who was rightful king! Spare me your lies, boy. You came for the same reason all of this marauding rabble came. The promise of riches. Now, the men you are with are counting our numbers and thinking, 'Maybe our new noble captain will lead us into battle and we will still get to sack the town.' But that would be very foolish."

"You think so, old man?" said Oldrik, trying to sound brave. "They are right. We do outnumber you quite handily. What prevents us from killing you and taking what we want?"

Holger cupped his hand to the king's ear and whispered until Calder's face split into a wide grin. "I will tell you," said Calder. "Because some of the men you are with are very cunning. None of them thought I would kill Elof without even drawing a heavy breath, and yet that is exactly what they saw. Our force is smaller, but how can they estimate our power? Perhaps nothing is as it seems."

"It sounds to me like you're bluffing," said the prince.

"All right, I'm bluffing then. It does not matter now," said Calder.

"And why is that?"

"Because the men with you are done counting and reckoning and they know what to do. The goal is to have riches and to live long enough to spend them. If they attack us, whatever the outcome may be, many of them will die and never taste the riches. But on the other hand, if they had a stupid princeling who was pretending to be a warrior that they could hold for ransom, one whose rich father would pay dearly to save him, and none of them would have to die..."

Asmund felt somewhat sorry for the young prince as the Vikings led him away at swordpoint. He definitely knew a thing or two about being young and naive and getting in way over your head. Thanks to Holger's whispered counsel, Calder had turned the larger force away without commanding Asmund to call down the fire of the gods or some other nonsense that he could not do. He knew he should feel relieved, but he could not. For now the time was fast approaching for him to ask the king to honor his bargain. He could not help dreading that Kolga had been right when it came to trusting the king's word.

The troop turned for home and a celebration. Calder instantly began regaling his men with a blow-by-blow retelling of the events they had just witnessed, complete with how he had recognized Prince Oldrik and devised a way to get rid of the marauders and destabilize the neighboring kingdom all in one fell swoop.

Asmund noticed that Holger was the loudest to cheer the king's brilliance at this point. He found the absurdity of it all exhausting and longed to be gone from this place. He had truly delivered on his promise of powerful magic, and it had cost him days away from his quest. He had earned his and Kolga's freedom.

As they arrived in the courtyard, the festive mood was increased by the cheers of the household, who were assembled up the stairs at the threshold of the fortress doors.

"My Lord!" Asmund shouted, trying to be heard over the din of celebration. "My King!" He dismounted his cart and drew closer.

The king caught sight of him and called, "Ah, my wizard! Thanks to my strength in battle and my far-seeing wisdom, I had no need of your magic today."

"True, My Lord!" replied Asmund, stepping into Holger's act instantly. "My magics are not needed by a king as powerful as you."

This made Calder stick out his lips even farther than usual and look around to satisfy himself that everyone was listening to the high praise.

"My King, my cart is already hitched and ready. Now is the perfect time for me to leave on the important quest." Asmund saw the corners of the pursed lips turned downward in a frown, but he pressed on. "If the woodcutter's girl can be sent down from her room, then I can be on my way."

"Nonsense!" the king said. "You can't miss the feast! It's going to be the biggest feast you've ever seen!"

Asmund was now wishing he had spoken to the king privately. He knew getting the king to change his mind in front of everyone would be next to impossible, but he longed to be on his way. "My Lord, I have served you well, and the quest is very important."

"Enough! I will hear no more of this!" the king snipped testily.

"My Lord, I must insist."

"You insist nothing!" the king screamed, instantly enraged. The king's startling outburst made all his merry subjects fall silent at once.

Asmund took a step back in shock. This had escalated from bad to terrible in an instant. "My Lord, there is no need for this. Simply release Kolga, and I will trouble you no further."

The king nodded to someone behind Asmund, and before he could turn, his arms were grabbed and twisted behind his back. His walking staff went clattering to the ground. He opened his mouth to shout, but another set of hands appeared from behind and pulled a gag between his lips. The angry king stepped forward, drawing his magic sword. "You think I'm afraid of you, wizard? If you can't wave your hands and speak your spells, then you are helpless!"

Asmund could see the warriors who held him out of the corners of his eyes. They were some of the king's pouty-mouthed worshipers. He realized this action had been planned all along in case the king should grow angry with him.

The king addressed the crowd. "I give and give and give! I do everything I can for people and they all betray me! It seems I am not done proving my power this day. After everything I've done for him, the wizard still seems to think that he is too good to serve me. Very well, I will release him from my service. Bring down the woodcutter's ugly little daughter, so he can watch me slit her throat before I cut his guts out." The king stepped in close and whispered so only Asmund could hear, "The best part is that I'm going to use the sword, my sword of invincibility that you made for me, to kill you."

Asmund jerked at the hands that were holding him fast, but the men were much stronger than he was. He scanned the crowd. Everyone was caught up in the show, hungry for a bloody spectacle. All but one. Holger stood watching with sad eyes as Asmund struggled vainly against his captors.

A few moments later, Kolga was led into the courtyard, cursing and struggling. She caught sight of Asmund. "I don't forgive you for this!" she cried.

This caused a roar of laughter to erupt from the bloodthirsty crowd. The king laughingly called, "Bring her over so the wizard can see her die."

Her guard dragged her over and the smiling king turned to Asmund. "Are you ready?" Asmund locked eyes with him and calmly nodded his head up and down, very clearly stating that he was. This made Calder's smile disappear and he hesitated. Slowly, he turned toward his victim and equally slowly rose the sword for the kill. Then, to everyone's surprise, he buried its blade in the head of her guard. The man dropped like a sack of rocks. The king jerked back toward Asmund and struck down both of the soldiers holding his arms. Asmund spun and looked at the shocked man who had been holding the ends of his gag as the king struck him down as well.

The king whirled and fell upon the crowd of warriors, his sword slashing so hard and fast that two or three fell dead with each swing. The king staggered this way and that, hacking them to bits. The ones further back screamed in terror and ran from the carnage, fleeing the gates of the fortress and not looking back.

In no time at all, the king was standing in the middle of a pile of bodies, bathed in blood from head to toe. The only people left alive were Asmund, Kolga and Holger, who no longer looked sad. Up the stairs at the great doors stood the shocked servants of the house, including the girl Asmund had last seen sitting bruised and drunk in the King's bedchamber. Asmund stared at her for a moment, then looked back at the king. "Turn and face me, you rotten pile of dung."

Calder slowly turned, his face a mask of confusion. "I don't understand."

"What do you not understand?" Asmund asked. "I told you when I gave you the magic sword that it obeyed the thoughts of its master. I never told you that you were its master."

Calder shook his hand and pried at his fingers with his other hand, trying desperately to drop the sword.

"No. It cannot fall from the wielder's hand if its master does not will it so. I do not will it. Not yet. It has one more person yet to kill, so it can own its true name."

"What's its true name?" the terrified Calder asked.

"Kingslayer."

Asmund waited a moment until he saw the king's eyes open wide with realization. Then the king stretched out his arm as far as it would go and struck himself with the sword, snapping his own collarbone and staggering back a few steps. He was now blubbering and crying as he watched the sword stretch out before him again, then come rushing back straight between his eyes. Then he saw nothing more.

Everything was quiet for a few moments. Then Asmund called out, "Kingslayer." The sword slipped from Calder's lifeless grip and flew to its master's hand. He turned to Kolga. "Are you all right?" She nodded, looking stunned. "Holger," Asmund called.

"Yes, My Lord?"

"Get Kolga's belongings so she can return home. We have both been held up long enough."

"At once, My Lord." Holger moved quickly to obey. He also commanded the servants to fetch more provisions and load them into the cart. Calder's belt and sheath were brought, and Asmund slung Kingslayer from his hip.

When all was ready, Asmund mounted the cart and looked at Holger. "You have not asked why you alone were spared."

"I think I understand," answered Holger. "I know I do not deserve to be spared. It is my fault that you were brought here in the first place. But someone will seize power with Calder dead, and you know if it is me, I will not have men robbing travelers or taxing the poor until they starve or stealing their daughters anymore."

"Speaking of that, see that she is taken home and cared for," Asmund ordered, glancing up to where the girl still lingered above the courtyard.

"I swear it will be done, My Lord," answered Holger, bowing deeply.

Then Kolga climbed up and sat next to Asmund in the cart. "And go to my father, Scald the Woodsman, and tell him I am safe. I am traveling with the great wizard on his quest."

Asmund turned toward her with surprise. But then he smiled. "The road awaits. Let's ride."

The craftsman walked along the road to Hel, trying to collect his thoughts. He felt like so much of himself had been left behind, and with each step, everything felt farther away. There comes a day in each person's life, and it comes in many different ways, when they know their life will never be the same as it was, nor will it be exactly what they imagined or hoped for.

This is what he was thinking when he heard the sticky, wet paws running up behind him. He turned and saw the dog towering over him, fur dripping blood, ears flattened back against its head. It growled, bearing razor-sharp teeth, and stared into his eyes.

"Oh, hello, Garmr," the dwarf said absently. The dog ceased its growling at once and looked baffled.

"'Oh, hello, Garmr?'" it echoed in disbelief. "Garmr, the gore-soaked hound of Hel, appears before you and you say, 'Oh, hello, Garmr?'"

"I meant no offense."

"That's not the point! I mean who the *here* are you? You sneaked into the underworld without passing my gate!"

"I came through the tree of life."

"You came through Yggdrasil?"

"Yes," answered the dwarf peevishly.

"Like a god?"

The craftsman shrugged.

"You escort animals to Valhalla. You fight Valkyries. You take casual strolls on the road to eternity, and faced with the agent of your bloody, screaming, doom, you say, 'Oh, hello.'"

"Well," started the craftsman.

"Well, what?"

"Well, it's just..." he began again.

"Just what?"

"It's just that I looked into your eyes, and saw that you didn't want to kill me."

"I didn't?" asked the dog, sitting down heavily.

"No," replied the craftsman.

"Well, it's my job," protested Garmr.

"That's as well may be. But I'm a dwarf of the Great Hall. I can look into someone's eyes and see what they desire. It mostly comes in handy when making something for someone and hearing them gasp and say, 'Oh my, that's perfect! It's just as I imagined it!'"

"Well, maybe I do not want to kill you," admitted Garmr. "I mean... You were so kind to the boar."

"Trufflesbane," the dwarf said helpfully.

"And you were so stupidly brave trying to fight the Valkyrie, and, well..." The guardian of Hel lowered his head, looking embarrassed. "And, well, you are interesting! It's so boring here! Hardly anything ever happens. Then you march in and everything happens. I can't remember the last time anyone interesting was here."

The craftsman smiled. "Well, I'm glad."

"But I still have to kill you."

"I don't understand," the dwarf said, smile fading.

"I swore an oath," said the dog solemnly.

"What oath?"

The dog sat up straight, cleared his throat, and recited:

If before his time he walks this road,
Thus breaking peace in death's abode,
The fool doth seek to meet the beast
And provide for him his favored feast.

"That's it?" asked the craftsman.

"Yes. But don't you see? If you sneak into Hel I must feast!"

"Oh, well, if that's all." The craftsman cheerfully sat down in front of the shocked beast. He reached into his purse and pulled out a long strand of sausages, two flat loaves, and a little stoppered pot of honey. "Let's feast."

CHAPTER EIGHT

Kolga fell into the role of driver. This gave Asmund the opportunity to relax. He was displaying signs of a weariness that went deeper than merely physical. She knew he had worked on his magic spells for days, seeking to free them from their captivity. Then when the final showdown had played out, the absolute carnage had been gut-wrenching.

Was that really only a couple of hours ago? she thought to herself. Perhaps there was something magical about traveling. It felt like with every passing league, the past became less and less real.

She was glad she had come. She had felt certain that he would question her on her sudden change of heart, and she knew that she would not really have a good reason to give him. She had deeply regretted her sensibleness the first time she had watched him drive away without her. She would have regretted it even more if she had watched him leave without her again. It had not been a decision based on careful thought.

It still made no sense to jump into a cart with someone she barely knew and go who knows where to do who knows what. It made even less sense when she was standing in a courtyard filled with death and destruction and a vague sense that wherever he went, there would be more of the same. She could not tell him that something inside her simply told her that she needed to be by his side, and she did not really care where they were going or what would happen when they got there. To her relief, it appeared that he would not ask for any explanation at all, and that would suit her just fine.

It was now the height of midday. Asmund withdrew the brown disc with the mirror inside that she had first seen in the stables back in Brekka. He held it high above him and said some words she did not understand. She waited for some effect, but nothing happened. Apparently that was as it should be, because he wore a satisfied look on his face as he put it away and took out his map. After studying it for a moment, he re-rolled it. "We will have to camp out tonight. I'm counting on your woodcutter skills to build us a cabin."

"Of course," she replied. "I am rather tired however, so I can only promise one that is two stories high. Maybe three if I get a second wind."

"That's what's wrong with young people today. No pride in their work!" he said, wagging his finger at her.

"It's sad, really," she agreed with such an earnest look of disapproval that he had to start laughing.

They rode on through the afternoon into the evening, not talking much. But it was comfortable. She felt like she had known him forever. Maybe if you spend a few days with knives pressed to your throat, the threat of death looming ever-present, and someone kills a king and all his warriors to save you, you get to skip the awkward 'getting to know you' process. Maybe it's more that once you've gone through those things, asking questions like, 'Do you like cheese?' just seems silly.

"If I read the map correctly, there are some lakes or ponds that we will make it to this evening. I think we should stop when we see the first of them. We are already behind schedule, but squeezing out a few more leagues before dark won't make so great a difference. If we can set up camp quickly, there is some magic I would like to perform. Something that might aid us."

They had rolled on for another three quarters of an hour when they crested a rise that looked out over a picturesque valley. Ahead, the road led between two crystal lakes. "What a beautiful place to make our camp," she said, smiling. "In fact, let's just live here forever."

"It's settled!" he laughed. "We each get a lake of our own."

They reached the lake on the right-hand side. A turnoff was clearly visible where the hooves and wheels of past travelers had gone before. Kolga drove past it, paying it no heed. "Not this one?" he asked her, confused.

"No, the smaller one up here on the left. It has a nearby copse of trees with some big boulders running through it. Didn't you see from up on the hill?"

"No, not specifically," he answered, sounding a little lost.

"Well, we don't want to camp and build our fire out in the open next to a big lake. We'll use some natural shelter and – what?" she snapped crossly when she saw he was smiling at her. "What are you smiling at?"

"Nothing. I'm just really happy you're with me. I don't know any of this stuff."

"Oh," she said with surprise. Now she felt sorry she had been so quick to take offense. She was accustomed to having her thoughts dismissed or ridiculed, and it was a sore spot. She had automatically assumed that Asmund's question and smile was a form of condescending disagreement, but she knew he was not like the men she had grown up around. She felt ashamed and embarrassed.

They found the turnoff for the second lake and she drove to the spot she had picked out from the hill above the valley. They came to a stop. Asmund began to dismount. "I'm sorry!" she said in a rush.

He stopped and sat back down with a confused look on his face. "For what?" he asked.

"Snapping at you when I was explaining the campsite. I misunderstood." He shrugged his shoulders. She could tell he didn't really understand what she was talking about. "I'm happy I'm here with you as well." This made him smile at her and bump his shoulder into hers playfully.

"I'll take care of the cart and pony, if you want to start making camp for us," he said, climbing down from the cart.

"One cabin coming right up," she said, hopping down as well. She took inventory of what was in the cart. In addition to the bedding and shelter cloth that Asmund had brought, there was some additional bedding and skins the servants had added at the fortress that morning. This gave her an idea of what she wanted to build. She selected a spot amongst the boulders and paced off a square, making a few marks in the ground with her heel.

She went to the copse of trees that was more like

a cozy forest in miniature. She could see that she would be able to gather what she needed mostly from deadfall with minimal cutting required. She drew her handaxe and spun it around so the blade was facing her, then entered slowly, placing each step carefully and quietly. A dozen steps in she stopped and listened. She had just decided that there was nothing to hear when a rustle came from the left. She strained her ears, trying to pinpoint the origin. A few moments later the sound was repeated. Slowly she turned, creeping forward, scanning the carpet of fallen leaves, seeking the source of the rustling sound. The hare took a tiny hop. The movement caught her eye. Instinctively she loosed the axe, watching it turn smoothly in the air and strike true. The throwing of handaxes was the one art at which she excelled above her older brothers. They did not grasp the finesse of it like she did. They never learned to respect the weight and design inherent in an axe. They added too much power and spoiled the throw.

Kolga rushed to the hare so she could dispatch it swiftly and keep it from suffering. She found this was unnecessary, as it had died instantly. She dressed it on the spot. Within five minutes, she emerged from the trees with a rabbit ready for cooking.

The pony was unharnessed and drinking from a bucket while Asmund brushed its back and flanks. "You made good progress," she said.

"Getting him out of everything isn't too hard for me. Now the opposite is another matter altogether. I see you found a butcher shop doing business behind the trees."

"That's right," she said, holding up the hare for his approval. "Their prices were outrageous! But I thought, how often do we treat ourselves?"

He laughed. "Give it to me. I'll make a fire. Where shall I build it?"

She handed him the hare, then used her heel again to mark the ground, tracing a rough circle in front of where she had marked out the shelter.

When she returned, dragging her first load of deadfall timber, he had finished arranging a circle of stones and was gathering some sticks and small logs from the edge of the trees. When she returned on her second trip, a fire was already going. When she returned a third time, he was arranging the rabbit on a spit over the flames. She dropped her load and said, "Wait a minute! You say you don't know what to do, but you build a fire like there is nothing to it!"

"Well to be fair, the hardest part of it, the producing of flame, I do with magic."

"Even so, it is still impressive," she said, wiping her brow. She set about laying out their shelter.

"I'll gather some wood to keep the fire going, and then I will start my magic work," he announced.

She watched him return to the copse of trees, walking with some difficulty without the aid of his staff over the uneven terrain. He had played off her complement about building the fire, but she was truly impressed. She could see that these labors took great effort on his part.

She laid out the frame where she wanted it and then turned back to watch his progress. He was inside the tree line now. He drew his magic sword, finding a dead tree that was still standing, leafless and without a top. She watched as the sword flashed and felled the tree with ease. The force of the blow felled Asmund as well and sent him tumbling to the ground like a ragdoll. She started to rise, wanting to run to him, but stopped herself. As a woman in a traditionally male job she knew personally what that felt like. The nice people always stepping in to help because they knew you could not be capable of doing it for yourself. She refused to do the same to him.

He got up on his knees and bundled the trunk and a couple of fallen limbs together. He produced a cord from his purse and lashed them snugly. Now she was confused. She did not see how he could lift any of the pieces alone. How could he possibly budge them all together? He stood up slowly and started to walk back towards the campsite. She noticed that he appeared to have forgotten the sword as well. Perhaps he was coming to ask for her help. That would be fine, as long as it was his idea.

She realized that she had just been sitting watching him. She scrambled back to her work before he saw her. She selected her two Y-shaped poles. Four perfect strokes from her handaxe turned them into sharpened stakes. These she drove into the dirt with the back of the axe. She finished sinking the second one as he arrived back to camp. "How's it going?" she asked with a smile.

"Good," he answered. "It only looks like I'm empty-handed. The firewood is going to deliver itself, if all goes to plan." He turned back toward the trees and held out his hand. "Kingslayer," he said. The bundle of wood came bounding out of the forest, hovering two or three feet in the air. It bobbed up and down, scraping a couple of times against the ground, but never stopped until Asmund lowered his hand and ceased willing it to come. There before them was the bundle of wood with Asmund's magic sword lashed tightly to it. He turned and smiled at her. "I was hoping that would work."

"Impressive! I'm surprised that cord held."

"It's charmed. A giant could swing from that cord and it wouldn't break. Magic items are my specialty. Well, that and foot races," he laughed, loping around in a circle, his tongue sticking out of the corner of his mouth, his brow knit with mock determination.

She howled with laughter at the vision of him circling around with that ridiculous look on his face. He completed another loop shouting. "Out of my way, I'm going to win!"

Her sides were splitting, tears standing out in her eyes. "Stop! Stop!" she begged, doubling over, trying to catch her breath.

He came to a stop, his cheeks flushed from exertion. "There, now you know all my secrets," he said, laughing. "Oh no, the fire is going to die soon. I was so busy showing off my athletic prowess that I forgot to finish my work." He knelt and untied the cord from the bundle.

She watched him with a big smile on her face, quakes of laughter still rippling through her. He had told her once that she was comfortably herself. But she thought that applied far more to him than to her. He was brave and smart and secure in who he was. She looked at him kneeling in front of the logs, using the sword to chop them. He seemed to be experimenting with his control, to find if he could use it without the speed and force being too great to handle. He caught her watching and smiled.

At that moment a knowledge began to dawn

deep inside of her. Before her mind could articulate that knowledge, she shut it down, turning back to her work. She hammered the second stake further into the ground. Why did she have to be so silly? He would never feel the same way about her, and she would only end up looking stupid. And that was the one thing she could not stand.

She set the cross pole, then began propping the slanting roof poles across it, not bothering to cut them to length for a single night's use. She finished by tying the shelter cloth over them. She would cut some pine branches for the floor and the gaps at the sides before they slept. But otherwise, it was finished. She heard Asmund gasp when he looked up from his work.

"I was joking when I asked for a cabin. I never thought you would actually build one!"

"It's nothing, really," she said. "With the fire here, it will catch and hold some heat for us, and if the weather changes, it will protect us from the wet."

"It's amazing! So is the rabbit. Trust me, without you I would be eating cold porridge while the wind off the lake blew my soggy shelter cloth into my sputtering campfire. I would be so miserable that only one thing would console me, and you know what that is, right?"

"No, what?" she asked.

"Why, naturally, the knowledge that I was still the fastest runner in the world."

He delivered the joke with such a straight face that when it landed she was surprised by her own laughter. She had never laughed so hard in all of her life. Any other time, this would have been a source of joy, but this time it seemed to strip away her defenses, to pull down her guard. Her face changed into a frown, laughter into a sob. Two hot tears raced down her cheeks. She spun away from him and hid her face.

"What's wrong?" he asked, standing up and coming around to face her.

"Nothing! I could never explain it! Don't worry. Everything is fine," she said, trying to stop crying.

"I'm sorry if I said something wrong. I was trying to say how happy I am that you're with me. How good you are at making a camp."

"I know! I'm happy to be here," she said raggedly, wiping her face.

"I realize now that it's insane for me to be making jokes. Because of me, you were kidnapped with knives pressed to your throat. Your life threatened for days. You watched that scene of death and carnage that would make a troll weak in the knees and then you traveled far from home, a thing which has frightened you for a very long time, and instead of respecting all that, I dance around like a jester telling jokes. I am so sorry," he said miserably.

"None of that is bothering me! I know it should, but it doesn't. I've never been happier or felt more alive! You have to trust me. I can't explain why I cried. It's stupid, I wouldn't want to be anywhere else but right here with you."

She could see that he was still confused, but he smiled, rocked forward as if he would hug her, then looked uncertain and put his hand on her shoulder instead, saying, "I feel the same way."

They stood that way for a moment, and then she said, "Let me finish the firewood so you can work on your magic."

"Yes, thank you," he said sounding relieved. He went to the cart and began to pull things from his bags and arrange them. There was still much to do to prepare the firewood, and this pleased her. She wanted to throw herself into the work. She cut and set aside a good-sized round of tree trunk to serve as a work surface. She could use it for splitting the other wood, and then it could be her table for preparing the rabbit. As she chopped the wood to length and began splitting, the haft of the axe in her hand helped to center her and give her back possession of herself. This axe was her magic sword. Its familiarity, its sureness of movement and tangible effectiveness banished all of the new feelings that had ganged up on her before.

She stacked new wood into the fire to make the type of flame she wanted and rotated the hare on its spit. Being busy felt good, so she kept working, drawing more water for the pony, finishing the sides of the shelter, and tending to the cooking of the hare.

After a couple of hours, Asmund returned. He was carrying two leather cords, each suspending a disc of wood shaped from an elm sapling and bearing burned runes.

"This one is yours," he said, handing one to her. She took it and began to slip it over her head. "No, it's not for you to wear."

"It's not?" she asked, confused.

"No, it's for me to wear."

"Then why give it to me?"

"So you can own it." She raised an eyebrow at him, and he hurriedly continued. "Just hold it and look at it. Say to yourself, 'This is mine.' Give it a name if you want."

She did as he asked, and could see him doing the same with the other one. "Now place it around my neck, and I will do the same," he said. They stood face-to-face and exchanged necklaces. "There. Now we can't lose each other."

She gave him another confused look. "Are we soul-bonded for all eternity? Because if so, I think my father owes me a goat and my mother's cooking pot."

Asmund laughed. "No, I don't plan on tricking you into a mystical love spell for at least another two or three days."

"Oh, my mistake," she said. "So then how does exchanging necklaces mean we can't lose each other?"

"Wherever the necklace goes, you will find it. Simply close your eyes and concentrate on it. You will know the path to it. When we were held in the fortress, I thought about trying to release you. But on top of everything else stacked against that plan, the fact was I just did not know where you were. That's what made me think about making these."

"I want to try it!" she said excitedly.

"All right, put your hands in front of your eyes and count until fifty. I shall hide, then you can follow the amulet to find me."

In answer, she smiled broadly and threw her hands up before her eyes. "One, two," she began. She heard him scurrying away, seeking a place to hide. When she reached fifty, she took her hands away and listened. She heard nothing but the crackle of the fire and a sizzle as some grease from the hare fell into the flames.

She looked all around, scanning the tree line and crouching so she could see under the cart. Then she stopped. This was not just a regular game of hiding and finding. It was a test of the magic amulet. She closed her eyes and pictured the wooden disk in her mind. She turned around and opened her eyes. "Oh, you're behind the line of boulders," she said, and struck out, following the pull of the magic amulet, feeling acutely where it would be.

She rounded the far end of the stones and came to where the feeling told her she would find him. But he was not there. "Well, so much for the magic working," she said, and turned around, scanning the scenery on this side of the stones. She could not see him anywhere.

She took a step forward, and the strange feeling inside of her gave a tug. It seemed to say, 'It's right behind you!' She turned back and stared at what was before her eyes. All she saw was the backs of the boulders. A thought occurred to her. Perhaps to play a trick on her, he had hidden the small amulet right here and gone off somewhere else himself.

She looked at the stone, but it was smooth and unbroken. She examined the ground to see if it had been buried, but the ground was undisturbed. She backed up until she could see the top of the boulder, but nothing was there. She clenched her fists and stormed off in frustration. She only got four steps away when she stopped and turned back abruptly. The feeling inside would not be denied. The amulet was right there!

She closed her eyes and stretched her hand out in front of her. She crept forward inch by inch, the feeling growing stronger and more certain. At last, her hand came to rest on something. She had been expecting it to be the surface of the boulder, but that was not what it was. She opened her eyes. Her hand was resting on Asmund's chest. He was grinning from ear to ear. She pulled her hand back and saw that it had been resting on the amulet itself.

"Where were you?" she demanded.

"Standing right here the whole time!"

"You were invisible?"

"Not really invisible. It's called a glamour. I made you see something else."

"You have the power to make people see what you want?" she asked, astonished.

"In theory, but practically speaking, it's easier to get them to see what they want to see, or expect to see in the first place. You didn't know if you truly believed in the magic amulet yet, so part of you expected to just see the back of the boulders. So that is what I made you see."

"Well, if you wanted me to trust the magic, you should not have deceived me," she said, feeling aggravated.

"No, don't you see?" he countered. "Now you will always trust the magic. Even when your eyes told you it wasn't there, you knew that it was. If we ever get separated, now you know that we will find each other again."

That actually was reassuring, she was thinking to herself, when the thought was interrupted by a growl from her own belly. "Let's eat, I'm famished," she said, and started for the camp.

"Best idea I've heard all day!" he said.

They ate the freshly roasted rabbit and washed it down with cold water from the lake. She realized that she had been eating in her usual manner of tucking in and devouring her sustenance with no etiquette or polite conversation. When she looked across the fire she saw Asmund nodding, his empty bowl almost dropping from his fingers. She came over and took it, setting it aside for him, then she took him by the shoulders and stood him up. "What?" he said, as if in reply, although she had not spoken.

"Time for sleep," she said.

"Wait, now that is the best idea I've heard all day," he said groggily.

She helped him crawl into the bedding under the shelter. Then she tidied the camp, disposing of the remains of dinner to discourage any nighttime animal visits. She drove two stakes at an angle into the edge of the fire and arranged a stack of logs against them. If it worked correctly, it would feed the fire through the night. The sun had not long since gone down, and already the chill was biting. She slipped quietly into the shelter, fearful of waking him, but he was softly snoring, lost in a deep sleep.

She awoke in the early hours of morning and looked at the fire. It was still burning well. Her log stack had worked, but now only two logs remained. They were burning both together along with one of the stakes she had put in to hold and guide them.

Asmund's body jerked beside her and he made a wincing noise. She rolled over to look at him. His sleeping face was filled with fear. He trembled in the flickering firelight. She heard another sharp intake of breath and saw him flinch. She saw his lips move as if he were speaking but could hear no words. Almost on a whim, she closed her eyes and searched for the amulet. It felt both close and far away.

Following an instinct, she wrapped her arm

around him and held him tightly. She felt his trembling subside and his breathing begin to normalize. He still seemed to be somehow far away but all the panic had left him. At one point, he turned his head to the side and said the word "Kalbaek" in a dreamy voice. A short while later, he began to tremble again, she held him tighter and kissed the side of his face, still operating on pure instinct. His trembling ebbed away again. A while later, he spoke once more in the dreamy, faraway voice. "Yes, children, I'm coming. I will help you." After this, she could feel him sleeping deeply again and she dozed back to sleep as well.

The dog erupted in laughter, nearly choking on a sausage.

"That's right!" the dwarf said merrily. "It sank – right to the bottom! We had to build another one in only half the time." He finished his tale, wiping tears of laughter from the corners of his eyes. A strange look crept over his face.

At this, Garmr stopped laughing. "Why do you wear that face? Has the flavor gone from our feast, Dvalinn?"

"Not at all," replied the craftsman, finding his smile again. "It just struck me that they are all gone. Those in our stories. Mothers and sisters. Fathers and brothers. Bosom companions. Either passed on or gone away. But thinking of them now, and knowing that we all must become memories that live in each other's hearts, I am surprised to find that they bring me joy and not sorrow.

"This was not so when I was younger. I spent half

my time looking back, longing for what had been, and the other half looking forward, always wanting more than what was mine. This day, I have lost so very much. Just an hour ago my heart was so heavy that I wept, but now my heart is so full that I laugh. It is all so very strange.

"I had kept hoping that old age would impart some great knowledge to me. I thought perhaps I would become a greater craftsman. But still, try as I may, I cannot form the corners of a little golden box quite to my liking. They just refuse to be perfect. Is it the skill I lack? Or is it the wisdom to appreciate it for how it is already?

"Yes, that must be it. That is the knowledge that age has brought me. I must go on loving those who have left without bitterness. Everything must leave, and no one can decide when. And even while you mold and shape and wish for something other, you can't forget to love things as they are now. Savor each cup of wine you are given. Its taste, its smell, its feeling. For every cup that is filled must be emptied, and every beginning must meet its end."

Garmr nodded his head. "Yes, some things can only be seen clearly when looking back. I abide here among the eternal dead. I exist as they do. Nothing marks the passage of one day to the next. They exist as shadows. The time for them to plant and reap, to love and to build is passed. They spend eternity remembering the things they did in life. The gods of the south punish or employ their dead. Ours just pleasantly continue to exist. What a shame that, when they owned hands that could touch and feel and move the world, so many of them were already just continuing to exist."

Dvalinn was much moved, and in a moment of understanding, he said, "The present moment of your life is a treasure chest. Do not let it be robbed by deep regrets for the past. Neither ransom that treasure for dreams of the future. If the past holds a wrong to be righted or forgiveness to be asked for, then rise up and make it so. If there is a better future that you can see, make a plan and follow it to that future. But do not find yourself walking this road one day only to learn that instead of living like a king in the richness of each moment, you starved, poor as a beggar, throwing all your treasure at any 'where' or 'when' but the one you were in." Then he fell silent, a wistful look on his face.

The dog looked at the dwarf for a long while. At last he stood up and drew in a deep breath. "We were well met this day, my friend. I am guardian of this realm, not its prisoner. I will not lie sleeping among the shadows this night. I shall once again run the mountains. I shall feel the wind in my fur. My cup of wine will be the great north mere from which I drank as a pup. I will taste its sweetness and bay at the moon. And as for you, the last son of Ivaldi, when we met, you rightly said that I did not wish to kill you. But what you did not say was that at that moment, you would not have been especially bothered if I had."

The craftsman opened his mouth to object, but instead, he simply nodded.

"And now that you have searched your soul and almost found your way again – now I will kill you! Had I killed you before, the victory would have meant nothing, and your meat would have tasted dull and bitter. But now you have regained some of your spirit."

What deceit, thought the craftsman. *How could*

such treachery be true? He had believed that as they feasted, they had opened their hearts to one another. He stood still, looking down at his feet, feeling as though he wanted to cry.

Garmr reared back, growling, and bared his razor teeth. He stalked forward slowly, preparing to strike. The dwarf felt cold and sick in the pit of his stomach. He knew the huge dog was bearing down on him.

"It's really quite silly, come to think of it. The thought that you could escape me and complete your quest. Now no one can save the children. And now you die!"

"No!" Dvalinn sprang back, drawing the hammer.

"Ah ha!" Garmr pointed his forepaw triumphantly at the dwarf. "Why 'no'? Tell me. Better yet, tell yourself!"

The craftsman drew a deep breath and held it in for a handful of heartbeats, then let it out slowly. "Because I no longer mourn or self-pity. No longer am I plagued by regret or held hostage by dreams of what might have been. This is my path to tread, and I must tread it to the end. I will not dishonor those whose memories I hold so dear by doing less than my utmost. I will not now disappoint those who love me by turning aside from what I have sworn to do." He met Garmr's eyes. "And lastly," he added, voice becoming grim, "because some filth climbed out from under a rock and is ripping children from their beds at night, is ripping families apart, and while I still have one breath in my body I will fight. I will use all that I have, all that I am, to stop this grave wrong. I will not lose heart again, Garmr, I promise you, and woe to him who stands in my way."

Garmr bowed to the dwarf. Then he rose and said in a mighty voice, "All hail Dvalinn, son of the Great Hall, Asger the Wise, Master of the Feast, who has defeated me this day with wit and will. I grant him the road." He touched his forepaw to the craftsman's chest, leaving behind a bloody pawprint which covered the coppery leaves of his armor. The print never dried; neither could it be wiped or washed away. "Be it known to all who see this, my mark and seal, that passage has been granted and none may bar his way."

They embraced and then parted ways, Garmr returning to the gate and the craftsman walking further into Hel. It was a sad parting, for their brief friendship had changed them both forever. But there was far still to travel, and much yet to be accomplished, and besides, they would meet again, soon enough.

The road to Hel was paved with good cobblestones. Often, things were certainly not as expected. The road was really all there was. To all sides, Dvalinn could see nothing but the rolling blackness. The dwarf made good time on the smooth, even surface, and he once again had a fire in his eye and a spring in his step. In the distance, he could faintly make out what seemed to be the din of a frenzied battle. He paused and strained his eyes toward the horizon, but they could not penetrate the misty darkness. In all the underworld, it seemed one could never see much more than a few dozen paces in any direction. The craftsman, knowing he had much yet to do and ever less time to do it, set out once again toward the sounds of slaughter.

The road took him around a bend, and the noise

grew louder. Within another score of steps, he was nearly deafened by the clash of steel on steel. The noise they made was such that he estimated the fighters must number in the thousands.

He drew the magic warhammer and readied himself for what he knew was coming. The sound was now a metallic thunder. He crept forward, knowing the edge of the battlefield could be mere inches away. Then the mists swirled and he saw it. He stood, dumbfounded, and lowered his hammer.

There before him flowed Gjoll, the river of Hel, broad and deep and flowing more swiftly than the flight of a falcon – but it held no water. Instead it contained every weapon that had ever tasted blood. Every sword, every axe. Every knife and every spear. Here and there through the torrent, even clubs and axes made of stone and wood could be observed. As the river rushed and eddied through the darkened valley, its countless waves clashed and rang in a ghostly echo of eternal conflict.

The craftsman stood for a time, gazing at the flood of blades. Once or twice, he thought he might even recognize one of the weapons. It would bob to the surface, clash against another blade, then dive back beneath the raging river of steel before he could remember its name or who had once wielded it.

He tried to make out the other riverbank, but could not. It was so far away that it might as well be on the far side of the moon. *The moon,* he repeated in his mind. The new moon was swiftly approaching. A spike of urgency pierced his heart. He paced up and down the riverbank. He must get across; so much depended on it. But how? *If only someone could help me,* he thought. He sat down with a grunt and stared balefully at the river of razor-sharp blades. "If only someone could help me!" This time he said it out loud.

At that moment, he looked down and saw the favor of silver hair given to him by Lagertha, the woman of the hideaway that had been toppled by the rock from the sky. He did not know how long he had been holding it. He had no memory of having taken it out. He heard her voice clearly over the cacophony of ringing steel. *It's not that you have need of it. Its that it is precious to me and I sacrifice it. Besides, who knows, maybe it will hold a touch of the wisdom of old women.*

The craftsman stood up and affixed the favor back onto his belt. *It's not that it is needed. It's that it is precious to me and that I will sacrifice it.*

He drew Scattersoul from its scabbard, the blood of a long-dead king still clinging to its length. He raised it to his lips and kissed the maker's mark, the name Ivaldi, which his father's hand had graved there while forging his masterpiece. His heart split in two as he reared back and hurled the blade with all of his will. He fell to his knees and watched as it sailed through the dark sky and plunged into the center of the river. It was instantly swallowed up in the jumble of blades and disappeared. There was no sound of thunder, no earthquake, no flash of light to mark the event. It was simply gone. He closed his eyes and bowed his head.

When at last he opened his eyes, he was kneeling at the foot of Gjallarbru, the great bridge of stone that spanned the river of Hel. The craftsman stood and gazed upon it. The bridge was gargantuan. An army could march over it at stride. Its path rose before him and disappeared into the mists far above. He hastened forward without hesitation. As he walked, the bridge rose so high that the sound of the river far below grew distant. After a time, he felt himself nearing the apex of the bridge. He knew he would soon begin his descent.

Without warning, a sound like a storm wind shook the very structure beneath him. "WHO DARES CROSS MY BRIDGE WITH MORTAL FEET?"

The sound swept the craftsman onto his back. He scrambled back to his feet and grasped his hammer. Standing before him, at the top of the bridge, stood Mooguor the Giantess. She was at once both terrible and beautiful to look upon. The acres of her pale skin were bare, save for a tattered dress, stitched from the sails of a hundred sunken longships. Her long hair was black as soot, her eyes the green of a deep, stormy sea.

The bridge, which had seemed so massive to the craftsman, was the perfect size for the giantess. "YOU DO NOT BELONG HERE," she boomed. "WHY DO YOU, THE LIVING, INVADE THE REALM OF ETERNAL NIGHT?"

The craftsman was unable to answer.

"SPEAK!"

At last, his trance was shattered. "I seek a name, t-to fulfill a quest," he stammered.

"AH! YOU SEEK TO MAKE A NAME FOR YOURSELF BY QUESTING."

"No. I seek to learn a hidden name and-"

"FOOLISH ADVENTURER!" she cut him off. "YOU WILL CURSE THE DAY YOU SET OUT TO SEEK RICHES AND RENOWN. YOU WILL ENJOY NO SPOILS. NO ONE WILL SING YOUR NAME, FOR I WILL CAST YOU INTO THE RIVER BELOW, WHERE YOU WILL DIE ONE LONG DEATH FOR ALL ETERNITY."

The dwarf stepped into the center of the bridge and raised his hammer on high. "I do not quest for glory or riches. I've had them both and found that their luster is soon tarnished. I seek to defend the defenseless, for if I do not, no one will, and if I must slay giants to do so – then so be it."

The giantess's scream shredded the dark sky, and she charged.

In the dwarf's hands, the magic warhammer glowed brightly. As it did, it illuminated the front of his armor and revealed the bloody red pawprint displayed thereon. Mooguor stopped in her tracks. She dropped to one knee. "THE ROAD IS YOURS, MY LORD."

The craftsman was confused for a moment. Then, remembering the mark and seal of Garmr, he lowered his hammer and stepped forward. "Which way to the gates of Helheim, My Lady?"

"DOWNWARD AND NORTH, MY LORD. THE WAY IS ALWAYS DOWNWARD AND NORTH."

When Kolga opened her eyes again, it was light out. Asmund was lying beside her. Her arms were still loosely holding him. When he saw that she was awake, he smiled and said "I haven't slept that well in weeks. The dream always makes me restless. I always wake just before dawn, feeling hounded. But this time was different. There was a presence there, letting me know I was safe and that everything would be all right. I told the children I was coming to help them and slept on through the dawn, feeling at peace."

Asmund mixed them up some porridge with berries as she hitched the pony to the cart. The pony gave out a loud whinny. She thought it was just a general greeting to the morning until a moment later when it was answered by another horse. Kolga looked toward the road, but no one was coming in either direction. She turned and saw Asmund shielding his eyes against the rising sun, watching a cart and horse following a path from the hills beyond the lake.

As it drew nearer, she saw that a boy of thirteen or fourteen was its only occupant. Its cargo consisted of three wooden barrels. The boy pulled up to the lake and dismounted. He waved a greeting to Asmund and her, then took a bucket and began transferring water from the lake to the first of the barrels. He poured carefully, trying to get the water in the hole, but much of it missed its target and sloshed to the ground.

"That looks like it will take him a very long time," said Asmund. "We have a bucket. Let's help him."

Kolga looked back at the boy splashing his second bucket down the side of the barrel and a thought occurred to her. "I have an idea. Give me a few minutes." She hurried into the trees without waiting for reply. She had seen a tree with a good-sized trunk which must have fallen somewhat recently. She found it again easily in the tiny forest.

She took her sharp axe and made a shallow two-foot slash straight down its center. At both ends of the cut, she made similar cuts going around the trunk's circumference. She used the edge of her axe to chisel and scrape, peeling the outer bark. She went in both directions until it cleanly separated. She switched to using her hands, carefully pushing and pulling and peeling. After a few minutes, she gave a final tug and had a perfect rectangle of flexible wood. She set the sides against the now-stripped surface of the downed tree and used her axe blade to trim them to the taper she wanted.

When she emerged from the trees holding the flap of bark she saw Asmund waiting with the bucket. He saw what she had made and looked confused. "Ready?" he asked.

"Yes, let's go," she replied. They walked around the lake to where the boy was busy at his toils. He stopped when he saw them approach.

"I am Asmund, and this is Kolga," Asmund called out when they had nearly reached him.

"I am Kael." the youth responded in a friendly tone.

"Do you have to fill all the barrels on your own?" Kolga asked.

"Yes!" Kael answered, sounding overwhelmed.

"Where are you taking the water?" asked Asmund.

"To my family's farm further up the valley. The well has gone bad. I have had to come and do this for three days now."

"No one in your family comes to help you?" Kolga asked sympathetically.

"It's only me, my father and my mother. My mother is very sick. My father stays by her side nursing her as she fights the sickness. She is too ill to travel. If I do not come and get water, we and our animals will not survive."

"Asmund, are you able to help?" she asked him hopefully.

"Maybe," he replied. "Sickness is harder for magic to heal than injuries. It's hard to explain. When a body is injured, it's simple, the body should be in its natural state but now it is not. You must simply restore it. But sickness is different. It lives in us, is part of us. Most sicknesses are not actually unnatural. Often, a wizard can heal the damage that the illness is causing and give a person strength to fight it themselves. But I can make no promises. I may not be of any help at all. However, I do have extensive spells to help farmers, including ones to purify and restore wells."

"Are you a wizard?" the boy asked, astonished. Asmund nodded. "Will you come and help us? I do not know what we could pay you, perhaps a goat. I will have to ask my father."

"You don't have to pay us. We are in haste to be somewhere, but we could not go with the thought that we could have helped you weighing on our hearts," Asmund said. "Now, we will help you fill the barrels the rest of the way. Your mother and the animals will be needing fresh water. Even if I can heal the well, it will take me some time." He turned to Kolga. "Also, unless I am mistaken, Kolga has devised some way to make the task less arduous."

"Oh, it will still be hard work," she replied, stepping over to the cart. "But now at least all the water will be going inside the barrel." She gave the piece of bark a roll and stuck the new funnel into the barrel's hole.

"Are you both wizards?" Kael asked in wonder.

"It would appear so," Asmund answered.

The bark funnel and two buckets made the job whiz by in no time at all. She enjoyed the looks of admiration she observed in her companions' faces as she handled the heavy buckets. She directed Asmund to hold the funnel while Kael dipped the buckets in the lake and passed them to her so she could hoist them up and pour them evenly and efficiently. Once that was finished, they watered the horses and themselves, making sure to fill their leather flasks to the top.

They followed Kael on the cart path further into the valley. She saw Asmund glance back at the road, then rub his right hand over the back of his curled left hand, a mannerism she had observed in times of stress. She knew he could not leave this family in need, but he must be very frustrated to again be delayed after only just getting back on his path.

The trip to the farm was not far, but the slow progress of the heavily-laden cart the boy was navigating along the rough track made it take a long time. When at last they arrived, Kolga saw a good-sized pen containing around a dozen spotted goats of various sizes. She saw chickens busily pecking here and there around the farmyard. A tiny cottage and simple barn completed the picture. She had an intimate knowledge of what unpainted wood looked like as it aged. She could see that none of this had been here very long. "The farm doesn't look very old," she said.

"We've only lived here for about eight months," Kael replied as he led them toward the cottage.

Asmund stopped walking abruptly, and Kolga nearly collided with him. She opened her mouth to ask him why he had stopped when it hit her. A cloud of stench rolled out to meet them. Her brain scrambled to identify it, to compare it, to do anything to try and understand the unmitigated assault on her olfactory senses. But it failed. It could not be identified or compared. It was the single most disgusting stench she had ever encountered.

Kael realized they were no longer behind him

and turned to see them clutching their noses and cowering at the edge of the farmyard. "Oh! I'm so sorry!" he said, rushing back to them. "I was so excited you came, I forgot to warn you."

"Is that the well?" Asmund asked, his voice muffled by his gray sleeve.

"Yes. It's over there beyond the goat pen," Kael said, pointing.

"How are you not affected?" Kolga asked, blinking her watering eyes.

"Oh, I am. But after the second day, I just learned to live with it."

Asmund turned to her. He fished into his purse and pulled out a handkerchief, which he handed to her, then pressed his sleeve over his face again. She covered her mouth and nose. Her stomach was doing flips. She squeezed her eyes shut, concentrating, trying not to vomit. "Lead us to your parents," she heard Asmund say. She opened her eyes just a slit so she could see to follow. They hurried across the yard and into the cottage, quickly pulling the door shut behind them to block out the stench.

Kolga took in the one-room cottage at a glance. Her attention quickly focused on the pale woman covered in sweat. Her half-opened eyes looked milky and they focused on nothing. The only thing indicating that she was still alive was the ragged breathing which moved her chest up and down. A tall man stood up from her bedside and turned toward them.

"Father, I brought–" Kael began.

"A wizard!" his father finished in an astonished voice. "I know the robes of a wizard when I see them. But how?"

"They were camping at the lake when I went for water. They can help!"

"I do not know if I can help," Asmund said, moving toward the woman. "But I will try."

"We would be grateful for anything you could do. I am Fahim, and this is Hana, my wife. We do not have much, but whatever we do have is yours if you will help us."

Asmund was examining the woman with a doubtful look on his face. Kolga began to dread the fresh heartbreak the father and son would suffer if he were unable to ease her pain. It had not occurred to her until now that perhaps they would have been better off not even coming.

Asmund straightened with an astonished look upon his face. "When did this sickness befall her?" he demanded.

"It was four days ago, at the same time that the well soured," answered Fahim.

"Of course!" hissed Asmund.

"I awoke in the morning to find Hana as you see her. I rushed to the well to get her water and found it befouled. Kael has been bringing water from the lake to keep us alive. We thought that perhaps an animal had fallen into the well and died, but it is something worse than that."

"Yes, it is," Asmund agreed, stroking his chin thoughtfully. He withdrew a book from his purse and studied it for some time. Everyone watched him and waited expectantly. At last, he put it away. "This will be unpleasant, but it's our only hope. Do you have something made of iron?"

"Yes. We have farm tools and cooking tools."

"A cooking spoon?"

"Yes," said Fahim. He retrieved it swiftly.

Asmund examined it and nodded his approval. "This will be difficult. Fahim, you will need to remove her nightdress and hold one of her arms. Kolga, you will need to hold her other arm. We must not let her rise."

Fahim turned to Kael. "Go and start watering the animals, son."

"I'm not a child! I can help!" protested Kael.

Asmund looked to Fahim and saw him give a small nod of assent. "Very well. You must hold your mother's legs. She will struggle, but her life depends on us keeping her still. Do you understand?" The nervous boy answered with a rapid nodding. "Very well, let us begin."

Fahim and Kolga tugged the limp woman into a seated position and managed to pull the sweaty nightdress over her head. Her ribs were beginning to stand out from the days without sustenance. Her skin was unnaturally pale and translucent. Ragged spiderwebs of blue veins stood out on her thighs and chest. Fahim and Kolga each took an arm and held her down.

"Kolga, can you crouch down and still hold her? I need room to work." Kolga switched positions, hunkering down and holding the arm from behind, and Asmund nodded.

Kael reached out and gently placed his hands on his mother's ankles. Seeing this, Asmund said, "Get closer, and be prepared to use all your strength if necessary. Sit on her legs or lie on them if you must. Do you understand?" In answer, Kael moved closer, grasping her ankles more firmly.

Asmund took a deep breath and closed his eyes.

He stretched out his hand and held it palm down over Hana's limp torso, a finger's breadth above her skin. He moved it up and down her chest and abdomen, until finally, it stopped just a little to the right of her navel. He opened his eyes and saw where it was.

He took the iron spoon from his left hand, gripping it tightly in his stronger right hand, with his eyes never leaving that spot, not even to blink. He brought it down and touched it to her skin. Kolga was not ready for the effect this would have. Hana let out an ear-shattering scream and tried to lurch out of the bed. Kolga tightened her grip and leaned back, pinning Hana's shoulder to the bed. Fahim leaned in, pinning the opposite shoulder down, but he let out a pained moan as he did so. Kael bent over, driving his weight into her legs.

Sweat broke out on Asmund's forehead. He began speaking in a strange tongue Kolga could not understand. His words sounded angry and commanding. The spoon inched up slowly, causing Hana to moan in pain and writhe against the hands which pinned her to the bed.

The whole scene seemed like madness to Kolga as she held tightly to Hana and watched Asmund sweating and shouting angrily in some guttural tongue while moving a kitchen utensil across a sick woman's belly. She tore her gaze from Asmund's face and looked at the spoon. She saw for the first time, right above the spoon, being chased by it – something was there. It was underneath the skin, but protruding. She saw it move to the side, trying to evade, but Asmund moved the spoon and shouted at it, keeping it moving where he wanted it to move. She lost sight of it when he reached the sternum, but the movement of the spoon let her know it was still there.

She looked back at his face and saw that he was soaked with sweat. She wished she could reach up and wipe his brow, but she knew she could not. She looked down and caught sight of the thing again as it reached the woman's throat. Halfway up, it appeared to fight back even harder.

Asmund's spoon halted, but his angry words turned into a gale as he screamed at the top of his lungs. Over the sound of Asmund's hoarse words, Kolga heard Hana gagging. Her face was turning unhealthy colors. Kolga could imagine the thing saying, "Let me back in, or I will kill her right now!"

Asmund pushed the spoon upward, howling at the lump. "Sit her up! Sit her up!" he shouted. Kolga pushed the shoulder and arm while Fahim, on the other side, pulled. Hana was lurched into a seated position. Kolga held her breath as Hana began to cough. A round, reddish ball of fur tumbled out of her mouth.

She fell back limply and Asmund scooped the lump of fur into the bowl of the spoon. Kolga cringed as it sizzled and let out a high-pitched screech. He carried it carefully to the hearth and cast it into the fire. They watched it as it burned, still screeching. Once it was quiet, he came dragging back to the bed, looking exhausted.

Fahim was bent over his wife, trying to wake her. The color in her face was still unnatural and her breathing was shallow and labored. Asmund ordered him to back away, and Fahim obeyed. Asmund examined her, then turned to Kolga. In a cracking voice, he said, "I have to take the hurt that was done to her and use magic to dissipate it. But my failing as a healer is that my body is weak. I get overwhelmed by the pain and lose consciousness. If that happens, then I will die from the hurt that was killing her. If I faint, please try to wake me. Slap me or splash water in my face, try whatever you can. Do you understand?"

"Yes, but-" she started, but he raised his hand and shook his head, silently asking her to speak no more, and reluctantly she complied.

He turned back to Hana, who now had small streams of blood coming from both corners of her mouth. He placed his hands upon her stomach and his body stiffened. He began to say the words Kolga had heard him say that first day in the stables, when he had healed her bruise. He nodded, saying confidently, "I can do this." He moved his hand to her chest and jerked back as if he had touched a flame. He repeated the words, then nodded again, repeating, "I can do this."

Kolga saw the color returning to normal in Hana's face. The twin streams of blood reversed their crimson streams and drew back into her body. Asmund began to repeat the words frantically, his voice now sounding desperate. His hand left her body and curled up next to his stomach, looking like an imitation of his withered left hand. His face turned to the ceiling, his neck cocked at an unnatural angle. Two streams of blood rolled from the corners of his mouth, painting both cheeks. He fell to the floor beside the bed.

Kolga screamed and tried to sit him up, but his face was frozen in a strange rictus and he could only lie as he had fallen. "Asmund!" she shouted, tears rolling down her cheeks. "Asmund!"

She slapped his cheek, turning the blood there

into a splattered handprint. She pulled at the leather bottle, fumbling to unlace it from his belt. Tearing it free, she unstoppered it and splashed his face, shouting, "Asmund wake up! Don't do this to me!"

He didn't stir.

The road wound its way through the eternal darkness. On and on the craftsman walked, seeking his destination. After one bend of the road, he began to worry. He walked on, waiting for the path to wind its way back, but it did not. He no longer walked downward and north. *Well,* he thought, *I cannot see what strange countryside lies out in the ebony mists. Perhaps I am walking around the base of an impassable mountain. I will just have to trust that the path will bend again, taking me back in the right direction.* He walked on. After much time, he heard the sounds of a mighty battle ahead.

At last, something. He drew his hammer and moved forward cautiously. After a few paces he stopped and lowered his hammer. *Oh, Dvalinn,* he chided himself. He put his hammer away and walked on. When the mists swirled away, he saw exactly what he knew he would. Somehow, that did not prevent his heart from sinking at the sight of it.

He stood again at the foot of the massive stone bridge, the deafening chorus of war rushing past below it. How had the road led him back to the river of blades? He turned slowly, like a sleepwalker, and looked back up the road. There was no evidence of another road, no loop he could have followed. It was as if he had simply turned around and walked back. The underworld did not want him here. It was not going to let him get where he needed to go.

How much time had he wasted with his wandering? How much time remained? He could not say. What if time worked differently here? Garmr had told him that the passage of days went unmarked. It would be nice if he returned to the land of the living to find but a single instant had passed. But what if he emerged and found himself a thousand years later? He sighed with exasperation. He was being foolish. He must hurry and complete his tasks, and not worry over things he could not control.

The craftsman strode back up the road. It was bitter to be retracing his steps. But it felt good to be heading downward and north again. The road wound its way through the darkness, just as before, and it once again turned back, heading in the wrong direction. The craftsman stopped walking. If he were a human, he probably would not be able to discern that this particular bend led the wrong way. But dwarfs? Dwarfs had carved the labyrinthine mines of Kiruna which spanned all the way from the Fjorm to the Sylgr. No dwarf can lose his direction. He looked all around at the darkness. But that could not help him here. This was the only road he could see, and it was going the wrong way.

He stood on the road just before it doubled back and scratched his head. *So the road ends?* he thought. He looked down the road he had just traveled, then turned his gaze to the bend in the road and looked down that path. *So then my only options are to go back... or go back.* What was he to do? The road was supposed to take him to the gates of Hel. But it was not cooperating.

He spun around. He squeezed his eyes shut, then

opened them again, peering at the inky darkness ahead. There was nothing but nothingness.

"Hello?" he called. "Can anybody hear me?" No one answered. The silence of the underworld was impenetrable. What was he missing? What must he do?

He thought back to all that had happened, trying to decide on his next move. Had Garmr told him anything useful? Well, yes, the dog had given him the road. He bore the mark on his chest. He cleared his throat and called out again. "Behold! I bear the mark of Garmr!" He puffed out his chest, pivoting it this way and that, presenting it to the surrounding darkness. "He has given me safe passage! Show me the true path!"

He waited. Nothing happened. The silent darkness was not impressed. He stamped his foot and made an indistinct noise. He was choked with exasperation. *Calm yourself. Think!* There has to be an answer. What had the giantess said? No, that was no help. He had asked her the way and she had told him to follow the road downward and north. Well, that's what he had done! He was following the road downward and north and then the damned road just...

Wait, that's not what she said. She had never said anything about a road. *Oh, what a fool I am! She only said downward and north. She said very clearly, it's always downward and north.*

The craftsman stared straight ahead into the void. A great feeling of unease gripped him at the thought of leaving the road and stepping into the nothingness. This had to be the right answer. It was the *direction* he must follow, not the cobblestones. This must be the right thing to do. But if so, why did it fill him with such dread? His mind conjured up images of himself wandering in the darkness for eternity. He shivered, but inched forward anyway. Right or wrong, he knew he must try. The dwarf lifted his foot slowly from the edge of the cobblestones and stepped toward the unknown.

"I would not do that if I were you," said a quartet of voices from behind him. He whirled, grasping for the hammer, but his hand stopped before he reached it, and fell back to his side. Before him stood a woman wearing a wrap that was as dark as the darkness that surrounded them – no, it was made of that same darkness, he realized. Her face was that of a small child, a young, a middle-aged, and an elderly woman all at once. He found himself turning his head this way and that. If he angled his eyes toward her, he could see each of the faces more clearly. A scent of mingled roses and decaying flesh permeated the dank air. He spent some moments regarding her. At last, she spoke again, with one voice that was four voices at once.

"I said, 'I would not do that if I were you.'"

"But that is the direction I must go," he replied.

"You can go that direction. But I would not advise it."

"Oh," said the craftsman. "Why not?"

"Here on this road, you are in my realm. It belongs to me. It is named for me."

"The goddess Hel," the craftsman whispered.

"Those who die deaths of note while doing heroic deeds join the king and queen of Asgard. But everyone dies. Some die of sickness and old age and accidents. And for those, I make a place."

The craftsman fell to his knee and lowered his eyes. "Goddess, I beg your pardon for coming here. But my cause is noble. I seek-"

"I know what you seek, Dvalinn, son of Ivaldi. And you will not find it here."

"I mean no disrespect. But I must try."

"You must do nothing but what I command you to do! You do not belong here, and as you can plainly see, the road is no longer open to you! You must turn back and quit this place."

"Please, Goddess, I cannot turn back now. If the road will not take me, then I will leave it and keep going north."

The goddess threw her head back and her four faces howled with laughter. "As I said, this road upon which we stand is my realm. But out there – that place is Niflheim, the mist world. That which was long ages before the forming of the world. It's the place you saw deep below the rainbow bridge. If you pass into that realm, you will forever be lost."

The craftsman looked back into the darkness and shivered. To think, moments ago he almost stepped into it. "Goddess, please, I implore you. Tell me how I may reach your sacred city of Helheim. I must complete my quest. Please help me."

"Help you?" she raged, her form growing and expanding. "I would never help you!" Her voices battered down on him from above and forced him onto his hands and knees. "You disobedient halfling! Help you? Ha! If I could, I would kill you!"

The dwarf squeezed his eyes closed while she raged at him. His heart was gripped with icy terror. He prepared himself for death and then... His fear faded. "Um, excuse me," he said, opening his eyes and sitting up. "You would kill me?"

"Of course! Your friend the battleswine slew my

father to save your miserable life, and now you have the gall to invade my realm, making a mockery of my power!"

'If you could?" he continued.

"Queen Frigg, instead of seeking vengeance for a son, or upholding a granddaughter's dominion, decrees that no god may strike at you."

"Did she decree that you protect me?" he asked.

"No, that she would not ask, for then your quest would be meaningless," replied the angry goddess. "I was expecting the dog or the giantess to have torn you to pieces, and that's what I should do to them for failing to do so!"

"I understand," the craftsman said. Then he stood, turned around, and walked straight into the blackness.

He could not see. He raised his hand before his face, but all was darkness. He reached out in front of himself, the way anyone instinctively does when they cannot see, and stepped forward cautiously. He could feel that his feet still trod upon the same cobblestones going gradually downward and north.

The voices hissed close by his ear. "Here it comes. The edge of the abyss. If you do not turn back now, you will tumble to your doom."

"That's not true, goddess," the craftsman said calmly, "because you would not help me. You wish me dead, and you do not have to prevent me from being harmed, and so I know that I draw closer to your gates with each step I take."

He could not see her there in the pitch black, now in her true form of a towering giantess whose right side was beautiful and fresh with youthful life, her left a rotting corpse, her mighty hand raised up to strike and crush him. She shook silently with barely contained rage. Then he heard her voices say: "You are protected now, but you..." There was a pause before a little girl's voice said, "will," a young woman's voice said "not," a middle-aged voice said, "always," followed by the elderly croak, "be." A cold wind blew the dark away and the gates of Helheim loomed before him.

Hana sat up and saw her husband weeping. She followed his gaze to a strange girl on the floor who was splashing water in a young man's face and shouting for him to wake up. "What's happening? I've never seen you weep, husband."

"Oh, Hana," he wailed, hugging her. "You were dying, and the wizard has traded his life for yours!"

"What? I don't understand," she gasped.

"He has taken what was killing you and was using magic to banish it from himself, but the pain has made him unconscious and she cannot wake him. So he will die."

"What? If he wakes he can live?" Fahim answered her with a sad nod. "Kael," she shouted. "Go to my medicines and bring me the pot labeled deer's horn. Husband! Cut me a cloth from somewhere -- just a small square."

Fahim was handing her a ragged square of blanket just as Kael returned. She came around the bed and shouted, "Move!" Kolga scrambled out of her way. Hana knelt by Asmund, dumping some of the liquid from the pot onto the cloth. The odor was like the urine of a thousand barn cats and struck like a slap in the face. Hana thrust the rag to Asmund's nose and he sat up instantly, his eyes confused. He looked at the naked woman kneeling beside him holding a piece of cloth. This seemed only to confuse him further. His hand shot up and clutched at his throat.

"Magic the hurt away, Asmund," Kolga urged desperately. His mouth began to move, blood dribbling from his lips. "Good! Good!" she said, coming back and kneeling beside him where he could see her. His eyes began to roll back in his head once more. Hana thrust the rag beneath his nose, jarring him back to consciousness. "Keep going," Kolga pleaded.

He kept repeating the spell, his words becoming audible as the hurt fled. They trailed off and his breathing became normal. He looked around, seeing the assembled onlookers watching him expectantly. "It is passed," he said, holding up his hand. "All is well." Everyone let out a sigh of relief and Kolga hugged him tightly.

Hana rose and put the stopper in the deer's horn. "Why am I so hungry? I feel absolutely famished!"

"You haven't eaten in four days," said Fahim.

She shook her head in wonder. "That would also explain why I desperately need a bath."

Kael brought his mother her nightdress and said, "Unfortunately, the well is poisoned."

"What?" she demanded. "I've never been more lost in all my days."

"Don't worry about the well. I know what's wrong now, and I can fix it," said Asmund from the floor.

"You are certain you will be all right now, wizard?" Fahim asked, his face still red and wet from crying.

"Yes, I am quite well again," Asmund answered.

Then Fahim, to the surprise of his wife and son, who had never known him to show strong emotions, knelt and kissed both of Asmund's feet. "I know I could never speak what is in my heart. I can only pray that you understand." Asmund could only nod.

The chicken watched as the dwarf emerged from the darkness. She saw him stop with a relieved look on his face and gape at the giant walls. She clucked once and went back to pecking, catching a juicy grasshopper. It crunched in her beak. She tilted her head back and shimmied it down her throat. She liked to come here and roam just inside the walls. There were always lots of nice things to peck, and she could watch the new people while they arrived. This one was different somehow. People here never looked cautious or apprehensive like he did. They just came down the path and walked right in. They belonged. This dwarf reminded her of a cat she had once seen that had fallen into a river. He did not belong here, and he knew it. She stopped pecking and tilted her head to look at him again. He was standing just outside, looking in.

Dvalinn stood looking in at the sunny countryside beyond the gates. The skies were clear but for a few fluffy clouds. The scene looked peaceful and serene. He saw a road leading away to a normal-looking village. There was even a white chicken, with a black spot on one of her wings shaped almost like a triangle, pecking for her breakfast by the gate. He was uncertain of what to do. He looked all around, but could not see anything that might be of use. He saw movement at the edge of the darkness. A moment later, a man emerged. He was old and gray, dressed in a woodsman's cloak, and he bore an aged and worn axe upon his shoulder. He strode forward as if he were off to work.

The craftsman walked out and met him. "Greetings, master woodsman."

"Greetings, master dwarf," the man replied. "Are you on your way to Hel as well?"

"I am, but I can go no further. I am still alive and wish only to visit. But any who enter the gate can never leave again."

"What you say is true, master dwarf. I don't know how I know that, but I do. I wish I could be of service, but I cannot. I must enter the gates; I belong there." The man kept striding toward his destination.

"You can be of help," the dwarf protested, having to jog alongside to keep up. "If I might borrow your axe?"

"My axe?" the man echoed. "I could not. It is somehow part of who I am. It must go with me. No. I am sorry."

"If you could wait but a minute, I would use it and then return it to you."

The man started walking again. "That is a problem, though. You see, I cannot seem to stand still and wait. I have somewhere to be. I do not understand it any better than that. I must get where I'm going."

The craftsman ran ahead and stopped the old woodsman again. "Please! I can pay you." He pulled the empty scabbard from his belt. "Behold the richness of the silver, the design chased into the metal by the master of all masters. The emeralds and garnets, the clearest ever cut, set to perfection in their shimmering mounts."

The old woodsman looked at the precious scabbard, then into the hopeful face of Dvalinn. "I'm sorry, master dwarf. But I find that I want for nothing. I am somehow incapable of wanting for anything. Now, I wish you good luck, but I must be off." He walked around the craftsman and headed for the gate once more.

The craftsman stood for a moment, already hating himself for what he was about to do. He once again ran to intercept the old man. Then he snatched the axe from his hand. The old man watched it leave his grasp. He stared at it, a confused look on his face.

Dvalinn asked the man, "Is something wrong?" The man shifted his gaze to the dwarf's face, but could not answer. The craftsman tucked the axe into the back of his belt. "Is there something... you want for?" Dvalinn pressed the end of the scabbard into his hand and rested the body of it on his shoulder.

The old man's mind seemed to clear. "No, I do not want for anything. I cannot."

"And is there not somewhere you need to be?"

"Yes, I have to get where I'm going."

"Very well, I will not keep you."

"Yes, right then. Farewell, master dwarf. I am sorry I could not help you."

"It's all right," Dvalinn said quietly. "In the end, we all do what we must."

The woodsman nodded and passed through the gates. The chicken fluttered out of his way and clucked indignantly.

The craftsman withdrew the axe from his belt, and at its touch, his shoulders slumped. In his mind, he watched the old woodsman's father shape the fine cut of ash into a handle and fit it to the axe head when it was new. He thought about himself kneeling on the banks of the river Gjorm, watching Scattersoul disappear. His face grew grim with sorrow.

He focused all his belief and took action. He unslung the rope that was not really there and tied an end of it to the middle of the axe that was not really there either. The axe in his hands showed him another vision. At this moment, the dwarf could see the son of the woodsman he had just met. He was carrying the axe proudly on his shoulder as he strode to work in the eastern forests. He did not know that when he returned in the evening, his elderly father would be gone.

The craftsman stepped back, looking up at the tall wall that was called Nagrindr, the fence of the fallen. Its logs were shaped into long points at the top. He would aim between two of them. He stepped into place and spun the axe tied to the rope. When he judged the moment was right, he let fly. The rope paid out so swiftly through his cupped hand it heated the tough skin of his palm. He watched the axe as it sailed high above the wall and hit the top of its arc, then disappeared behind the wall. He imagined the rope laying precisely between two timber peaks, and so it did. He pulled carefully until the axe caught between the points of the wall far above. He tugged a few times to make sure it would bear his weight, and then he ascended, slowly, hand over hand, so high that the world below grew small.

At last he reached the top. He wedged himself

into the tiny perch between the spires. It was precarious. He was short, but his limbs and the set of his shoulders and hips were the opposite of small. He balanced himself and, with some difficulty, reset the rope and axe for his descent. He then tied the loose end of the rope around the swell at the end of the axe's haft. He scanned the land from his high vantage, straining his eyes to find what he sought. "There!" he declared, locating the dwindling dot in the distance. Knowing where he must go next, he hurriedly descended the rope.

When at last he reached the ground, he took the slack out of the tail end of the rope he had tied to the haft swell, letting the axe fall down a bit out of its seating high above him. He deftly maneuvered both ends of rope so that upon pulling, the axe gracefully slipped handle-first over the wall and tumbled down. The craftsman stood watching it fall with satisfaction. *Quite ingenious,* he thought to himself. He then shouted, "Oh no!" and dove to the side a second before the plummeting axe would have struck him.

The chicken walked over and pecked his boot once. "Bock bock bock bock," it said.

Nothing like lying in the dirt being laughed at by a chicken to keep you humble, he thought. He stood and gathered up the rope and axe. "No time to lose," he said out loud, and started up the path.

Dvalinn ran as quickly as he could. As he did he considered the list of great dwarfen runners, and how that list would never be written. He pumped his short legs as his tangled hair flowed behind him in the wind. He dashed into the village and tore down its main road. Startled villagers made way before him. He came to the turn he sought and bounded around it, his boots thundering like a rockslide. He lowered his head and pounded down the straightaway.

He took the next turn so quickly he nearly left his feet. Managing to keep his balance, he looked up and saw his goal ahead. Before him walked a man with an empty scabbard resting upon his shoulder. He was walking toward a deep green forest. The craftsman had spied which way the man had gone from high up on the wall. Now that he knew he would catch up with him, he bent over, hands on his knees, and breathed deeply for a few moments.

Ahead, another man came out of the forest and beckoned to the woodsman. "Come along, son," he called. "Your mother has brought us a pot of stew, that we may continue working through the day. Help her carry it from the cart."

The craftsman saw that the stranger was holding the same axe he now held in his own hand. He rushed ahead to catch the woodsman. "Excuse me, sir."

The man turned at his approach. At first he was a stranger to the craftsman, but he quickly realized that the woodsman had grown young and vibrant. "Oh, master dwarf! I see you made it in after all."

"Yes, thanks to your help."

"My help?"

"Yes, I came to say thank you, and to give you this." He took the scabbard and replaced it with the axe. "Do not forget your axe."

"No, I mustn't. It's a part of me," said the young woodsman, walking away to join his father.

"I know," said the craftsman.

The craftsman wiped his brow with the back of his hand and watched the father and son disappear into the trees. He smiled, and then thought a bit enviously, *They will eat stew prepared for them by loving hands and chop wood for eternity. Not a bad end.*

He made his way back to the village. All around, people were going about their busy days. He heard the ring of a hammer in the smith's shop nearby. That sound was his favorite music. He smelled fresh bread baking and followed his nose to a garden in front of the public house. Tables had been set up there, and folks sat around them, drinking ale and eating bread and cheese and fruit. They paused their singing and welcomed him as he approached. All were in the bloom of youth. "Join us! Eat! Drink!" they called, waving him in.

"Oh, I would dearly love to, but I mustn't."

"Did you catch up with Snorri Oleson?" asked one of the men.

"What?" asked the craftsman, confused.

"The woodsman. We welcomed him as he came through, and then a little while after, you came running through as fast as a rabbit. We figured you must be trying to catch up with him."

"Yes," replied the craftsman, now understanding. "I was bringing him his axe."

"Oh, yes, he will be needing that," said a skinny man dressed in old-fashioned furs. "His family have been woodcutters here since we founded the village. It was so long ago, I know not how much time has passed. We were only seven families then, but now look; the village grows bigger and bigger each year."

"And which village is this?" asked the craftsman.

"It is Forsfjoror," answered a woman with berry-stained lips.

"Forsfjoror that is just a morning's ride from

Einarshofn by the sea?"

"The same." She belched, then took a pull of ale.

"Oh no! That is too far away!" he cried. The diners looked at one another and then erupted into laughter, dropping food and sloshing their ale. Dvalinn thought for a moment, and then he laughed too. "Thank you, my friends. I wish I could stay, but I must be gone."

"Here," said a big, smiling woman from the doorway. "If you must go so soon, take this with you, and never let it be said that the village of Forsfjoror is second to any in hospitality." She hurried over, tying up a bundle containing some bread, salted fish, and a pot of ale.

The craftsman dipped into his purse, and to the woman's surprise, tossed her a piece of hacksilver. "Don't spend this all at once." Again, laughter rang out, and the villagers hammered the tables with their cups. The dwarf threw his head back and laughed along, caught up in the mirth of the dead.

He hurried back along the road. He needed to get to the gate. He now surmised that the gate would lead to wherever the person who entered was going. His fear was that should someone new enter, he would be trapped here, far to the east of where he needed to go.

The gate came into view just ahead, but as if in answer to his fears, he sensed the shadows shifting behind him. The clouds began to rearrange themselves in the sky. His view of the gate grew hazy. He broke into a run. Some sort of aperture seemed to be swiftly narrowing before the gate. He propelled himself forward with all his might and launched through the closing portal, tumbling in a heap at the foot of the gate.

He rolled over and beheld a completely different countryside. No longer was the village of Forsfjoror nestled in the distance, surrounded by its lush forests. Instead, he saw a panoramic view of high mountain country. It was early evening, and lantern lights dotted a hamlet at the foot of a nearby mountain.

He was still lying propped up on his elbows when a chicken walked up, clucked twice, and pecked his boot. *This is my life now,* thought the craftsman wryly. *I just lie on the ground by this gate while chickens peck at my boots.* He focused on the bird, and then corrected himself. *Not chickens – chicken.* Unless all chickens here had triangular spots on their wings, then this was the same one he had seen before. *It must have moved with the gate when someone new arrived.* Someone new... This thought gave him pause.

He jumped to his feet. The chicken fluttered away, clucking its disapproval at the commotion. He peered through the gate and saw a man emerging from the darkness, trudging toward him. He looked to be of middle-age. His hair was thinning and his face was lined from long years of worry. He looked pale and seemed to be shivering. The craftsman watched as he stepped through the gate. In an instant, his hair was thick and yellow, his face smooth and young.

"How do you do, sir?" greeted the craftsman.

"Quite well," answered the man, then seemed to consider for a moment. "I can remember suffering from a horrible chill – but it now seems very far away. And how do you do on this evening?"

"I am well, very well, but I fear I may be lost. Tell me, what hamlet lies at the foot of that mountain?"

The man looked out at the little houses with their twinkling lights. His face was so young and serenely happy that it was hard to remember the lines of worry that had etched it just moments before. "That is Horsfell, the village of my birth. I am going home. Won't you come with me? I can sense that my kin await me there. They will welcome us and build a fire and we will sip warm spiced wine."

"That sounds lovely," said the craftsman, looking wistfully at the distant cottages with their smoking chimneys. "But that is too far from where I need to be, and so I must wait here and watch for another traveler. Your kinsmen await. Go, my friend, but when you get there, if you can remember, drink a toast to me. Wherever I am, I will know and feel the warmth of it."

"I will remember," said the man. "Good luck on your journey, and may you find what you seek." They clasped each other's wrists and the man set off into the gathering dark.

The craftsman sat, resting his back on the wall next to the gate. He ate his bread and fish and sipped the ale. A short while later, he watched as the heavens above the mountains started to spread their glowing fingers of ghostly green. No matter how many times he saw the magic lights of the northern sky dance and frolic, they still made him feel like a child, just as he had been the first time, held in his father's arms, watching the pinks and greens and purples blossoming in the dark. As he watched, he felt the unmistakable sensation of a drink of warm wine inside him, and when he opened his mouth, he tasted spice on his lips. "And here's to you," he said, lifting his pot, and quaffing the last of the ale. The white chicken nestled down beside him, and he felt contented.

The craftsman awoke with a start as someone

spoke. He opened his eyes to broad daylight, then squinted. He shook his head to clear it. Remembering where he was, he bounded to his feet. Who had spoken to him? The mountains were gone. In their place he beheld vast, untouched wild lands.

He could see the figure of a boy walking toward a distant farm with a rough-hewn house and matching barn. The boy was already some distance from the gate. Dvalinn did not like the idea of having to stray so far, for he knew that if someone entered the gate while he was away from it, he would remain there while the gate shifted to another place. He made up his mind quickly and ran to catch up with the youth. "Hello," he called as he came up beside him.

"Oh, hello," said the boy. "I greeted you as I entered the gate, but you were sleeping."

"Yes, I must have dozed off." Dvalinn glanced back nervously at the gate. He must find out quickly where he was, and if it was not right, he would run back as quickly as he could. "Where is this place, young man?"

The boy walked a few more clumsy steps and stopped with a bewildered look on his face. He was at an awkward age, around fourteen winters, and the length of his limbs outraced his muscles. "Where is this place?" he repeated. "Why, it's here."

"No," the craftsman tried again, "I mean, what's it called?"

"It's our farm," answered the boy.

The dwarf felt himself becoming exasperated as he gauged the distance back to the gate. Maybe this whole strategy was just a waste of time, maybe he should just stay here, get a mount, and begin journeying where he needed to go.

The boy said, "I am sorry, sir, but I really must be on my way. I was up in the top of the barn moving the hay when I think I lost my balance. I really must get back and finish my chores."

"Of course, son. But first, tell me, is there a village or town that your parents have taken you to?"

"A settlement," said the boy, apparently happy to finally know an answer to one of the strange questions.

"A settlement! Good! Do you know what it is called?"

"Eystribyggo. Of course I know the name. It's the only one."

The dwarf cocked his head to one side and looked up at the sky, thinking, *I know that name.* Eystribyggo. *Why, that's in...* "The green lands? Is this an island? This is called the green lands, isn't it?"

The boy scrunched up his face and shrugged.

Getting a mount and journeying from here would not be an option. "Farewell, boy. I must go. Oh, and be careful up in the top of the barn." He spun as the youth waved and bolted for the gate. This adventure had turned into far more running than really seemed fair. He made it back and leaned against the wall, panting. While he caught his breath he thought to himself, *I didn't even have to run so fast – nobody came through the gate.* As if in reply, the world began to change around him as someone new stepped from the darkness outside.

The craftsman watched as the figure came into view. It was a young woman. A touch of sadness clutched at his heart, for he saw that she cradled a small figure in her arms. It was what it was. An everyday tragedy. He knew how often mother and child came to this place, instead of the arms of their loving families. He knew, and yet knowing did nothing to stop that feeling of pressure in his chest.

He could see her clearly now. She had not yet been given twenty winters. Something was odd about her face. It was a light purple and covered with soot, much of which was concentrated into diagonal lines coming from her nostrils. That was strange. Instead of dying while trying to bring forth life, it looked more like she had...

"Hello," the young woman said as she stepped through the gate.

The craftsman saw her face brightened with health and vitality. He opened his mouth to greet her, but was interrupted when the figure bundled in her arms barked with delight, and sitting up, began to lick her face. The craftsman laughed with joy at the little golden-red puppy and reached out to pet its head. This delighted the puppy, and it licked his hand. "Oh, it's a dog!" said the craftsman.

"He is that," said the young woman. "And so much more. He is a part of me."

"Do you remember how you came here?" asked the dwarf.

The young woman stopped and thought. As she did, her eyes grew distant, as if gazing at far-off things. "Yes," she replied slowly. "I can watch it all happen, as if it happened to someone else. Which, in a way, I suppose it did.

"I had been dreaming that I stood close to a roaring furnace and it frightened me. I wanted to leave, to get away from there. I heard my little dog, Ulf, barking at me, telling me to run to him. Then I awoke, and Ulf really was barking at me, the walls of the house were engulfed in flames. The thatch was raining down little droplets of fire from above. I screamed, 'Help! Help!' but I knew no one would hear. Father was not there. He was away at his work. Little Ulf barked and barked for help as well, but we were all alone.

"I tried to reach the door, but the flames would not let me. I turned to the window, but it was the same. Drops of flame tried to ignite my hair. Little Ulf tugged at my skirts, and made me follow him. He had found a hole crumbled in the stonework next to the hearth. He ran through it, then stuck his head back in and barked, beckoning me to follow him.

"I tried pulling at the stones to make the opening wider. I kicked at them, but they would not move. I tried forcing my way out, but to no avail. The heat was growing intolerable. More of the thatch was raining down. It was harder and harder to breathe in the smoke. I sat back, away from the hole, and cried. Ulf barked at me from the little opening. 'I can't fit!' I sobbed at him.

"I saw him disappear from the hole. I could hardly hear him over the roar of the flames. But he was barking, trying to find someone, anyone to help. I knew that father would not return for many hours, and there was no one else to hear him. 'Poor father,' I cried. With mother gone and now me, he would return from his working to find himself alone in the world. This made me weep even more.

"Ulf came in again and crawled onto my lap. 'I know, Ulf. I know you tried. Thank you. You must go now.' He sat down and licked my hand. 'No!' I shouted, 'you have to go!' My lungs were burning. It was getting so hard to breathe. I grabbed him and thrust him through the hole. I could taste a little hint of fresh air outside the opening. 'There. You can live.' He tried to come right back in. I pushed him out and held him out. But a drop of fire from the ceiling hit my leg, and I let go of him to pat it out. I was growing very sleepy then. The smoke was making it so hard to breathe.

"I sat back again, and Ulf climbed onto my lap once more. I cried. He was just a puppy, he did not know what any of this meant. Then he stood on my lap, and putting his little paws on my shoulders, he pressed his head against mine, and then I knew. Of course he understood. He knew that when he went out the little hole he could breathe again and he was not hot. He understood what everything meant. He understood, and he was telling me he would not leave me. I lay back and hugged him to my chest. He licked my face, and I said, 'Maybe we should just sleep.' And so that's what we did."

When she finished speaking, the craftsman was silent. He reached up and pet the happy puppy again. "Love is the strongest magic," he said. "It will outlive every other kind."

The woman's eyes came back as if from far away. "I really must apologize, but I feel like I need to get where I am going."

"Of course," said the dwarf, remembering himself. "I wanted to ask you, where is it you go?"

"My mother is waiting for me. Our lands are not far from the village of Holbaek."

"Is that not also called the Village of the Lakes? Unless I am mistaken, that is not far from the Village of the Two Rivers."

"Yes, I have heard the old folks call it the Village

of the Lakes. It is to the east of Essetofte, but that village does not have two rivers. Then her face brightened. "Could you mean Kalbaek, to the north? In the Valley of Rivers! That's it, that must be where you mean!"

"Yes, that is it! Kalbaek, where the two rivers meet. May I walk with you, my lady?" the craftsman asked with a bow.

She smiled and put down Ulf, saying, "Lead the way, bravest of dogs." He trotted to one side briefly and sniffed at the white chicken who was still pecking nearby. Then he circled twice and ran ahead, barking gleefully. The young lady stretched out her hand and the dwarf took it in his own. They struck off into the bright countryside, breathing in the cool fresh air.

"Thank you for seeing us home safely," said the young woman, holding the little puppy. "Good luck on your quest."

"Thank you, my friends. And thank you for the use of this fine pony," called the craftsman, as he rode away to the north.

CHAPTER NINE

Kolga sat watching over Asmund as he slept. Hana sat at the table, drinking water and eating small bites of porridge. When she had first tried eating, she had gobbled the food quickly and made herself sick. Now she was pacing herself, but Kolga could tell that she felt frustrated and impatient to regain her strength.

Fahim and Kael returned from tending to the farm. Although the cottage door opened and closed quietly, the sound was enough to wake Asmund. "How long have I been asleep?" he asked.

"Only a couple of hours," Kolga replied.

"I am sorry to have awakened you," said Fahim.

"Not at all," said Asmund, sitting up. "I just needed a little rest."

Fahim smiled with relief and said. "The chickens have given us a bounty. A good meal will give us all some much needed strength."

Hana rose and reached out for the basket full of eggs, but he evaded her outstretched hands. "No, you sit and rest. I will cook." She looked as if she might protest, but then thought better of it and sat back down.

The midday meal seemed to lighten everyone's mood. After they had eaten, Asmund sat back and said,

"Kolga, if you are willing to brave the smell again, I could use some help healing the well. We need to gather some plants from the forest."

"As long as I can tie your handkerchief over my nose, I am at your service."

"I may be able to help in that regard as well," said Hana, rising.

Kolga could see that she stood with greater ease and that more color was coming back into her skin. She went to the cabinet where Kael had retrieved the pot of deer's horn tincture earlier. She took out a bundle of dried leaves and placed them in a small iron cauldron. Going to the hearth, she used the same iron spoon Asmund had used to save her life to scoop some embers into the cauldron. She held it up and gently blew into it. A moment later, a thick smoke began to emanate, fragrant with the scent of sage. "Here," she said, flipping the hanging handle up and passing it to Kolga. "This should help some."

"What can we do to help?" asked Fahim.

"It really shouldn't take more than Kolga and myself. I'm sure you have chores that need your attention," Asmund said.

Hana spoke up. "I am feeling better, husband, and long to show our guests proper gratitude. If you and Kael will take your bows into the forest and bring back a brace of pheasants, then I can roast them for a feast tonight."

"Are you sure you feel up to it?" asked Fahim doubtfully.

"Yes. The wizard has healed me completely. All I needed was food and water to find my feet again. Please let me do something. It's not every day that someone is willing to lay down their life to save yours. I know it would be impossible to truly thank them, but I must try my best just the same."

"A feast it is, then!" proclaimed Fahim. "Kael, go and gather vegetables for your mother and I will string our bows for the hunt!"

Even with the handkerchief tied in place and the sage smoke wafting in her face, it was miserable in the farmyard. Kolga was pleased, however, to find that much of the assistance Asmund needed fell very much into her field of expertise. He had her strip the sticks from spruce boughs and weave them into a ball twice the size of a man's head, which they suspended from the well rope. Then, using a spade from the barn, she dug a deep hole out in the forest.

Asmund set about preparing the large spruce ball, frequently consulting his book of spells. He spoke a quiet incantation while writing on a small slip of parchment which he then rolled and slipped into the center of the ball. He spoke a few more words while sprinkling some of the sage ashes from the cauldron onto its surface. Then he directed Kolga to lower it slowly into the well.

Once the ball had reached the water below, he placed his hand on the rope just in front of hers. He began speaking in the same language she had heard him use when moving the iron spoon across Hana's body. The rope began to vibrate and grew warm to the touch. The farm animals grew restless and noisy. Asmund's words became angry and commanding, just as they had done earlier that day.

She knew he was once again expelling something malicious that did not want to go. She could hear the rope hum with the vibrations. The heat was intensifying. Asmund shouted in the strange tongue with a defiant rage animating his sweating face. Kolga's palms were stinging. She began to fear that she would not be able to hold on much longer. She squeezed her eyes shut and held on determined not to let go. Then, suddenly, everything ceased. The rope went dead in her hand no longer humming and burning. Asmund's angry words were gone and the restless animals were soothed.

"Pull it up, please," said Asmund. She began pulling the rope, but her hands were numb and she fumbled.

"Use care!" he cautioned urgently. "Do not let it touch the sides of the well. Once it's out, let it touch nothing, especially not us!"

She took turns removing each hand and shaking it to return feeling. Then she braced herself and carefully lifted. Once the ball left the water, she noted that it weighed much more than it had before. As it rose, the stench, which had already been horrendous, intensified. She allowed herself no reaction to this renewed assault on her senses. The caution she had heard in Asmund's warning had impressed upon her the importance of her actions right now, and she devoted all of her attention to the task.

Once the ball was out of the well and dangling before her, the stench was so great that tears streamed from her eyes unchecked and her stomach clenched in revulsion. The wooden ball was no longer visible. All that could be seen was a pale yellow glob of glistening, viscous slime. Swiftly, Asmund drew his belt knife and sliced away the excess well rope, leaving her with only the last few feet suspending the unwholesome pendulum.

"Now to the hole waiting in the forest," said Asmund. "Carefully."

She started forward cautiously. It was not too heavy, but it did hold some weight, and she carried it with her arm extended, terrified of it touching her. Thus, by the time she reached the hole, her arms and shoulders were screaming with pain.

"Place it in the hole," he directed. "Go easy."

She lowered the ball of slime gingerly. Once it made contact with the bottom of the hole, the substance oozed away from the spruce sticks, becoming a sloshing puddle of putrescent filth. This was more than she could endure. Kolga dropped the rope into the hole and ran deeper into the woods. She had made it a dozen steps or so when she fell to her hands and knees, and ripping off the handkerchief, she deposited her midday meal onto the ground.

It was some time later that she was able to rise and rejoin Asmund. He was still shoveling dirt into the hole, but the liquid horror was hidden from view and the smell was already fading.

"I'm sorry," she said.

"No, I am sorry," he replied. "I had no idea how bad it would be. I couldn't have done it without you, though. So thank you."

She felt drained as she watched him fill in the rest of the hole. He could not use the shovel in the conventional way. He held it in the center of its handle with his right hand. The rest of the handle was braced along the underside of his forearm. He leaned over, tossing half scoops of dirt into the hole until it was completely filled in.

Returning to the barn, he traded the shovel for a bucket. "Let's draw some water from the well."

How could one ever trust this well again? she thought. She followed him back to the well and had to admit that with the smell gone, she was feeling more optimistic. When the first bucket of clear water was hoisted up, her optimism grew a little more. When she watched Asmund cup a hand of water to his lips without hesitation and slurp it loudly, she became a believer. She used the cool, clean water to splash her face and rinse her mouth out. This helped to chase away the memory of having been sick, and the success finally struck her full force. "You did it, Asmund!"

"We did it!" he replied, returning her smile.

Kolga's mouth watered as Hana laid out the feast -- the greens and honeyed turnips, the nuts and berries, the roasted pheasant. Hana apologized that there had not been time to bake breads and churn butter. They all assured her that they were not missed.

Hana looked exhausted. This task had definitely been too much for her in her still-weakened state. But everyone understood how important it was to her to express her gratitude. Once everything was laid out she sat down, squeezing between her husband and son. They all sat virtually shoulder-to-shoulder. The little table could barely contain all the boards of food.

Fahim rose from the cask that served as his seat (the only three chairs they owned were occupied by his wife and their two honored guests) and picked up his cup of ale. "Drink with me. We thank you, Gefjun, goddess of the farm, for sending Asmund and Kolga to us. And thank you two," he added, holding his cup toward the two of them, "for chasing the sickness from the farm. If I lived a thousand years I could never repay you for your kindness." He drank, leaning back and gulping until little rivulets escaped and ran down his beard.

Kolga quaffed her cup of ale, matching Fahim's gusto. It was delicious! She could taste the hint of berries that had helped to sugar the fermentation. *I could travel around for the rest of my days,* she mused, *sampling every farmhouse ale, and never taste the same one twice.* She fell upon her food in her accustomed predatory manner and devoured it.

Everything was scrumptious, especially the pheasant, which had been roasted with garlic and thyme. She finished off her meal with a handful of berries. She sat back and thought, *I can't remember being happier than this.* Good food, merry company, and for the first time in her life, adventure! Adventures that seemed harrowing and desperate at the start but all worked out for the best in the end. She knew that much lay ahead of them, but in this moment, everything was perfect. Nothing could spoil that.

"Now that Hana is healed and the well is clean, I have such plans for our little farm!" Fahim said, beaming and pouring himself another cup.

"You can't stay," Asmund said.

"What?" Fahim asked, still smiling, certain that he had misheard.

"You must leave this farm," Asmund repeated somberly.

"But why?" Fahim said, all joy draining from his

face. "Everything is fine now! The way it was before!"

"This was no accident," Asmund said. "This was an attack designed to drive you from the land. Haven't you asked yourself how the well would be poisoned at the exact time that Hana fell sick?"

Fahim did not reply. He just stared miserably at the pheasant carcass in front of him.

"Who attacked us?" asked Kael.

"It was a Brunnmigi." Asmund replied. "A mystical beast; a shapeshifter who likes to take the form of a monstrous fox. They are very territorial. They often slumber for long stretches of time. I think it was probably sleeping when you arrived, but then awoke to find that you had built your farm in its lands, so it urinated in your well and cursed the woman of the house."

"Oh, no! I did not need to see that image in my head!" Kolga said, making the face of someone who has tasted sour milk. "It pissed in the well?"

"Yes."

"So that filth we removed from the well was..." She stopped speaking and put her hand over her nose and mouth, remembering the unholy stench.

"Why did it attack me?" asked Hana.

"To exterminate something from its land, it strikes the life-giver, the woman. Then the numbers cannot grow and the spirit of the men will be broken. It is the easiest way."

"Well, can we guard against it, or fight it?" asked Fahim.

"No. You must flee," said Asmund gravely. "This is a magical creature, ancient and powerful. It employed these tactics so you would leave and not even know of its existence. When it returns and finds that you have defeated its curses, it will be enraged. I do not think it will return until the new moon, but I am not certain. You must be gone as soon as you are able."

Fahim's shoulders slumped and he bowed his head. Hana put her hand on his arm to comfort him. "All we built is gone," he sighed.

"I wanted to wait until after the feast to tell you. You have already been through so much," said Asmund.

Everyone sat silently now, all of the joy from earlier forgotten. At last, Hana broke the silence. "The sun is down. I think everyone could use a good night's rest. You, our guests, will take the big bed, and we–"

"No, that won't be necessary," interrupted Asmund. "Kolga and I can sleep in the barn. We had been expecting to camp out every night on our journey, so the roof of the barn over our heads will feel like a luxury. Hana, you are still not fully recovered from your ordeal. You need to rest in your own bed."

It was clear that it would be of no use to argue with him. "It will be nice to rest in our bed, while it is still our bed," admitted Hana. "I will fetch you some blankets for the barn."

"No need," said Kolga. "We have all of our bedding in the cart." She rose from the table and Asmund began to slowly rise as well. She could see that he was bone tired. She placed a hand on his shoulder. "Sit, rest for a few minutes more by the fire. It is dark and the bedding needs to be put down. Give me ten minutes to prepare, then you can come to the barn and go straight to sleep."

He smiled up at her. "Thank you. You are better to me than I deserve."

"Truer words have never been spoken," she replied with a wink.

"Speaking of the dark," Fahim chimed in. "I will light you a lantern, but you must be cautious in the barn. There is a lot of dry hay."

"I have just the thing," Asmund said. He drew his belt dagger and spoke a word. Instantly the blade began to emit a white light that brightened the tiny cottage. "Here," he said, passing it to Kolga.

She took it from him gingerly. Careful to touch only the handle, she held it out away from herself. Observing this, he said, "No, it is light only, no heat. I mean, yes, still avoid the blade; it's magically sharp. But you can put it on a pile of hay or stick its point into a plank while you work and there will be no danger of fire."

She shook her head in wonder. "All right, give me ten minutes. I will make a nice bed in the hay and then we can all put this crazy day behind us."

The dwarf bobbed along on top of the gray pony as it trotted past a crystal clear lake. Every league behind them would have taken ages on foot. He was in a fine mood, but it was a fine mood tinged by a vague sense of unease. How much time had passed since he entered these realms? How long did he have until the new moon? He looked ahead and said to the pony, "The ground is good here. Let us run," and so they galloped.

The pony never seemed to tire as the leagues fell away. In any other circumstances, the coming of night would have served as their clock, informing them when to stop and rest. But darkness fell and on they rode. Many times had the dwarf reached down and felt the pony's neck. It was always dry, the breathing always unchanged, and the speed never seemed to falter. Only a dead pony thundering across the Helheim could be so swift and tireless.

The pony whinnied triumphantly as he cut through the dark. This infected Dvalinn with a sense of exultant pleasure. Leaning forward, he held on as his hair flew back in the rushing wind. His blood pumped through him like fire as he howled out, "Freyaaaa!" He watched as the journey of two days was hacked away under the tireless hoofbeats of his valiant steed. At this rate they would arrive in under a day. That is, if he did not give out first. *No!* He would not give out. If the pony could run forever, then he would ride for just as long.

They streaked into the Valley of the Rivers under a midday sun. He saw the first of the farms on the outskirts of the village. It was one of these farms that he had come to find.

After moving so swiftly for so long, coming to a stop felt strange. The stillness was almost panic-inducing. The craftsman dismounted and held onto the pony's neck for a moment until they both felt normal again.

"Farewell, my friend, and thank you. If I succeed and save the children, it will be because of many who have helped me. Among their number will be a pony, who I now name Shadowfoot the Gray. Go with my gratitude. Return and watch over the girl and her dog." Shadowfoot gave one last whinny and was away.

Kolga carried their gear from the cart to the barn. She arranged their bedding on a layer of hay, using all of the blankets and skins they had. The barn would keep the wind and the wet off of them, but without a fire, they would need to cover up to keep warm. She went behind the barn and relieved herself, then used the glowing blade to cut two sticks for them to clean their teeth with.

When she returned to the barn, she expected to find Asmund, but he had not yet arrived. She used one of the sticks and rinsed her mouth with a swallow from her water bottle. She removed her belt and sat down on the bedding, then watched the door impatiently for a time. With a sigh, she took her smooth river stone from her belt purse and dressed the edge of her handaxe. It had not really seen enough use to get dull yet, but it seemed a useful task to occupy her time.

Asmund must have fallen back into conversation with our hosts, she thought while she worked. Once the axe's edge was perfect, she put it and the stone away. She rose and peeked out of the barn door. She saw the lights of the cottage glowing through its tiny window. The sliver of moon had not yet risen very high, and the rest of the farm was lost in shadow.

She stuck the tip of the dagger into the door frame and left the door ajar. *That should be enough light to guide his way,* she thought, coming back to the bedding and lying down. She lay in the dark for another twenty minutes or so. The wind grabbed the barn door and dragged it wide open. A chilly breeze blew in, filling the barn. She rose and went to the doorway.

The cottage now was standing dark and quiet. "That's not right," she said out loud. *Perhaps he is off doing his necessaries before bed,* she thought. But the thought did not satisfy her. She strapped her belt back on and pulled the glowing blade from the door frame. Stepping into the night, she turned in a circle, holding the light aloft. She could see the goats all huddled in one corner of their pen. She saw their cart pony standing next to the farm horse in its corral. She could make out the well a little further away. "Asmund, are you out here?" she called, not expecting an answer.

She walked to the cottage and knocked. A moment later, she heard someone moving within. She saw a candle's light begin to glow through the window. Fahim opened the door. "Is Asmund still here?" she asked without any greeting.

"What?" asked Fahim, confused. "He left a little after you did. Did he not make it to the barn?"

"No, I never saw him!" she answered, panic rising in her voice.

"That doesn't make sense," Kael said, rising from his bed. "When I opened the door to see him out, you were waiting just outside."

"I was not!" Kolga protested.

"You were!" Kael insisted. "As I closed the door, I saw that he was following you out past the well."

"Are you sure?" asked Hana, joining them at the door.

"Yes," answered Kael. "I could see them clearly by the light of the torch."

"But I don't have a torch, I have this!" Kolga cried, holding up the dagger.

Everyone was struck silent for a moment. Then Hana gasped, "The creature!"

"Asmund!" Kolga shouted, then spun around. She began running for the woods beyond the well.

Fahim called after her, "Wait, I will get dressed and come with you!" But she was passing the well by the time the words had left his mouth. She ran for a few minutes, the dagger lighting her way into the pitch-black forest. It dawned on her that she did not know where she was going. She was in a panic, desperate to find Asmund.

"It's hopeless!" she cried, panting from her headlong dash. *If only there were some way...* She froze midthought, her frenzied mind finally remembering the amulet. She closed her eyes and focused. Instantly she turned and opened her eyes, knowing exactly where to go.

She set off at a fast jog. The light of the magical dagger did not keep her from stumbling again and again in the shadowy forest. This pace was reckless on terrain such as this, but she would not allow herself to slow.

After stumbling along for several minutes, she narrowly avoided plummeting into the darkness as she came to a drop-off leading down into a rocky ravine. She could feel that the amulet wanted her to continue moving straight ahead on her current course. It made no allowance for impassable obstacles. Her panicked impatience flared at the thought of having to travel either one way or the other looking for a safe way down into the ravine.

She knew she was very close to him now. She raised the dagger over her head and looked to her left and right, trying to decide if one direction looked more promising than the other. To her right, she saw a tree growing at the edge of the ravine. She moved her eyes up its length, judging the height of the tree, then looked down, mentally measuring it against the depth of the ravine. She had an audacious idea that would either work brilliantly or prove to be the waste of time that would cost Asmund his life. *That is, if he's still alive at all.*

She shook her head violently to banish that thought.

She placed the dagger on the ground so that it would provide light where she would need it and drew her axe. She would have to fell this tree with precise technique for two reasons. First, to make it fall very quickly, and second, to make it fall exactly how she needed.

Anyone who was not a woodcutter would guess that a flurry of powerful chopping would be in order. But Kolga knew that it would require a series of careful and deliberate cuts, removing wedges in exactly the right places. She set to her task, moving with precision. Her father's patient voice echoed in her memory, directing her movements just as it had done when he first taught her. A few minutes later, she pushed the tall tree. It toppled into the ravine. A splintered joint remained attached to its stump. The peak of the tree now rested on the ravine floor far below.

"So far, so good," she said, sliding her axe back onto her belt. She clasped the knife between her teeth. This did not strike her as a particularly safe idea, but she needed both hands free to climb, and still needed the dagger's light to see by, so to her view no better alternative presented itself.

The first twelve feet of tree were difficult to descend. She hugged onto the trunk and slid down painfully, leaving a good portion of the skin on her forearms behind. Once she encountered the limbs of the tree, she had handholds and footholds, but she also had a series of obstacles blocking her path. She shimmied and contorted, making her way through the tangle of limbs. After what seemed like an age, she stepped down onto the floor of the ravine. She was skinned and battered.

She removed the knife from her mouth and felt a trickle of blood run from one corner of her lips.

Kolga concentrated on the pull of the amulet and followed it along the ravine. Her progress was not as swift as she had hoped. The ground was strewn with stones of various sizes, and here and there some dead-wood had fallen into the ravine, creating barriers that needed to be traversed.

The glowing dagger did not reveal the intersect-ing side ravine until she was already passing it. When she saw it, she closed her eyes and felt for the amulet, then opened them and hastened into the side passage. She had to squeeze past a dense pile of fallen limbs.

Ahead, she could see a distant torchlight bob-bing along. She could not make out anything else. She tucked the dagger behind her back and focused on the bouncing light. Now she could see the glowing outline of two figures. She knew that if she called out as loud as she could they would hear her, but she hesitated to do so. *No, I must follow them without announcing myself,* she thought. The torch flame disappeared, but a lin-gering glow remained. She began moving forward, and she saw the glow get stronger. Now it was a circle of diffused glowing firelight, but with no sign anymore of the flame that was its source.

Once again using the dagger for light, she picked her way through the rocky terrain as quickly as she could. About halfway to the circle of glowing light, she brought her right foot down on a shifting stone. She hadn't been testing her footing -- she was simply taking steps in her desperate scramble to reach Asmund. All her weight came down on her ankle. She stumbled and fell to the ground. Her brain informed her of an injury, but she ignored it. She rose instantly and strode on. Each step of her right foot was a shout of pain inside her head. But she did not pause for even a moment to consider the wounded joint. She must reach Asmund at any cost.

She came to a space of clear, even terrain and hurried forward with an almost hopping gait, planting her throbbing right foot, then quickly jumping ahead with her left. This made her think of the way Asmund walked. It must have been his belabored steps over the rough terrain that had allowed her to catch up with them. To her right, she could see a pathway that led gradually down from the top of the ravine.

She kept moving, drawing close to the circle of diffused firelight. She scrambled over some small boulders, but only allowed her brain to vaguely register the excruciating explosions in her ankle. The circle of firelight was looming larger ahead of her as she drew near. She skirted more fallen limbs. She could see now that her destination was the mouth of a cave. The two figures with the torch had entered it, but their light was still shining out.

The ground before the mouth of the cave was clear and even. She drew her axe in her right hand, gripped the glowing dagger in her left, and crept forward. She could hear her own breathing loud in her ears. As she entered the cave, she tried to slow it down. Her heart was pounding so hard that she imagined it was like a drum announcing her arrival.

She edged in along the stone wall, being as stealthy as she could, trying to employ her lifetime of hunting experience. She remembered stalking the hare at the campsite last night. Had that only been last night? So much had happened since then, it almost felt like a year ago. She tried to re-create those silent steps she had used in the forest. She cringed as her injured right foot disobeyed her will and scraped against the floor.

The cave narrowed and curved around to the right. She followed the curve. It opened into a larger cavern. Her eyes were drawn to a large fire, the source of the light she had been following. Someone was arranging a large spit for something like a boar or a deer. They looked almost like... She could not quite say. She inched forward a little further around the bend, her right foot scuffing along the floor once more. The figure stood up from the fire and spun toward her.

"Kolga, it's you!" Asmund said. "I was just building up the fire. It's cold in here."

"Asmund?" she said, stepping into the main chamber. Relief washed over her and she wanted to run to him and embrace him. Then she hesitated, remembering the danger. "Where's the Brunnmigi?"

"Oh!" said Asmund with a smile. "I let it lead me here, believing it had fooled me. I didn't want to confront it at the farm, where you or the farmer's family could be hurt. Also, I wanted to see its lair so I could be sure it was the only one. It was careless because it thought I was deceived, so I killed it easily. My, am I glad to see you!"

She looked into his eyes and knew instantly everything was all right. She felt so grateful, she stretched out her arms and limped forward to embrace him. His face lit up and he stepped forward to return her embrace. She had set her emotions aside in her haste to find him, but now they came rushing toward her.

Tears began to well up and she squeezed her eyes shut. As soon as her eyes broke contact with his, she felt a familiar magical tug. Eyes still closed, her arm moved in a smooth blur. She hurled the axe and heard it strike true. She opened her eyes and beheld Asmund standing with a shocked look on his face. The entirety of the axe's blade was sunk into his forehead. He reached out for her, took one step forward, then fell back and was dead.

Kolga spun and followed the magic pull toward the back of the cave. The air grew rank and moist. The light of the fire was not reaching back this far. She lifted the dagger and used its glow to probe the darkness. She saw a vast pile of bones. She could identify horse and boar and deer and... A chill clawed at her heart when she saw a pile of human skulls grinning mirthlessly in the gloom. Her feet clattered through the carpet of bones.

The magic sense pulled her to the left. She lifted the dagger higher and caught sight of something bundled against the cave wall. She hurried to it and found herself staring down at Asmund's motionless form. His pale face was peaceful and his eyes stared at her lifelessly. She fell to her knees and gathered him into her arms. "No!" she wailed. "Asmund, please don't be dead! I love you! Do you hear me? I love you!" She squeezed him to herself, tears running down her face and onto his. She rocked him back and forth, her wails echoing off the cave walls and becoming a chorus of grief.

"You're crushing me," Asmund's muffled voice croaked into her shoulder.

She sat back and looked into his eyes. He started to say something else, but was interrupted by her lips on his as she gathered him into a long, deep kiss. He reached up and wrapped his arm around her neck. They lay together for some time, and even though they were lying in a dank, rotting pile of bones, in the charnel pit of a demon's darkened cave, they both felt they had finally found a home. A place their hearts truly belonged.

After a while, Asmund gasped, remembering where they were. "Where is it?" he whispered tensely.

"Dead," she answered, brushing her fingers through his hair.

"You slew a Brunnmigi? How?" he asked, astonished.

"Thanks to you," she replied. "After the test behind the boulders, you said that no matter what I saw before my eyes, I would trust the magic of the amulet, and you were right."

She saw understanding dawn on his face. "Thank you, Kolga." He said, looking into her eyes. "Oh, and one more thing, I love you too."

CHAPTER TEN

The craftsman found the farmyard he sought and entered it. Voices floated to his ears from the house. He passed it and headed for the field. As he rounded the corner of the house, the barn came into view. He saw a woman and a man inside working. "Hello," he called.

"Hello," they replied. The woman was sewing a tiny shirt and the man was carving a stave for a half-completed crib. They both gazed past him toward the field. Toward *it*. They seemed somehow different than everyone else he had met here.

"Do you want for anything?" he asked.

"No," they answered, both shaking their heads. The man looked at the dwarf and opened his mouth to speak again. The craftsman waited anxiously. But then the man closed his mouth and shook his head. Again, they both glanced out toward the field before returning to their tasks.

The craftsman found a shovel in the barn, then walked out into the field and approached the big stone. He read the old runes carved on it. They said exactly what he knew they would.

He circled the stone, looking for the proper

place, and then he dug. The task would take many hours. That is, unless you were a dwarf. None could dig like dwarfs. It was dwarfs who had dug the vast mines beneath the Trollheimen and had lived there in their marbled cities.

He set the shovel aside a short time later and stood before the remnants of an ancient door, crumbling with decay. A sickly glow lit his way as he descended the wet stone stairs into the barrow.

Halfway down he heard a scuttle on the stones below and froze. For a moment, he was tempted to go back up and quit this place. The moment passed and he drew his hammer, clenched his teeth, and continued down.

At last, the steps ended and he entered into a round chamber. He took it all in with a glance: the skeleton laying on the big stone slab in the center, the pale green luminescent algae that clung in patterns to the walls, the sickly damp that dripped from the ceiling and formed filthy puddles on the floor. Most of all, he saw all hundred glowing eyes of the giant spider that peered at him from the dimly-lit far end of the chamber.

With an earsplitting screech and a blur of eight legs, it charged from out of the gloom. He leaped to meet it, swinging his hammer down to strike a blow on top of it – only it did not land on top of it. Instead, the hammer smashed into the stone floor. A huge crack formed along the floor from one side to the other, and half of it sagged deeper into the earth.

He realized now that the spider had moved sideways the very instant before his blow had landed. It ascended the wall and scuttled upside-down across the ceiling, as if unaware that it was the size of a large elk-hound and weighed just as much. As it passed above him, it cast a line of web across his back and shoulder.

It began to run down the wall on his other side. But he was ahead of it and struck as it reached the center of the wall. But no – again, it was not there. His hammer smashed into the wall, shattering the stones where it landed. The whole barrow shook. Part of the ceiling collapsed, and the far end of the chamber disappeared under falling stones. The instant before his blow would have fallen, the spider had leaped from the wall and sailed past him. A new line of web now encircled his upper thighs.

The craftsman tried to shake free of the web, but it held him firmly. The spider moved too quickly for him to strike it, and if he continued to miss his mark, he would demolish the chamber and bury them both beneath the earth.

The spider moved around him in a blur. He felt the web tangle him further down on his legs. It jerked the web, causing him to fall to his knees. He tried to stand, to get away, but he could not. He looked up and saw it straight in front of him, inching closer. It jittered up and down rapidly and let out another horrible screech. Two long dagger-like fangs unfolded and a drop of milky venom dripped from one.

The craftsman knew he had but one chance, one strategy that might preserve his life. Unfortunately, the major component of the strategy was sheer luck. The spider's legs blurred once more as it charged, and Dvalinn began to swing the hammer straight down. There, that was all he would need. The hammer had only moved half an inch when he twisted his body with all of his might, redirecting the blow at the empty air to his left.

Half of a racing heartbeat later, a crunching noise filled his ears and a jolting pain traveled up his arms. When his eyes could catch up to everything that had happened, he saw the hundred surprised eyes of the dying spider. He watched as the eight furry legs turned up to the ceiling and stopped moving. He had known that the lighting-fast monster would dodge his blow to one side or the other. Luck had saved him when the spider had moved to the left.

Once his breathing returned to normal and his heart was no longer thundering in his chest, he tried to break the web that was entangling him. Struggle as he may, the strands felt like ropes made of iron. If only he still had Scattersoul. It would surely be able to cleave this web. What was he to do? Was there nothing here that could cut this web? He felt a panic rising as he imagined himself lying here, legs tied, for all eternity.

Calm yourself. Think. He looked all around him. There was nothing. Nothing but himself and the dead spider. Then a thought struck him. *Well, anything is worth a try.* He dragged himself over to the spider. Fighting his revulsion, he grabbed one of the spiders dagger-like fangs. He was careful not to touch the tip, still glistening with venom. As he maneuvered the fang to cut the web, a terrifying image filled his mind. Maybe the beast was not dead, only knocked senseless. Any moment now, it would lunge forward, digging the poisonous barb into his leg.

The craftsman worked with a sickened look on his face. The tip of the fang was razor-sharp and sliced easily through the web, passing a hair's breadth from his skin, where the merest poisoned pinprick would cause him an agonizing death. Upon slicing through one strand, the entire web seemed to die, and it fell away from him in a big coil.

He stood and began to explore the chamber. As he headed to where the floor was tilting and the ceiling had caved in, he felt the ground shift beneath his weight. He retreated to the center of the room and instead examined the skeleton lying on the slab. A pair of old, rusted iron shears lay open upon its chest. He looked down at the bones of the feet, lying flat on the stone. The big toes had been lashed together with a silver wire.

"So you are the cause of all this trouble. What kind of miserable creature were you in life that they needed to bind you so in death? Tell me your name," he demanded of the grinning skull. "No, I know you will not tell me. I did not come to ask you. But where are they? I thought they would be here with you."

He spun around in a circle, examining the walls, fixing his eyes on the ruined side of the chamber. "Are they hidden? Did I collapse a secret passage while fighting the spider?" He walked along the circle of walls. Stopping here and there, he pushed on some stones and pulled on others. He tried looking very hard at the walls and then looking away from them to see if the corner of his eye revealed anything. *Curse it!* He had thought he would find them here.

He stood in a puddle of filthy water next to the dead spider, his hands hanging uselessly at his sides. "Where are you?" he asked the emptiness. Then in frustration, he shouted. "Sassa! Sassa Baldersdottir!" The sound echoed through the chamber and more of the ceiling crumbled in. "Sassa Baldersdottir!" he called again. Then he hung his head and was silent. "I thought you would be here," he said sadly. Then reluctantly he turned and started up the steps toward the daylight.

"Hello," a voice called faintly, as if from far away.

He stopped and listened.

Nothing.

He shook his head. For a moment he had imagined that he had heard a...

"I'm here."

"Sassa?" he called. He spun and rushed back into the chamber. "Where are you?"

Nothing.

"Speak again, I beg you!"

"We are here."

The craftsman's eyes opened wide with understanding. "I'm coming!" He ran to the slab. He pushed, but it did not budge. He threw his shoulder into it and pushed until tears sprang into his eyes and ran down his reddened cheeks. "Thor, give me strength!" he called out, but still the slab would not move. He stood back, muscles aching. He looked at the skeleton lying smugly on top. He shoved the old bones vindictively. They did not move.

Of course, Dvalinn! he chided himself. *Slow down and think.* He touched the old iron shears. They thrummed with energy. He stepped back, and taking up his magic hammer, he aimed and then swung with all of his strength. As it struck, both the hammer and the shears sparked brightly in the gloom. The skeleton, shears still in place, slid a bit to one side. He struck again. It slid further.

He struck again and again. When he stopped, the

skeleton, still lying stiff as a plank, hung suspended in space, its feet and lower legs the only thing still resting upon the stone platform. Once again, Dvalinn put his shoulder to the stone slab. This time it moved. It slid over until the skeleton rested once more in its place on top.

"We are here! Down here!" called the voice, no longer faint.

"Come up!" the craftsman called back.

"We cannot. Not while he binds us."

"Then I shall come down. Wait for me," he called. He could see stone steps leading down into total darkness.

He retrieved the discarded lengths of spiderweb and wrapped them around his scabbard, fashioning a makeshift torch. He set the torch next to the iron shears, and using his magic hammer, he struck showers of bright, angry sparks on it until a flame bloomed and crackled to life.

Holding the torch before him, he descended carefully into the pit. At the bottom of the steps, gazing up at him, stood seven ghostly children. They were different ages, but they all stood upon their own feet, even the smallest infant. They returned his greeting when at last he reached them.

A girl of three, with honey-colored hair, stepped forward and said, "I am Sassa Baldersdottir. Who are you, sir?"

"I am a friend to you. Your father sent me to find you – to find you all. Do not fear any longer. I will defeat the Draugr and free you. But first, you must help me."

"No!" shouted an infant boy. He was the youngest of them all, and had been here the longest. "We must not anger the again-walker, or he will punish us. He is the evil that death and time cannot defeat!"

"No, he will not punish you!" replied the craftsman. "You must give me the final ingredient for that which I build. Then it is I who shall punish him! It is I who shall defeat him once and for all, and I will free you!"

"Is this true?" asked another boy, who was the tallest of them.

"Yes, it is. I swear it on my life," said the dwarf.

"But what do we have that we can possibly give to you?"

"A name," answered the craftsman. "When he speaks the words that bind you here, he says his name. Now I want you all to tell me it. But whisper it to me very close to my ear, so that he will not hear." He knelt, and they gathered close around him and whispered. He nodded and rose. "And now I must go."

"Go? Without us?" the children wailed. "Do not leave us! Take us with you! We want to go home!"

"I cannot, said the craftsman, his heart aching. "Not yet. I must finish making that which can defeat him. I must destroy him and break his bonds over you. Only then can I bring you home."

"You don't know what it's like!" cried the boy who was the youngest of them. "He torments us and feeds on our fear and pain! If you leave us now, we cannot survive."

"You will survive. Do you know how I know?" he asked.

None of them spoke. They just looked at him and shook their heads.

"I know because of how much stronger than him

you are!"

"You are wrong!" said the tallest boy. "My father is very strong, but when he tried to grapple the Draugr, he could not lay hold of him!"

"This is true," confirmed Sassa. "When it came for me, my father tried to cut it with his axe, and my mother tried striking it with her fists, but it could not be harmed."

"Yes, I know, children, but you are still stronger than it is. Because each one of you has your own human heart, and that is the strongest thing there is!"

The children looked at each other with confused expressions. "The human heart?" asked Sassa.

"Why, yes," answered the dwarf. "The Draugr has no heart. But each and every one of you has one, and it makes you very, very strong! It is the center of you. It is who you are. You can want. You can create things. You can give and receive love. Your heart can understand the *why* of life. These are all powers the filthy ghoul does not have. Remember, waiting for you up above is the Village of the Two Rivers, your home. Very soon you will walk its fertile land, you will swim in its waters and grow tall and strong. When the Draugr comes again to torment you, remember your heart. Go into it and look at all the things that await you, and in no time at all I will come back for you, and I will be wiping the dust of your tormentor from my boots."

The craftsman spoke these words with great conviction. They were chosen carefully to give the children heart; to convince them that he would be victorious and save each and every one of them. This was, after all, his goal, and even if he had known then that it was not true, and indeed it was not, he would have still told them exactly the same thing.

"Now one last thing, children." He uncoiled the rope from around his shoulders.

"What a fine, strong looking rope," said Sassa.

"Thank you. I made it myself. When first I began making it, I knew that it was destined to be made, but I did not know why. I thought I was making it to save miners who were trapped in a hole. But then I learned that was an illusion. Then I used it to climb into the land of the dead. I thought that this must be what it was made for. But as soon as I was done, I knew that was not its purpose either. But now that I am here I see it clearly. It was intended for you. Now, children, help me tie it where it needs to go." As they worked, he whispered instructions to them. When they had finished, he turned to go. "Remember, children. Soon."

He hurried up the stairs just as the last of his torch sputtered and died.

The craftsman emerged from the darkened barrow and squinted in the bright sunshine. His eyes slowly adjusted to the light, and he was able to make out the man and woman sitting in the barn. Still they worked slowly, dreamily, at their tasks, gazing over toward the stone. He knew their son was the youngest of the children he had just met down in the darkness. Somehow, it seemed that they had some vague sense that he was trapped in the twilight between life and death. The craftsman clenched his fists with determination. The living, the dead, and those who could neither live or die were all depending on him. He had gotten what he needed from the underworld. Now he must hurry back and complete his work before it was too late. He had to seek the hidden path down here that mirrored the one above, and find the tree of the world. Even now he lay there in the grace of Queen Freya, she who had forbidden the goddess Hel from striking him down.

"Why?" he asked. "What have I done for her to notice me? Well, it is not for me to ask that. Who am I to know such things? But now, whenever the hot blood is in me, it is her name I shall call, just as I did when I rode upon Shadowfoot the Gray!" Then a thought struck him. "Even now does she watch over me?"

He stepped forward and raised his arms to the sky. "My goddess, Queen of the Gods. Time grows late and my quest is righteous. I have nothing to offer you but these hands. All that the gods owed to my house has now been paid. But if you still watch over me, and if you still care, please show me the way."

His prayer finished, he lowered his arms. All was still and quiet. After a while, he nodded his head. "No, I do not think you watch over me anymore," he said, and turned around. There, sitting on the stone was the little white chicken with the triangle spot on its wing.

"Bock bock," said the Queen of the Gods.

The craftsman opened his eyes and sat up. He stretched his back and wiped sleep from his eyes. He was all alone at the foot of the world tree. He stood and beheld the white door, still hung on one hinge, a bloodied boot print yet marking its surface. He strode over to the skeleton of one of the warriors slumbering in the circle of the dead and drew its sword.

It was Dreamtaker, forged by Brokkr and his brothers, the same dwarfs who had forged the hammer of Thor. He returned to the tree, and catching up his beard and holding it in his fist, he called out, "Freya!" at the top of his soul. He brought Dreamtaker slashing down and hacked his beard off just below the chin. He placed the beard at the roots of the tree and stepped back, looking up to the boughs above. He placed his fist over his heart and stayed still for some time, that she might see and understand. "It is not that you have need of it. It is that it is precious to me and I sacrifice it."

The craftsman's heart was thudding in his chest. This was a thing that no dwarf would do, a thing that a dwarf could not do. Not that it was forbidden – for how could a thing never conceived be forbidden? It had just never been done.

Dvalinn turned, and sheathing Dreamtaker, he stumbled out of the presence of the tree. He tripped passing through the circle of the dead, but rose and continued. He was almost all the way through the hallway of elms by the time he learned the new balance of his beardless body and could walk steadily once again.

The craftsman lifted his torch to the north and his lips moved, speaking the words quietly. He turned to the south and repeated the process, then followed it with the east and then finally west. Then, solemnly, he lit the forge one last time.

As the stand of oaken sticks began to burn amongst the coals, he reached out and grasped the rope that hung down. He pulled slow and steady, pressing the giant bellows, blowing a stream of air into the heart of the fire. The bellows looked like the ones someone might hold in their hands to ignite a fire in their home fireplace, but these bellows were the size of a small ship, and the forge they fed was the legendary birth-place of the tools and weapons which had helped shape the fate of the universe.

He knew that he must hurry to complete his work. Much depended on it. He had given his word; he must not fail. But as he worked he also felt a sad sense of dread for the moment he would be finished. He thought of the heat slowly leaving the forge and then it resting cold forever. He looked all around the huge workroom. He could imagine he still saw his father and brothers bent at their toils, shaping the destinies of those who would receive their wares.

He smiled to himself. *Take heart. You have had many tremendous yesterdays. You have a hot forge today and a reason to swing your hammer, and soon you will... Well, "soon" will take care of itself.*

He retrieved the last piece of the rock that had fallen from the sky, the rock he had used to forge the chain, the stake, and the collar. With it he had also forged the chisel he had used to shape the troll's flesh once it had become the iron stone, and now he would forge this final tool.

As he worked, he sang.

> *Sing out the deeds just and meet,*
> *Blow the flame and metals heat,*
> *Grasping tongs and hammers beat,*
> *Things are made when songs repeat.*

Thus did Dvalinn work and sing until at last he had shaped a fine graver. He heated it and left it to cool six times. He put it into the forge a seventh time and pulled the rope, pumping the bellows again and again, causing the graver to glow brightly.

Then he took up Dreamtaker and lay open a small cut on his forearm. He caught the flowing blood in the empty shell where old Gudrun the turtle had once lived. He thrust his tongs into the fire and withdrew the glowing graver. He mouthed the sacred words and then brought it down to quench in his blood.

He went to his father's workbench. Everything was covered in dust except for one box. It was pale green and cunningly carved to look as if it were adorned with scales. He opened it and reverently lifted out what it contained. It was a long, curved spike, and it appeared to be some sort of aged ivory. In reality, it was a fang from the dragon Nidhug, the great serpent who gnaws at the roots of Yggdrasil. It had been brought back from Nastrond, the corpse shore, in another age of the world. This was one of the only things capable of doing what now needed doing.

With infinite care, he used the fang to hone an edge on the new graver. He worked slowly, meticulously, dressing the forever edge onto it. When at last he sat back and beheld the little hand tool finished, he smiled.

This was a pleasure only a craftsperson would ever feel. To make a special tool, whose purpose was to make another tool, was a thing unknown to most. Tools such as this were made for the making of great weapons, and great weapons were often given names. Names that were remembered in song and story. Weapons that became linked to great heroes, great battles, great deeds. Their images painted and woven. They would live on in legend. "But tools such as you," he said, picking up the little utilitarian masterpiece, "no one will ever know of you. No songs will be sung, no paintings ever made. Only I will ever love you."

Finally, he selected a delicate hammer from his tool bench and deeply chased the old runes onto the striking face of the magic Ironstone hammer. That done, he quitted the workshop. He selected the proper hallway and reached the vast treasury room. He came to the biggest, tallest treasure pile. Winding his way up the encircling path, he ascended the mountain of gold and jewels.

When at last he reached the top, he found the golden box, the one with the imperfect corners. The box he had toiled over for so many, many years. He held it carefully and returned to the workshop. The box was, in truth, the most perfect thing any hand had ever formed. He just could not see that because he knew what it contained. He would never be able to regard the box without asking himself if it was worthy of its use, for what it held was so exquisitely beautiful that in all his lifetimes only once had he seen it surpassed.

A vision of a single crystal tear falling from an amber-colored eye filled his mind and he was overcome. He had to leave the golden box sitting on the workbench and stand next to the embers of the dying forge, looking into the lingering glow among the coals with its rippling halo of heat.

He had assumed for so long that his last thing to build must be the golden box. He had only known for sure that the last thing that he was meant to make before he could lay down his tools was the thing that would contain this treasure, the treasure which was stowed in the box on the bench behind him. Now he could see clearly the true reason why he had always felt the box was never quite right.

He took a deep breath and steeled himself. He walked over to the bench, opened the box and stared directly at it. He pulled it out, forcing his hands not to shake. A flare of midsummer sun flashed into his eyes as he held the delicate strand of Lady Sif's perfect golden hair. At its touch the room grew brighter. For miles around, fields of wheat sprang up and stretched toward the sky. Dvalinn's already iron-corded muscles doubled in strength. His beard, which he had cut in tribute to Freya, poured down from his chin, growing thickly past the buckle of his belt.

A vision took hold of his mind and he saw clearly how one day long ago, Sif had lain slumbering in a garden. The Trickster, filled with jealousy and hate, had crept up and shorn her legendary hair in an attempt to mar her perfect beauty. When Thor had learned of the treachery done to his wife, he was enraged. He caught Loki by the throat, and the only way that he would spare his life was if Loki could get the sons of Ivaldi to make a headdress for Sif to cover that which had been stolen from her.

The Trickster, in his fear, had brought her hair and all of his wealth to the sons of Ivaldi. The craftsman could see once again the crown that he had made from her hair. It was so beautiful that it made her twice as powerful as before, and her worship and glory rose among all creation. Left over from the making was this single hair, which in her pleasure and gratitude Sif had allowed him to keep. The Trickster had ever after hated Dvalinn.

The craftsman lifted the hair and said aloud,

"Goddess of earth and sky, sow your harvest in the mark of my plow, that we may reap one blackened soul. As you will, so shall it be." He set the hair into the runes he had carved on the face of the magic hammer. As he did, a spark of lightning welded it into place. The heat of it beat on his face and its lightning charge made his hair stand up on his tingling scalp. When he finished, he stood back and looked at his creation. *Yes, this is the one last thing I was meant to make.* This thing, not the box, was destined to contain the hair of the goddess.

Now he was done with his making. There was nothing left to prepare. Now he would face the demon. He would face him with this. He held up the finished warhammer, and it began to glow like a radiant sky. On the striking face now shone the gold that had been Sifs hair, set into the engraved name. The name that the children had whispered to him, in their prison beyond Hel.

CHAPTER ELEVEN

Ragna made her way through the rainy darkness to the barn where her husband, Balder, was hiding. He was sitting in the shadows, clutching his greataxe, eyes riveted on the dingy stone out in the farmyard.

"All is yet quiet," he said as she stepped in from the wet.

"Here, I brought you an extra skin for warmth," she said, wrapping it over his shoulders.

"Thank you, wife," he said, eyes not leaving the cursed stone.

"Are you scared?"

"Yes."

She leaned down and hugged him. "It will all end well or it won't. Only the gods know that now. We can only do our best."

He reached up and clasped her shoulder lovingly. "We all know our parts. We will give it our all."

She released him and said, "I will go check on Dag. Do you have your horn at the ready?"

In answer, he held it up for her to see. She nodded, and pulling her cloak around herself tightly, she stepped out into the rain once more.

The straightest path to where Dag was hiding was right across the field, past the stone. But especially now, as the night was growing late, she dared not approach it. She followed the path back out of the uninhabited farm to the road and followed it to the stand of trees where Dag was concealed. His makeshift shelter was fighting a losing battle against the wet, and in spite of his layers of cloak and blankets, he was shivering.

"Not long now, I reckon," he said as she crouched down beside him.

"Very soon, I would think," she agreed. "You remember what to do?"

"Yes, it is simple. Only five houses with children remain in the valley, and I have my horn right here." He patted a bulge barely visible through the wet layers of cloth.

"Very good," she said, starting to rise.

"Do you think it will work?" he asked. She paused and crouched back down.

"Well," she began, choosing her words carefully, "if it doesn't, we won't let it be said we did not try our hardest."

The wooden cart rolled along the road. Asmund held the reins as the pony pulled them through the afternoon toward a cloudy gray horizon. Kolga was sitting with her arm around his waist and her head on his shoulder, eyes closed in a contented half sleep.

She was dreaming of the last three wonderful days. They had been the happiest of her life, which was somewhat strange since nothing much had happened. Since leaving the farm, the days had consisted of rising in the morning and traveling. At midday, they would stop and rest. They would eat, take care of the pony, and Asmund would hold his mirror up to the sky. Then they would travel on until evening. She would make them a simple camp and they would eat supper.

Lying in their bed, she had learned that if she fell asleep feeling his magic amulet close by, that she would be pulled awake when it began feeling far away. When this happened, she would find him in his troubled sleep, just as she had that first night. Just like then, she would hold and soothe him until he assured the children that he was coming and would be there soon in his hazy dreaming voice. Then he would relax and sleep on through the dawn.

Then they would rise and repeat the same day over again. That really was all the happiest days of her life consisted of. No more bands of street kids attacking. No more evil kings. No more well-pissing monsters. Just the two of them traveling together. She wished they could keep doing it forever.

But you can't, a voice in her head told her.

She knew the voice well. It was the one she had heard all her life. The one that came along and tried to keep her from enjoying moments of pleasure, by pointing out that they wouldn't last, or that they might be regretted. It was the voice that had talked her out of leaving with Asmund that first time. The voice had been wrong. When she had ignored it the second time and gone with him, she found the most happiness she had ever known.

I'm ignoring you! she declared in her most definitive mental tone.

That's fine, the voice replied. *But you know this*

journey cannot go on much longer. You also know that you are not on your way to pick flowers for spring festival. You are on your way to a demon who will kill the one you love.

Kolga's eyes snapped open. The sky ahead of them was dark and angry with faraway flashes of lightning. It filled her with an awful dread.

"That's not what the horizon looked like when I closed my eyes," she said, lifting her head from Asmund's shoulder and stretching her back.

"No, it has been gathering for the last hour or so," he replied.

"We should stop for the night around here then. I know that you have been pushing our travel later and later these last few days. But if we stop now I can build us a good shelter, like the one we had back at the lake. Then if the storm comes we can be dry and have a fire."

"We cannot stop," he said.

"If we don't stop before we reach the rain, then we won't be able to build a fire at all, and it doesn't matter if you try to put up a shelter cloth if the ground and all the leaves are already soaked."

"No, I mean we cannot stop at all tonight."

"I don't understand," she said, bewildered.

"The reason I've been pushing to make more leagues each day is that I wanted to reach the village by tonight. We are only five or six hours away by my reckoning. If we travel into the night we can make it."

"But why not rest where it's warm and dry? Then we can rise early in the morning and arrive in daylight, when there will be people to talk to," she countered.

"I fear by then it will be too late," he answered gravely. "When we were at the farm, I worked out what time of the month it was. I realized that tonight will be the new moon. I'm afraid that tonight will be the night that the children need me. In fact, I'm becoming convinced of it."

"Why is that?"

He looked up the road toward their destination and caught sight of the far-off lightning. "Because in my dreams, when I enter the town of Kalbaek, it's always raining."

The ancient hate rose from its dusty slab and went down the steps to where the children waited. It inhaled their pain and terror to give it strength for the work ahead. It was sorely disappointed with the amount. Surely they were not used up yet. Especially not the ones he had snatched more recently.

He saw them looking at him with almost a touch of defiance. This looked like a good occasion for the spider to pay them a visit. He reached out with his mind and called for her. She did not come.

His anger began to boil. He looked at the children and scratched his bony fingers across the surface of their minds. He saw a heavily bearded face. A dwarf's face.

"Aww, did someone tell you not to be afraid? How precious." Without warning, he grabbed up the little infant boy, the one he had snatched first. Tilting back his head and unhinging his bony jaw, he tore the child's body apart, stuffing bloodied chunks down his throat. The other children screamed in terror, filling the chamber with a murky vapor that swirled into the ancient Dragr's form, making it grow larger and more defined.

When at last the screaming had subsided, he looked around the chamber at the crumpled, exhausted children. That had worked a bit too well. Now some of the children were very nearly used up.

He felt so powerful now that he thought perhaps he would go and gather multiple children tonight. This thought pleased him, and he turned and moved out of the tomb.

Sitting alone in the silent barn, Balder felt a strange presence. It made the hair on his arms stand on end. He did not feel afraid; somehow the presence felt happy. Out of the corner of his eye, he thought he saw a man leaving the barn, leading a woman holding a baby in her arms, but when he turned to look he saw that he had only imagined it. He shook his head and turned back to the stone just in time.

Balder watched the Dragr emerge from the earth beside the stone. At first, it seemed as if the darkness were swirling in the wind, but then the shape of it grew darker and more defined.

His heart began hammering in his chest and sweat broke out upon his brow. He sat motionless, holding his breath for fear that it would hear him and come to devour his soul.

It began to move toward the center of the village. He crept from his hiding place and follwed at a distance.

The Dragr passed through the fence at the far end of the farm, the wooden planks sliding straight through its body unhindered as Balder's own axe had once done. Balder felt exposed as he crossed the open ground. His feet were squishing on the rain-soaked earth. He imagined the creature looking back and catching him at any moment. He climbed over the fence and peered into the darkness ahead. The demon was nowhere to be seen. He scanned the misty blackness, trying to find it. A jolt of panic stabbed at his heart. In his caution, he had stayed too far behind. If he could not follow it, all would be lost. He hurried ahead, straining his eyes to penetrate the curtain of night.

Dag the shepherd was creeping along the edge of the darkened road. He watched the demon gliding through the fields to his left. He saw it pass through a fence and cut diagonally through the crops. It came out on the road ahead of him. Dag glanced back and saw Baldur still creeping forward along its original path.

He lost sight of it! Dag thought in alarm.

He quickened his pace, knowing he must not also lose sight of it. As he stared at its shifting, milky form, the memory of it shattering his door and coming for his son came rushing back. He relived the moment of insanity when he had tried to grab it, tried to wrestle it. It made his heart feel sick.

He remembered telling the other men in the village how he had thrown himself at the wraith, how he could not hold it. They had called him a liar. Called him a coward. Well, where were those men now? Those who had not fled from the village altogether were hiding beneath their beds, while he was out here risking his life in an attempt to save another family from knowing the grief that his had known.

The creature moved quickly along the road, and

Dag hurried close behind.

Baldur came to a stop in the soggy field. He wiped the rain from his eyes. He had rushed forward for several lengths, but could see no sign of the Dragr. He spun, looking behind him, fearing that he might have passed it in the dark and it was even now rushing up from behind to attack. Nothing was there.

He turned again, scanning the road. He saw nothing until a timely flash of lightning lit the sky. He caught a glimpse of Dag moving forward along the tree line. Baldur began cautiously moving again, setting a course that would intercept him.

Asmund and Kolga hurried through the long shadows of the evening. The last light of day revealed a wagon heading down the road toward them. All the possessions of a household were lashed to it, piled up high and protruding from the sides.

A family of four inhabited the bench seat; a tired man at the reins, a little boy of eight or nine, and a plump woman with a toddler on her lap.

The man, seeing their cart approach, pulled his wide load over and stopped. He waved them on to pass.

Asmund brought the pony up beside and halted. "How far to the village of Kalbaek?"

"Only a few hours more," said the man in an impatient tone.

"Do not go there tonight!" said the woman. "Stop and camp for the night!"

"We see the storm ahead," started Asmund.

"No, it isn't the storm!" she said in a desperate voice. "It is the Dragr, the evil thing! It will come tonight!"

Icy fingers danced up Asmund's spine. "It is a Dragr?"

"Yes, an old evil, buried long ago, bound with a magic stone. That foolish lake-lander broke its spell and brought the evil down on our heads!"

"Please!" shouted the man raggedly. "Move your cart and let us back onto the road. The demon, it steals the children, don't you understand? We should have left days ago when the others went. But instead we prayed to the gods and believed in cursed Balder when he promised a dwarf would come and save us!"

"A dwarf?" Asmund asked excitedly as pieces of the puzzle fell into place.

"Yes, a mystical dwarf! If you can believe it. But he never came! Of course he never came! I have been so foolish!" the man shouted.

"Be quiet, husband! You're scaring the children."

The man turned to his wife hotly as if to reply. Catching sight of the little boy burying his face in his mother's side, he stopped. Regaining his composure, he turned back to Kolga and Asmund. "I am sorry, but please let us back onto the road. We must be on our way. If you young travelers are wise, you will heed my good wife's words. Do not travel on to Kalbaek tonight. There are still five houses with young children. Still five families trusting in the gods or in Balder's magical dwarf. That means that tonight the dead monster will rise again and claim another soul."

"Not if I have anything to say about it," Asmund

said, then rode on.

The man shared a confused look with his wife. Then, remembering their haste, he flicked the reins and pulled back onto the road.

The pitiless monster stood at the point in the road where Kalbaek's farms fanned out along the valley. He cast his thoughts out, seeking the little children. Five! Only five? There had been many more last time. They must be fleeing. He should have collected more of them when he had the chance. He would not make that mistake this time. He felt very strong tonight. He would not return without collecting all five. He felt two to the left side of the valley and three to the right. One was further down the valley than the others. He would start with that one and work his way back toward the barrow.

He chose the lane leading to it, gliding down it with a delightful anticipation. All was still and quiet at the farms he passed. He could feel the people inside the houses. They were awake, but huddling silently in the darkness.

Somewhere behind him, a horn sounded clearly. Three distinct blasts shattered the silence of the valley. He spun and reached out with his thoughts. He found two frightened minds hiding behind a bush.

He waited, motionless, but nothing else happened. Something moved far off in the darkness at the edge of the village. Was it circling, trying to get ahead of him? Perhaps this was a trap. He stretched his mind out toward the sound, but nothing was there.

He began to feel foolish. What was he worried

about? Even if a whole army were laying in wait for him, it mattered not. There was no weapon that could touch him. He was invincible. He continued down the lane toward his first prize.

He arrived at the cottage. The lights were glowing within. He probed it with his mind and felt almost disappointed. There was no army laying a futile trap for him. Only a mother and father sitting to the right by the hearth, holding their useless vigil through the night. Praying that he would not come. To the left inside the cottage he felt the little child laying in its bed.

"Yes, my precious little thing. Enjoy your last seconds of peace. They come to an end... Now!"

He smashed in the door, sending its splintered ruin flying into the back wall. He entered and looked to his right. The man and woman threw themselves into the corner and cowered.

What? No axes? No fruitless grappling attempts? he thought disappointedly. *Oh, well.*

He looked to the left and saw the bed. The child was lying still with the covers pulled up over his head. He was terrified! The Dragr smiled with delight. He moved slowly, savoring the moment. He could see the outline of the child's body. It was short but plump. He reached the bed, grabbed the corner of the blanket, and tore it away.

The little body sat up, a big smile splitting its bearded face. That face! He recognized it from the children's minds.

"You!" he cried as the dwarf lifted a glowing hammer. "Your puny weapons can't–"

That was all he had time to say before he burst through the roof of the cottage and sailed through the night, landing in a soggy turnip field outside.

The craftsman rose from the bed and said, "It's all right, you can come out now."

The little boy shimmied out from where he had been hiding beneath the bed, tears rolling down his face. His mother rushed to him and gathered him up in her arms.

"You were very good at being quiet. You are a brave little boy," the craftsman said. He peeked around the corner of the cracked doorframe just in time to see that the Dragr had risen and was fleeing back down the lane. Dvalinn flew from the house, running quickly to catch up.

Asmund and Kolga drove on in the darkness, the rain stinging their faces. Kolga was controlling the reins now. Her powerful arms were needed to guide the frightened pony. Asmund held the shining dagger aloft. Even with its light, they had nearly run off the road several times as it curved this way and that.

The road started descending into a large valley. In the mist they could see two rivers, converging then disappearing off in separate directions. Both rivers were raging. The spot where they met was swelling above the banks. The road ahead was nearly washed out.

"It must have been raining here all day," Kolga shouted over the sound of rushing waters.

As the road leveled off into the valley, they found

themselves struggling through a flooded landscape. They were fast approaching the spot in the road that was being washed away.

"Hold on!" Kolga yelled, urging the pony forward. "I'm going to keep to the high side of the road and try to make it through!"

Asmund braced himself as best he could. They rushed into the tumult and instantly began to sink and slide out of control. Kolga shouted, urging the pony on. The terrified pony found its footing and pulled with all its might. Something beneath them cracked loudly, but they came rolling free of the water.

"That's a relief," Kolga began once they had gained a safe distance from the flood, but then the cart fell to the ground with a crash as the axle gave way. They came to a jarring halt and could go no further.

The craftsman was careful to stay a short distance behind, trailing the Dragr as it fled through the night. He needed to let it get close to its destination before he struck again. His plan depended upon it. He knew the Dragr could only sense the thoughts of humans, so Dvalinn need only stay quiet and out of sight to stalk his quarry. It had now reached the main road, going back the way it had come.

Was the Dragr slowing down? The craftsman thought to himself, *I must not get too close.* It was too late, he realized. The glow of the hammer had reached his prey. It saw the light to its sides and its own shadow being cast on the road ahead.

Stupid mistake, he chided himself, lifting the hammer to defend. But he was too slow. The Dragr struck. It raked a bony claw across his chest and sent him tumbling, the hammer sailing from his hand. It landed out of sight behind the hedge.

The Dragr began to flee, then halted. It turned, seeming to reconsider.

The craftsman lay flat on his back, struggling to breathe. The pain was agonizing. This was like no wound he had ever experienced. Blood flowed from beneath the scales of his charmed armor. The armor itself was neither rent nor dented. The blow had seemed to simply ignore it. His clouded mind tried to focus. The Dragr was closing in on him. He would not have time to go searching for the weapon; he would not have time to retreat. He raised his hands up before himself, a feeble defense for the deadly blow he knew was about to land.

On the other side of the hedge, Balder had run up to the hammer, grabbing its haft. He lifted with all of his might. The hammer did not move. Dag came up beside him, grabbing it as well. They heaved together, every muscle straining, but with no effect. In despair, they realized they would never lift the magic weapon. It would take a strength from within, a deep well of belief that they just did not possess.

A person squeezed between them, pushing them aside. The newcomer grabbed up the hammer and charged through the hedge. On the other side the Dragr was beginning to bring its skeletal claw down. Before it could strike and end the dwarf, the glowing hammer smashed into its chest, sending it cartwheeling down the road.

"YOU - TOOK - MY - BABY!" screamed Ragna as the demon fell into a heap on the muddy ground.

Kolga looked back at the broken, inverted wheels. "We'll have to go on foot from here," she shouted over the sound of the waters.

"Wait!" yelled Asmund, putting his hand on her knee to stop her. He looked into her eyes and shouted, "I love you."

"I love you too," she replied.

He kissed her. When their lips parted, he hugged her tightly, speaking close to her ear so she could hear him. "I love you with all of my heart. I know what is waiting for us up there. You won't forgive me for this, but it can't be helped."

She began to pull away, confused. But he spoke quickly into her ear and touched his finger to her head. He lay her deeply sleeping body back in the wagon. He climbed down, and with a lump in his throat, placed a hand on her cheek. "I won't let you die because of me." He began walking through the rain. He knew he must make it to the battle.

Dvalinn found the strength to rise and stepped toward the farmer woman. She tried to lift the hammer and hand it to him, but now she could not move it. Just down the road, the Dragr stood and began to flee once more. The craftsman snatched up the weapon and ran headlong after it.

"Oh, how I wish you were here with me, Trufflesbane!" Dvalinn cried, struggling to close the gap. His boots pounded through the mud and the rain stung his eyes. He wiped his face, trying to clear his vision. He must not lose sight of the wraith! He had to catch up to it at all costs.

He saw it leave the road and pass through a farm fence. It was cutting diagonally across a field. The dwarf reached the fence and plowed through it, cracking it to pieces. He was running as fast as he could, but he knew he was losing the race. The Dragr passed through a second fence without slowing down. The dwarf could see that the dingy binding stone lay straight ahead of it. His plan had required stopping it at the stone, but being this far ahead, it would simply reach it and escape to the safety of the nether realms.

The craftsman stopped at the second fence and screamed, "Freya, guide my hand!" He hurled the magic hammer as hard as he could.

It was an insane last-ditch effort. He threw it at an upward arc to try and bridge the distance. His eye, which measured all things with precision, could see by its flight that it would sail harmlessly past the creature's right shoulder just before it reached the gateway to the tomb. His heart sank but he could not look away. He watched as it sailed past its shoulder, just as he knew it would. Then he gasped when a moment later, the hammer bounced off the magic binding stone and struck the Dragr dead in its chest.

The craftsman stood shocked for a moment, then jumped the fence and ran. *Why did I stand there watching? I should have already been running!* he scolded himself. His eyes were locked on the hammer. He had to reach it before the Dragr stood.

It began to stir, and he knew he would not make it. The Dragr stood, but its back was still to him. Dvalinn drew the sword from his hip, and without slowing, hurled it at the barn to the creature's right. It worked! As it clattered against the barn wall, the Dragr spun toward it, baring its claws.

The craftsman used the distraction to reach the hammer. He swung for his adversary's back. The Dragr turned, claws still raised. Their blows landed almost simultaneously. The craftsman crumpled to the ground, but managed to retain his weapon this time. The Dragr flew straight back, striking so hard that the little barn was toppled.

Fighting through the pain, the craftsman rose and charged toward the ruined barn. The Dragr emerged from the wreckage and met him in the open. Dvalinn swung the mighty hammer at its chest, already anticipating watching it sail back through the air. A moment later, the hammer smashed into the ground. The creature had evaded with ease, raking its claws down the dwarf's exposed flank.

Again, the armor served no purpose. He felt gashes open beneath it. Dvalinn launched a counterattack, but the ascending backhand swing found nothing but air. For his troubles, the side of his head was lain open. He staggered away, desperate for a little distance. The Dragr reached out, striking so swiftly that the dwarf had no chance at warding the blow.

The craftsman realized that every blow which had thus far landed on the creature had used some element of surprise. Fighting like this, out in the open, toe to toe, he was being swiftly torn to pieces. The craftsman knew he must attempt what swordsmen called a second intention attack. He needed to surprise it again.

The creature began to close the distance between them. He launched a feint attack which favored to his right. It had the desired effect. The wraith dodged to his left, raising its talons to strike. The craftsman's true attack met it coming forward and bashed it to the ground at his feet.

This time the angle of the blow prevented it from hurtling away. Every time the magic hammer had struck it, its smoky body had become solid. This time was no different. The craftsman moved swiftly, swinging the hammer down at the fallen monster. It rolled, trying to evade, but the hammer caught its right arm just above the elbow. A crunching sound could be heard over the sound of the rain, as could the shriek of pain. He saw the severed limb lying on the ground, wrapped in old, decaying cloth, its crushed bone protruding.

The craftsman took note of how the limb remained solid and tangible even as the rest of the body returned to its misty incorporeal form. It was at that moment that he realized his folly. He was leaning down, overextended, gawking, when it reached its remaining hand up straight into his stomach. The hammer fell from his grip and he stood regarding the arm protruding from his midsection. The Dragr twisted, then pulled, spilling the craftsman's guts.

Dvalinn fell back onto the muddy ground. *I'm sorry, children. I'm so sorry.* He closed his eyes and saw the porcelain face of the Valkyrie, a single beautiful tear running slowly down it.

He opened his eyes again and the sky was clear. No sign of the rain remained. He stood and looked around, finding neither the Dragr nor the farm. In their place, he saw a crowd of ghostly people. Some were standing, some were lying down. The one nearest him appeared to be a very old man who was lying in a bed. Dvalinn saw his lips moving, but could not hear what he said. He stepped closer and heard the man muttering, "I love you. I love you all." Then the old man exhaled a long, rasping breath and fell silent. The dwarf leaned in to regard him closely, and was surprised a moment later when the man's eyes opened. The craftsman stood back and saw that the old man was no longer ghostly and transparent. He was solid. He rose from the bed with an alert and focused look on his face.

"Are you all right?" the craftsman asked him.

The man tilted his head, looking for the answer. "Yes. I think I was very ill. I could not rise from my bed. But now I am well. If you will pardon me, I need to be getting home."

With that, the man strode away. The craftsman took a step and felt a strong pull, telling him to lie back down and shut his eyes once more. He shook this off and instead followed the man through the field. Ahead, he saw another ghostly figure lying on the ground screaming, "No! Get away! Please!" They were holding up their arms, trying to defend themselves from someone or something Dvalinn could not see. The figure fell back and was silent. A moment later, they, too, solidified. They stood and began walking in the same direction. He observed a similar sight to the other side as a man holding a sword stopped moaning and stood to join the procession.

The craftsman saw their destination loom into view. It was a huge stone gate. There were people entering it while Garmr, the giant dog, lay sleeping, paying them no heed.

When the craftsman drew near, he saw one of the

dog's big ears lift up, as if detecting something of note. Eyes still closed, it lifted its head and sniffed the air. "Patience," the dog said, sitting up and opening his eyes. "Your time will come." He fell silent as his eyes focused on the dwarf. "Is it that day already?"

"Oh, hello, Garmr," the craftsman said. "This time it looks like I'm here to stay."

"It is the way of all things, my friend," said Garmr. "I shall walk with you and herald your arrival."

"You honor me, Garmr. I am ready. Lead the way."

"It is not yet time. This field beyond the gate is where the mind goes when it has fallen asleep for the final time, but the body can linger for a little longer. Only once the final spark has left the body may you pass the gate and go to eternity." Garmr lifted one ear again and looked into the gate. "It appears someone else comes to welcome you."

The craftsman heard a familiar thunder of hooves. He looked in past the giant dog and saw the blur of reddish fur pounding up the dark road.

"Dvalinn!" Trufflesbane shouted with joy, clattering to a halt just inside the gate.

"Oh, Trufflesbane!" the dwarf cried excitedly. "I am so happy to see you again!"

"I have missed you so very much!" Trufflesbane said, trotting in place. "I want you to tell me everything that happened. I have been so anxious to hear!"

"Oh, yes, I have so much to tell!" replied the dwarf. He knew that this was true, but he could not seem to remember what these things might be. He focused with all his might, but he could not recall anything before opening his eyes in the field.

"Did you defeat the creature and save the children?" she asked anxiously.

At the sound of her words, memory descended upon him like a ton of stones. The craftsman stood motionless for a long moment, then fell to his knees, reliving everything that had brought him to this moment. "I was careless!" he sobbed. "The demon slew me when I was but moments from saving the children! Now it was all for nothing! Everything we did! Your sacrifice! I promised the children, I swore to them I would save them! How could I have failed them so?"

"Be gentle, my dear one," said Trufflesbane sadly. "You gave your life trying. No one can ask more than that."

"It hurts so much, Trufflesbane," the dwarf wept. "I looked them in the eyes. I promised I would save them. Poor children. Now who can help them?"

CHAPTER TWELVE

Asmund struggled across the muddy field, drawing closer to the battle. He saw the mighty dwarf hurl his magic warhammer, bouncing it into the demon's chest. He watched him knock it into the barn, leveling the entire structure. He was still terrified to be heading straight toward the conflict between these powerful creatures. But he was becoming more and more optimistic that good might prevail against evil. As he arrived within a dozen paces of the combat, victory looked more assured than ever. Then he saw the demon reach up with its remaining arm and gut the dwarf like a fish. Asmund froze in horror as he watched him topple to the ground, dead.

He was still standing frozen, looking at the fallen hero, when the Dragr rose and came for him. Snapping out of his trance, he fumbled in his purse. It had nearly reached him when he twisted the little mirror open and pointed it at the creature. Asmund's lips moved and the beam of pure, concentrated sunlight shot forth, striking the ancient nightwalker. It burst into blue flames. Its unholy howl of agony rent the night in two. At the sound of it, every child on the planet sat up in bed and cried. The creature turned and began to flee, only making it as far as the ruined barn before falling.

The last of the sunlight streamed out and all was darkness once more.

When finally Asmund could see again, he beheld the charred smoking form of the Dragr still lying where it had fallen. Relief washed over him. The mirror's magic had been his only hope. He knew the demon could snuff his life out with a casual swipe of its claw. And he knew that he had no other magic that could touch a shadow creature. This had been his one shot, and it had landed true.

He knelt down by the bloodstained body of the dwarf and placed his hand on the armored shoulder. "Farewell, noble dwarf."

"Yes, farewell," said a hollow voice. It was followed by an icy laugh.

Asmund saw the smoky figure sit up and look at him. The feeling of relief vanished, but he was surprised to find it was not replaced by his previous panic. Instead, he felt an instant calm despair. A tear escaped Asmund's eye and mingled with the raindrops on his cheek. The Dragr rose and came toward him.

Asmund pointed his staff and unleashed a fireball, which passed harmlessly through the ghostly form. The icy laugh could be heard once more.

"Is that the extent of your magic, wizard?" the Dragr asked.

"No," Asmund answered. "There is still one more magic left to try."

The craftsman felt a strange wholeness coming into his body. "Trufflesbane, I feel it happening." He stood up, tingling. "This is it, my friends. I am becoming solid. Now I can enter and we can be together forever!"

"Dvalinn," Trufflesbane said, smiling. "Make things right, and always remember that I love you! Now goodbye."

"Goodbye?" the craftsman repeated, bewildered. "I don't under–" Dvalinn watched Trufflesbane and Garmr flying away as he was ripped backwards through space. The last thing he could see was a youth in gray robes approaching the gates.

He opened his eyes and saw the Dragr standing above him, looking down at something that was lying next to him. The Dragr looked smaller and more transparent than before. Dvalinn moved his hand and encountered the handle of his hammer. Seeing the movement, the Dragr looked at him and gasped. "You? But how?"

The craftsman swung, striking the creature low in the legs, sweeping them out from under it. He scrambled up on top of it. Choking up on the hammer's handle, he set to work. This time he would not stop to admire his handiwork, nor would he bandy words with his adversary. Somehow, he had been given a second chance. He would not succumb to any distractions. He would carry out his plan.

His blows landed swiftly. Standing up, he gave it another brisk blow to the chest, keeping it solid. Then he grabbed the screaming creature whose arms and legs were all bashed away, picked it up and turned around. He now saw what the Dragr had been looking at. Lying there before him was the dead body of the youth he had seen at the gates of the dead. He recognized the robes. The boy was a magic healer. This boy, who he had never seen before, had traded his life for Dvalinn's.

The dwarf slammed the Dragr into the dirt at the foot of the stone, right where he knew the entrance of the tomb to be.

"Open it," he commanded.

The broken thing laughed. "Never! You can kill me, but I will never do your bidding!"

"Open it!" the craftsman repeated.

"I will never open it! Long after you have killed me you will live with the knowledge that those children are trapped for all eternity! You have no power over me!"

"Is that what you think?" the craftsman asked ominously. "That I have no power over you?"

The Dragr laughed again. "You know it to be true."

The craftsman grabbed the hem of his scaled shirt, running it across the palm of his left hand, cutting it open. He struck the Dragr with his hammer and squeezed the blood into its solid face. "I am Dvalinn, the last son of Ivaldi! I am the craftsman of the gods! I bind you, Brynjar the Defiler, and in the name of Freya, queen of Asgard, I order you to open the door!"

A loud sizzling sound could be heard and smoke rose from the demon's body. "Who told you my name? The gods themselves do not know it!"

"Open the gate. I command you!" thundered the dwarf.

"No! No! No!" screamed the writhing Dragr, but the ghostly door opened anyway. The craftsman saw the familiar stairway leading down into the darkness.

"How dare you! Make this agony cease!" the evil wretch howled.

The craftsman thumped his hammer into its chest once more. Then he tore its jaw from its face and tossed it aside. Its shock and indignation could only be spoken with its eyes.

The craftsman stepped forward to enter the barrow. He reached out his hand. It encountered an invisible barrier. He leaned his shoulder into it, trying to force his way through. He tried striking it with his hammer. No matter what he attempted, he simply could not enter.

He cupped his hands around his mouth and shouted. "Children! It's me! Come toward my voice!" He could hear his own voice echoing down below, but nothing more. He felt his desperation rising. Finally, when nothing worked, he stopped struggling and rested his face against the invisible barricade. It was maddening to see the goal right before his eyes but not be able to reach it.

Clack. Clack. Clack, the craftsman heard from below.

"Children? Is that you?" he called.

No reply.

Clack. Clack. Clack. Getting closer.

He peered down into the darkness, holding up the glowing hammer to pierce the gloom. He spied someone laboring up the stairs, leaning heavily on a walking staff. As the figure came closer, Dvalinn saw it was the young wizard who even now was lying dead not ten paces behind him. Shocked, the craftsman stammered, "Who... How... Why would...?"

"None of that is important now," the young wizard said. "The children are bound below. They told me you tied this around each of them." He held up his hand. Nothing was there.

"The rope, yes!" the craftsman said delightedly.

"Throw it to me."

The wizard tossed the rope that was not there through the doorway and the dwarf caught it. "I will go down and fight the binding spells. You pull them up," he said.

The craftsman watched the wizard clack back down into the darkness, then waited until he judged that he would have reached the lowest chamber. He turned around and arranged the rope for pulling. He examined the slash on his left palm. It was no longer bleeding. He tested it against the rope and found that his grip was still strong.

He dug in his heels and heaved with all of his might. The rope did not budge. He wrapped the rope around his hand and braced his feet on either side of the door. He leaned back, pushing with his legs as hard as he could. He pulled and pulled until finally the rope gave and he gained... an inch.

He paused, regaining his breath. "Come on, wizard, fight the magic," he said, taking a new grip and pulling once more. He strained for all he was worth, but felt very little gain. The frustration was maddening!

He felt the rope coming from the back of his hand lose its slack and go taut. Someone was pulling with him. All at once, the rope began to move. The craftsman dug in and began hauling hand over hand.

"Help us!" Ragna shouted. Balder and Dag stood with confused looks on their faces.

"But there is nothing there!" Balder protested uncertainly.

"Believe that there is a rope and that your children are tied to the other end of it and pull," shouted the dwarf without stopping.

"Pull, curse you!" commanded Ragna, straining at the rope that was not there.

Dvalinn felt the rope begin to move even faster. Looking down into the tomb, he saw the first child come jerkily into view. Misty tendrils clung to its ghostly form, trying to drag it back in.

"Believe with all your hearts!" he bellowed. "Believe!"

"Ahhhhh!" Ragna let out a war cry, and the child slid forward even faster than before.

The craftsman saw more children emerging behind the first. "Pull!" he yelled again, dragging massive handfuls of imaginary rope as swiftly as he could. He was straining so hard that even when the young rain-soaked woman with golden hair walked in from the darkened road and passed them without a word, he did not stop to wonder. He just kept pulling.

The first child finally reached the top of the stairs and emerged from the underworld, his body taking shape and solidifying as it passed through the doorway.

"Son!" Dag the Shepherd called when he saw him.

"Keep pulling!" Ragna ordered.

One by one, they hauled the children out with all the force of their wills, until at last there were six.

"The seventh child?" the craftsman cried out, confused.

Dag's son shook his head sadly.

Dvalinn picked up his hammer and stood over the Dragr with a grim look on his face. But before he could carry out his intentions he caught sight of the golden-haired girl once more. She was cradling the young wizard in her arms and weeping. The sight of it tore his heart in two. She rose, and with her eyes closed, began walking in their direction. Her hand was out-stretched as if reaching for something only she could sense. She passed them and approached the ghostly doorway.

"Young woman," the craftsman said, "you will not be able to–" He fell silent as she stepped through the doorway and into the underworld.

Kolga felt her surroundings change. She was in a cold, musty-smelling environment. She opened her eyes and saw stairs leading down into darkness. She could feel that same far-away sense of the magic amulet Asmund wore that she had sensed when he was in his troubled dreams. She knew he was right at the bottom of the steps. She began to descend. She had made it only three steps when the musty smell was replaced by another odor. It was a mingling of roses and decaying flesh. A face loomed out of the darkness below her. It was the face of a young girl. Kolga's first thought was that it was another of the children who needed rescue. But then it spoke.

"You do not belong here. You are of the living, and this place is for the dead!"

"I won't stay long. I just need to get to the bottom of the stairs. Then we can be on our way."

The little girl's face looked to the side and disappeared into darkness, only to be replaced by that of a young woman's. It said, "There is nothing for you here. Once the dead enter this place, they can never leave."

"That's not true!" Kolga replied. "This whole thing was started by a Dragr – a dead thing that returned from here."

The young woman's face rolled into darkness and was replaced by a woman of middle age. "That is different. It took a powerful hate to defy the laws of death!"

"It is not different, it is the same. But instead of hate, it is love!" said Kolga. "Love is more powerful than hate could ever be."

"I told you that there is nothing here for you. Now go!" the face thundered.

"Step aside! I must get down the stairs!" Kolga thundered back.

The face turned once more, and Kolga was confronted with the angry face of a gray old woman. "You dare say 'step aside' to me? What if I told you that you were addressing the goddess Hel, queen of the dead?"

"That would be different," Kolga replied calmly. "In that case, I would say, 'Step aside, your majesty.'" Kolga drew her axe from her belt and continued down the stairs.

"You must be insane if you think you can defeat me!" crowed the old woman's face.

"I don't think anything of the sort," Kolga said. "I'm simply not leaving without Asmund."

"Foolish girl! You have this coming."

Bock. Bock.

Kolga stopped walking. "Was that a chicken?" She looked back up the stairs and saw a little white hen with a black mark on one wing.

"No fair!" screamed the four faces at once.

The chicken gave one little cluck, as if in reply.

When Kolga turned back around, the queen of the dead was gone.

Kolga felt her way through the darkness until she detected a light source coming from further below. She found Asmund down another, narrower flight of stairs. The light was shining from his glowing dagger. He sat unconscious with his magic book open upon his lap. She had seen this depth of exhaustion in him before, when he had been struggling against evil magic to save people in need. She looked at him and it felt as though her heart were so full that it would burst inside of her.

"Foolish goddess," she said to the darkness. "Death cannot stop my love for this man!"

The craftsman stood at the doorway to the tomb, peering down into the darkness. His eyes grew wide when he saw the girl emerging. She was climbing the stairs with the wizard in her arms. He stepped aside when she reached the top. As she passed through the door and left the realm of the dead, the wizard disappeared from view. But she still walked slowly, as if bearing a weight in her arms.

Everyone fell silent, child and adult alike. They watched her as she passed. They observed as she reached her love and carefully set down her invisible burden on top of his dead body. They all saw the young wizard sit up, and, recognizing the girl, throw his arm around her and hug her tightly, as if never wanting to let her go.

Dvalinn looked down and saw that the Dragr was watching also. It looked from the young wizard to the children gathered around Ragna, then lay back and turned its hateful eyes to him. It watched as the craftsman lifted his hammer high above his head and brought it crashing down.

ABOUT THE AUTHOR

Joel Newlon

Joel Newlon is from the United States. Over the years, he has wowed audiences as a stuntman, brought them laughter as a comedy writer, and saved lives as a police officer. But his biggest passion in life has always been writing. He specializes in tales of fantasy and adventure that provide an escape from the everyday world. He lives on a small, secluded farm with his brilliant wife, Ashleigh, and insane cat, Pyewacket.

He can be found on Twitter @JoelNewlon or on his website, joelnewlon.com.

Made in the USA
Columbia, SC
02 February 2021